The Crush

The Crush

An Oregon Wine Country Romance

Heather Heyford

LYRICAL SHINE
Kensington Publishing Corp.
www.kensingtonbooks.com

LYRICAL SHINE BOOKS are published by

Kensington Publishing Corp.
119 West 40th Street
New York, NY 10018

All Kensington titles, imprints, and distributed lines are available at special quantity discounts for bulk purchases for sales promotion, premiums, fund-raising, educational, or institutional use.

Special book excerpts or customized printings can also be created to fit specific needs. For details, write or phone the office of the Kensington Sales Manager: Kensington Publishing Corp., 119 West 40th Street, New York, NY 10018. Attn. Sales Department. Phone: 1-800-221-2647.

Lyrical Shine and Lyrical Shine logo Reg. U.S. Pat. & TM Off.

First Electronic Edition: October 2016
eISBN-13: 978-1-60183-824-7
eISBN-10: 1-60183-824-7

First Print Edition: October 2016
ISBN-13: 978-1-60183-825-4
ISBN-10: 1-60183-825-5

Printed in the United States of America

Acknowledgments

As always, thanks go to Sarah Elizabeth Younger at the Nancy Yost Literary Agency for her support and advice.

With gratitude to my editor, Esi Sogah, for guiding me with her usual grace and humor, and to the rest of the staff at Kensington Publishing for all they do to make my books shine.

Warm thanks to my dear daughter and loving husband for their encouragement. And to my sphere of family and friends who listen to me prattle on about imaginary worlds and the angst and joys of being a romance writer.

Chapter One

Rap rap rap!

Juniper Hart was agonizing over which of her wine business's creditors would luck out and get paid this month when she heard a loud knocking at the door of her tasting room.

Her head shot up from her bills. She scrambled out from behind her desk, heedless of the papers she set sailing. Inches short of the threshold, she skidded to a stop to smooth down her faded T-shirt emblazoned with WE ARE PINOT NOIR. From the other side of the door, she heard a familiar voice.

"Last I knew, Lieutenant, you had women in, let's see—Fort Bliss, Fort Belvoir, and New York City. And that's just stateside."

Though the words meant nothing to her, Junie recognized the timbre of her old friend Sam Owens's voice. Sam had racked up numerous awards for his military service before moving back to his hometown. These days, he made a living ferrying tourists around in his Clarkston Wine Consortium van, introducing them to Willamette Valley wine. And now, from the sound of it, here he was, delivering eager wine enthusiasts right into the palm of Junie's hand.

She pasted on her best smile and threw wide the door. "Welcome to the pinot state!"

"Hey, Junie!" said Sam warmly. "Like the new greeting."

"Sounds way better than 'Welcome to Broken Hart Vineyards,'" deadpanned Keval, thumbing his cell phone without looking up.

Junie cringed at the innocuous-sounding nickname. Keval Patel might be the town of Clarkston's god of IT, but he could use some help in the tact department.

But wait—these weren't Junie's desperately needed new customers making a detour off the established wine trail. Despite their chins sporting some degree of hipster stubble, to her, these guys would always be the same fresh-faced, coltish boys they'd been back at Clarkston Middle School. Ever since her dad died and her brother left town, they were practically all the family she had left. All except the one with the Ivy League haircut, dressed more for a job interview at Brooks Brothers than a drive in the wine country.

"Thought you said Oregon was the *Beaver* State?" the stranger asked Sam, eyeing Junie up and down. "Because, *damn . . .*"

Heath Sinclair's burst of laughter was cut short by Sam's swift elbow to his ribs.

"Why else would I leave a city where women outnumber men to fly all the way across the country?"

"Thought it was to do a brother a favor, Lieutenant." Sam raised a weary brow. "Sorry, Junie. We've done two tastings already, and some of these bozos forgot how to spit."

"I had all good intentions of expectorating when we started out." Heath straightened, still clutching his side. "But I'm a beer drinker. Beer drinkers swallow. It's what we do." Heath should know—he was the founder of Clarkston Craft Ales.

"Juniper Hart"—Sam stretched out an arm toward the stranger—"this is Lieutenant Manolo Santos."

The lieutenant nodded in curt, military fashion. "Pleasure."

"Manolo's a construction guy from back east. Came out to give me some expert advice on the new consortium building."

Junie examined Manolo dubiously. Tall and broad shouldered with a flat belly, it was easy to imagine him in a sweat-stained work shirt, hefting a load of two-by-fours. But the quick gleam in his eye, the pride in his bearing, and his impeccable grooming pegged him as more than just your typical manual laborer.

"Construction guy?"

"Construction engineer, technically," he replied.

"What exactly does a construction engineer do?"

"The official U.S. Army definition?" He flashed her a blindingly white grin. "Someone who works a twelve-hour day/night shift seven days a week on a rotational basis in a remote location."

Sam gripped Manolo's shoulder affectionately. "What the lieutenant here does is solve problems. Converts ideas into reality. Manny's helped design roads, schools, and hospitals from Arizona to Iraq."

"Is that so?"

Manolo shrugged off Sam's compliment like a too-tight shirt. "Think of me as kind of a combination Jason Bourne and Bob the Builder."

"You're forgetting horndog," added Sam, to backslaps and shrieks of mirth.

Junie dismissed Manolo and slanted her eyes at those she knew better. "You guys sure you can handle another one?"

They straightened their spines, trying their best to look contrite.

Keval tsked and gave her an incredulous look. "Are you *serious*?"

"C'mon, Junie. Let us in," pleaded Rory, whose family's apple orchard adjoined Junie's land.

"I'm designated driver." Sam jerked a thumb toward his log-splashed van parked out in the field, some distance away.

She propped her hand on her hip and pretended to consider her options. If not for Sam roping them in, no tourists would ever find their way off the main road to her boutique winery. Junie owed Sam big-time.

When she figured they'd suffered long enough, she broke out in a conciliatory smile. "C'mon," she said, stepping aside.

The men shuffled past Junie into the tasting room in single file, with Tall, Dark, and Sketchy bringing up the rear.

"After you, ma'am."

His baritone was soft and deep. Arrogant eyes the rich brown of espresso made the back of her neck prickle. *A man who seems too good to be true usually is.* She brushed off her warning instinct, slipped behind the counter, and dealt out five generic white coasters. Those would have to do until the day she could afford to have them done right, custom-printed with her name.

Lieutenant Santos's head swiveled on his neck, absorbing every detail of Junie's humble tasting room . . . the unfinished ceiling, the plywood walls, the makeshift bar cobbled together from cast-off parts. The closer he looked, the more inadequate she felt. So what if it wasn't the Taj Mahal? She was doing the best she could.

She kept half an eye on him as he wandered over to the opposite side of the room, where a picture window would be someday, if she was lucky. His every movement was a study in controlled power. Wherever he went, the others followed, drawn to him like bees to a hive. He said something Junie couldn't quite decipher. Whatever it was, her friends found it highly entertaining.

Daryl Decaprio, Clarkston High's most notorious flirt. The resemblance was uncanny.

When the laughter finally died down, Daryl's twin drifted over to watch her work. The temporary bar served only four without crowding. But there was an eighteen-foot slab of live-edge white oak out in the barn just waiting for the right time to be installed.

"You wouldn't happen to have anything to eat back there, would you?"

"This is a wine-tasting room. If you're hungry, there're some restaurants in town."

He raised a palm. "Fair enough. No harm in asking."

She launched into her rehearsed pitch. "So, where're you from?"

"Born and raised in Hoboken, New Jersey. But I left there a long time ago."

Junie busied herself opening a two-year-old vintage. She felt the heat of his gaze travel over her hands, up her arms to her chest, her neck, and finally her face.

"What's a beauty like you doing hidden away in a place like this?"

Her hands paused where they struggled against the stubborn cork. Beauty? *Her?* He didn't just look like Daryl; he laid it on thick like him, too.

Stick to your script, Junie. What had they said at that free class for entrepreneurs at the Yamhill County Extension? She was the one who should be asking the questions. Marketing 101.

She gave the screw a vicious twist. The cork came out with a muted pop, and she began to pour the one-ounce servings used for sampling.

"How long will you be in the Willamette Valley?"

"Not long. I'm a traveling man. Just passing through."

Lieutenant Manolo Santos was a walking, talking cliché, thanks to his good looks and bad lines.

Be nice to everyone, they said in the class. *You never know who might turn out to be an ally.* She clenched the bottle tighter in her moist palm, determined not to fumble under his penetrating glare, ally or not.

Sam hoisted his glass and the others followed suit. But before he could make a toast, the stranger beat him to it.

"To the Beaver State," he said, eyes sparkling with mischief.

That brought more cautious chuckles, as her friends weighed their loyalty to her against the novelty of the suave newcomer in their midst.

Sam swirled his wineglass at eye level, checking for all the signs: color, viscosity, legs.

Rory downed his glass like cider and followed it with a satisfied belch.

Junie's heart sank. Heath was a brewer and Sam was in the wine business, like Junie. Keval was industry, too, if doing IT for the consortium counted. Was it too much to ask for them to appreciate what she was trying to do here? They'd tried her wine before. They knew word of mouth was everything. That's where sales came from. But they couldn't pass the word on about how great her pinot was if they persisted in chugging it like marathoners on Gatorade. Maybe they couldn't handle three tastings in one day, after all.

"Yummy." Keval licked his lips and picked up a battered copy of *Wine Spectator* from the bar. "Just think, Juniper. Maybe you'll be in here someday."

Yeah, right. She couldn't even afford to renew her subscription.

At least Sam had the decency to give his wine time to wander around his palate, letting it speak to his taste buds. "Your wine sings, Junie."

Junie swelled with pride. High praise, coming from Sam. But even he couldn't seem to find her a distributor, though he'd been looking for the past couple of years.

True to his word, he spat into the receptacle provided. "Now, how about that rosé?"

Junie poised the new bottle to pour, but there were only four empty glasses on the counter. She skimmed the room for the fifth, spotting it in the hand of Mr. New Jersey.

Thick, workingman's fingers cradled her fragile stemware. Dense lashes brushed against carved cheekbones as he lowered them to gaze at the ruby liquid. Then he glanced up over the rim, catching Junie staring. "Young, bright appearance."

He lowered his Roman nose into the bowl and sniffed, then looked up, his eyes landing in the vicinity of her chest. "Juicy plums." He swirled and sniffed again. "And some other fruit I don't think I've had the pleasure of tasting."

Junie forgot about the bottle she held poised, and it sank to the bar under its own weight. "Lingonberry. It's native to the Pacific Northwest."

Manolo drank then. But all the while he worked her wine around in his mouth, he didn't take his eyes off her.

The tasting room grew uncomfortably warm, despite the chilly April air. Lieutenant Manolo Santos had a politician's command of the room. Even the guys quit horsing around in anticipation of what he would say next.

"Soft and supple, yet structurally complex. I like that."

The breath Junie didn't know she'd been holding whooshed out through her broad grin. This vintage was her most ambitious effort to date, and that was exactly the response she had been going for!

"It's good in a wine, too."

While the guys cracked up, Junie's smile ebbed and her cheeks burned even hotter.

Manolo raised his glass. "To—Junie, was it?"

She glared daggers at him. He may have played her once, but she wouldn't let it happen again. Thanks to her experience with Daryl, she knew better than to trust guys like him.

"Could we, ah . . ." Sam motioned to the still-empty quartet of glasses.

Only then did she remember the bottle of rosé she still clenched by the neck.

After she set them up again, her usually levelheaded, sweet friends surrounded Mr. Big Shot.

"To Junie!" he exclaimed, eyes aglow with a fire that disconcerted her, despite her resolve.

"To a promising future," said Sam, with a nod of appreciation for her skill as a winemaker.

The others echoed with woozy tributes of their own.

Testosterone-fueled shoulder bumps were followed by more enthusiastic clinks. "One more?" Heath asked, holding out his empty glass.

More laughter, more rowdy toasting.

Then Junie shrank at the sound of crystal shattering.

"I'll get the broom." She hurried back to her office, adding the cost of replacing the broken stemware to her long list of expenses.

Chapter Two

M anolo reached behind the tasting room door to relieve Junie of the broom handle she clutched. "I'll get that, ma'am."

"I've got it," Junie snapped. The flame in her eyes would melt steel.

Dammit, he was trying to be a gentleman. He meant well. His behavior leading up to this mess was just his way of warning an attractive woman that he wasn't cut out for the long haul.

His hands flew open to grant her wish, but she wasn't expecting it. The long handle teetered on its bristles, then toppled over in slow motion, drawing their eyes downward.

He caught it mid-fall. But not before he saw the crimson ink on the statements scattered beneath the scarred old desk. What's more, she saw him looking.

Back out in the tasting room, Manolo made short work of the broken glass.

"Where's the trash?"

Mutely, Junie reached under the counter and held out the can. He dumped the shards, then snatched a length of paper toweling off the roll on the bar.

She leaned over the counter to see where he was wiping the last streaks of blood-red wine from the floor. "You don't have to—"

"Done."

"Sorry." Sam winced. "Can't take these guys anywhere."

"Yeah, sorry, Junie," aped Keval, looking genuinely remorseful.

"Having too much fun," added Rory.

"No," Manolo said, wondering how he was going to make up for his lousy first impression. *She must think I'm a complete assjack.* "This is my fault. I take full responsibility." He jutted his chin toward the others. "Pulling these guys out of work so I could do a little day drinking."

Sam slapped Rory on the back. "Just wanted Manny to get to know my homies, here."

The woman wiped her palms down the sides of her slim thighs and tightened her lips against a retort.

Manolo put the broom back in the office, then strode behind the bar, lathered up, and offered her his freshly washed hand. "Please accept my apology."

Junie hesitated. Even after she grudgingly took his hand, she kept inventing ways to avoid eye contact. She blew a loose strand of hair out of her eyes and, when that didn't work, shook back her whole shaggy mane... chewed her lower lip... looked at anything and anyone but him. Finally, she lifted her pointed chin and glared at him defiantly, as if she saw straight through his pretext.

Blue eyes. No, blue-green, like the turquoise drops dangling from her ears. Thankfully, that earlier wildfire in them had simmered down to a slow burn. Below the plane of the bar, her hand felt capable and strong, pressed against his. He brushed his thumb lightly across the base of hers. While he drew lazy circles on Junie's skin, he recalled the phone conversation when Sam had first told him that the pool of local vintners he'd started was crowding him out of his own house. He needed a real building. Sam's news had only confirmed the buzz back east: that this corner of the Pacific Northwest was fast becoming America's new capital of pinot noir.

From inside the bubble Manolo imagined surrounding them, Junie used her left thumb and forefinger to methodically pry his digits off her right hand, one by one. Short of being under enemy fire, nothing got Manolo's blood pumping like actually having to fight for a female conquest. For the sake of cover, he kept up their light banter while drawing out their private little game of handsies as long as possible. She had succeeded in peeling his grip away once, only to have him immediately retake his lost territory. One honest tug was all it would take to free herself from his covert caresses, if she really wanted to.

"Apology accepted, on one condition. I asked you how long you were going to be wreaking havoc in our neck of the woods."

"Six months, max."

She smiled ruefully. "Looks like I'd better stock up on glassware."

She was a good sport, after all. "Shortest lease I could find," he said.

"That'll be September. The crush. All the festivities start on the ninth this year."

"That's the plan," said Sam. "We need to have the new consortium up and running by then for the onslaught of tourists. Manny took a place on Main Street above the Radish Rose."

"Clarkston's best restaurant." She lifted an approving brow.

Finally, he'd done something right. Truth was, Manolo never went anywhere without first scouting out the area's best places for food and wine. "Speaking of which, what are you doing for dinner?"

Junie's hand snapped back to her side, and the bubble popped. "Working."

He waited for her to explain.

"I wait tables at dinnertime during the week so I can be here afternoons and weekends for customers."

Customers? In the nick of time, he bit back a laugh. They hadn't seen another soul since Sam's van had left the main wine trail.

Sam stepped up to the bar. "Junie's got a lot on her plate, now that—"

"I can speak for myself, Sam." She picked up her bar rag with a flounce and vigorously wiped the counter. "Budbreak is a busy time of year. I have to finish weeding and mowing and paying the bills—" Her mouth snapped shut again at the mention of bills.

Well played, Santos. You've just been shot down—in front of four other men.

Manolo waved away his dinged pride. "Don't worry about it. Good meeting you, Junie." He reached for his wallet. "Before I go, here, take this for the wineglasses. And I'll take six bottles of that pinot. Once word gets out, it's not going to last long."

Sam and Manolo lagged behind the others on their way back to the van.

"Don't take it personal, man." Sam always could read him like a book. But then, he'd been highly trained to spot people's vulnerabilities or, as they said in military jargon, "handle assets." "Junie keeps to herself. Ever since she got back from UC Davis, she's been working her ass off."

"The big winemaking school?"

Sam nodded. "Right after she graduated, her dad died. That left just Junie and her mom to run the place"—he glanced backward out of an abundance of caution—"by which I mean, just Junie."

"Shame."

Manolo's practiced eyes skimmed over the faded brown landscape, across a winding silver ribbon of water to the misty distant hills. Evaluating ground for its development potential came as second nature to him. "Hard to believe grapes'll grow here. Day's more than half gone and those hills are still shrouded in fog."

"That was the old way of thinking," said Sam. "Brendan Hart was one of the first to see climate change coming."

From where Manolo was standing, the Willamette Valley felt different from anywhere else he'd been—and he'd been to a lot of places in his thirty-four years. While the East Coast seemed suddenly tired . . . sedate, rural Oregon still epitomized the frontier spirit, fresh and thrumming with possibility, its people brassy and vibrant.

"Pinot noir's the polar bear of grapes. The wine gets flabby if it's too hot. People assume it's cold here because of the latitude, but the Willamette today is like Napa was ten years ago. Now Cali's fried, and we're more temperate, like the Med. These hills are ideal for pinot."

"So, what happened?"

Sam made a face. "Do I look like a climatologist?"

"Junie's dad, numb nuts."

They struck out again across the uneven landscape. "The Harts aren't originally from around here. Junie was in middle school when Brendan retired as an MP. He was still young, so he started a second career as a state trooper. First month on the job, he neutralized some wing nut with an AR-15 holding a farm family hostage. Overnight, Brendan Hart was a hero.

"But being a cop was never Hart's main ambition. He might have gotten an instant reputation as a badass, but in person he was kind of quiet, mild-mannered. He found this old farm where filberts used to grow, and somehow convinced his wife that this was where they were going to settle down, plant their family."

"Family?"

"Junie and her brother, name of Storm. Soup sandwich, you ask me. You know the type. Always looking for a fast buck without paying his dues. Back when we were in school, you could always find him and Junie out here working alongside their dad. Once he graduated, though, it only took one crush for him to realize what the next fifty were going to look like. Got out while he still had a strong back."

Manolo winced. He knew what it felt like to be saddled with someone else's dream. Like you were slowly suffocating.

"Last I heard, Storm was making money hand over fist running one of those cannabis outfits in Colorado."

Asking would only dredge up pain. But a deep-seated guilt made him need to know. "How'd the old man take it, his only son taking off like that, reneging on his family duty?"

"On top of a decade of tending grapes by moonlight after pulling eight-hour shifts busting drug dealers? Massive coronary, that's how. Junie found him one morning lying right over there, where he'd gone out to graft rootstock the night before." Sam pointed between long rows of stakes to where a flock of robins pecked at the thawing earth. Their chirps filled the resulting silence.

Neither Sam nor Manolo were strangers to death. Right now, Sam was probably reliving his own horrors from his time in Iraq. But, as for Manolo, he was obsessing over wayward sons and how they broke their fathers' hearts.

"Maybe the brother'll man up, once he matures a little."

"Doubt it." Sam pulled a blade of wild garlic and stuck it between his teeth. "Some say Storm got his mom's good sense and Junie's a dreamer like her old man."

Some were probably right. "What about her mom?"

"She's originally from down south. It's a wonder Hart ever got her to move to Clarkston in the first place. She never really fit in." Then Sam's detail-obsessed nature asserted itself. "Check that. To be fair, she's a surgeon. Could be she just never had the time to get in good with the locals."

"A surgeon. Impressive."

Sam gestured broadly. "You think you could raise two kids, put one through college, and subsidize all this on a cop's salary? Everyone in Clarkston says it's only a matter of time before Jennifer Jepson-Hart gets tired of throwing good money after bad and talks her daughter into moving back to civilization."

"Sounds like Junie's inherited some good genes."

"What Junie's trying to do takes more than good genes. Running a vineyard *and* a winery is like operating three businesses at once."

"Growing grapes . . . making wine . . . what else?"

"Entertainment. Junie's one of the most gifted winemakers in the valley. Hart Vineyards is starting to get noticed. But that's not enough. People want to be *entertained* as part of the wine-buying experience. If she falls short anywhere, it's there. I can't seem to get that through her head. But then, speaking of gifted, you know about the seven intelligences."

"Say again? I know what kind of structure works best on any given site and how to throw together a decent marinara. You're the smart one. Enlighten me."

"You just nailed it without even trying. Seven intelligences theory says the average guy has two or three things out of a possible seven in his wheelhouse." He counted off on his fingers. "Math, verbal, spatial, musical, interpersonal, intrapersonal, kinesthetic.

"Take you, for example. You see a piece of ground and you instinctively know what kind of building will work best on it. That's spatial intelligence. Me? Back in OCS when they gave me the aptitude test, I scored high in intrapersonal—knowing myself—and interpersonal—knowing others. On the other hand, I don't know a noun from an adverb, and I have zero chance of being drafted by the Seahawks. Junie? She might have kick-ass winemaking chops, but it doesn't automatically follow that she knows how to sell what she makes."

Manolo nodded in assent. "That tasting room's a disaster. Best thing that could happen would be to gut it and start over."

"Hart didn't see the point of a fancy tasting room, either. He invested the bulk of his hard-earned cash in the actual winemaking equipment. I suspect Junie's still paying for those French oak barrels. Nothing's lacking down there in the cellar. But as far as marketing, Junie's got her work cut out for her. She's strong, though. Strong and proud."

The image of Junie's late notices strewn across the tasting room floor popped into Manolo's mind. But he made it a policy to steer clear of women's personal business. Getting too close only made it harder to pull up stakes when the time came to leave.

He tipped back his head, inhaling the sharp tang of wood smoke and manure. *Ahh, the smell of springtime in the country.* That wasn't what Hoboken smelled like. The fresh air cleared his head, bringing him back to less disconcerting problems. Problems that could be solved using inductive reasoning and logic.

"That's some great pinot she's got. You're right, though. This property needs a major overhaul if she wants to turn it into a point of destination. For instance . . ." Manolo jabbed his bag of wine toward a slope just south of the tasting room. "Over there." He backtracked several steps. "That grade is just begging to be terraced." In an instant, the development crystallized in his imagination. "Maybe a pergola there, some tables *there*. Optimize the view while people are sampling the wine. Put them in the mood to buy."

Sam followed him a few steps to humor him. "It's not me you have to convince."

But Manolo wasn't listening. His head was exploding with ideas. He turned on his axis, pausing when the dove-gray siding and cheery yellow door of the main dwelling came back into view. "The house looks solid enough, except for that skeleton of two-by-fours on the north end. Is that an addition?"

"Junie hired some fly-by-night to start the side porch over a year ago, to be true to her dad's original plan. The guy promised her the moon, stayed a couple weeks, then disappeared with her partial payment in his pocket."

"That's the kind of jerk that gives my profession a bad name. Not good for the frame lumber to be exposed that long, especially in this climate. The wood's susceptible to mold."

Sam shook his head. "That's all Junie needs, to have to start the porch over on top of everything else."

"Nice-size house. Junie live there all by herself?"

Sam headed back to the path. "She's still got her mom."

There was a flash of wings as a hawk zoomed down on an unsuspecting robin.

"Kestrel," said Sam, as they watched the raptor fly away with his prey. He turned to Manolo. "Let's get something straight. We pushed the envelope today. No real harm done other than a few broken glasses. I'll take the blame for not stopping after two wineries—I like giving Junie business when I can. Just don't go getting any half-assed ideas. Junie's not hookup material."

Manolo almost ran into him. *"Hookup material?"*

"You know. 'Hit it and quit it.' You don't need to add Junie to your list of Tinderellas. And don't think I won't hear about it if you try to sneak in under the radar. Clarkston's a small town. We all look out for Junie. Same way her dad looked out for us."

They walked on. Behind Sam, Manolo grinned. "Now, that's going to sting for a while. I'm more highly evolved than that. Don't you know? I actually think of myself as a feminist."

"Hah!" Sam huffed without turning around. "I must've missed the memo."

"In fact—no disrespect, Cap'n—but I'm thinking maybe you got a bad case of the hots for Juniper Hart, yourself."

"Negative, Lieutenant," Sam replied without missing a beat.

A rush of relief surged through Manolo, surprising him.

"I blew my chances with Junie Hart a long time ago."

Now this was interesting. "Out with it. You can't leave me hanging after a line like that."

"If you got to know. Ninth grade, spring dance. You remember ninth grade. Hormones raging? Junie was still new, didn't have many friends yet. On top of that, she was kind of quiet. When it came down to time for the dance, I still hadn't gotten around to asking anybody, and she was one of the last ones left."

"So you asked her."

Sam nodded. "Strictly platonic. We danced, some with each other and a little with other people. I left the gym to get a Coke or something, and that's when I got kidnapped by Mona Cruz."

"Ah." Manolo nodded. "No mother should ever name her daughter Mona. That's just asking for it."

"Roger that. Mona was a sophomore, but she should've been a junior. A silver ring in her bellybutton, jeans so tight you could see the outline of her new permit in her back pocket. She'd been giving me signs all year, but I was too dumb to do anything. Finally she saw her chance, and dragged me around the corner and down the hall. I was supposed to fight that off?"

"A man's gotta do what a man's gotta do, even if he's only in ninth grade."

"Next thing I know, Mona's got her tongue down my throat, I'm copping my first feel—and Junie comes walking around the corner. Woody melted like a popsicle in an oven."

"Christ." Torn between Sam's predicament and Junie's hurt, Manolo's face twisted in a half grin, half grimace. "At least you *went* to your ninth grade dance."

"What?" asked Sam. "You couldn't get a date?"

If only Manolo could put a humorous spin on his own freshman dance. But even after all these years, there was nothing remotely funny about missing out on the cardinal event of his high school career to do what he did every Friday night, which was work. Even worse was when clusters of his classmates clamored into his family's restaurant after the dance ended. If he lived to be a hundred, he would never be able to un-see all the other guys and their cute dates, un-hear their exclusive laughter over all the fun that he'd missed. Scribbling down their food orders, scurrying to fill them, he had never felt so left out, before or since.

"I don't think I had a single date all through high school. My old man was unrelenting. All we ever did was work. My sisters didn't date, either. Two of my sisters ended up marrying the first guys that came along after graduation, for better or worse. I hightailed it in the opposite direction."

"You more than made up for lost time," Sam joked.

"You could say that." Manolo grinned unapologetically.

"Anyway, now I hear Mona's got kids by two different baby daddies," said Sam, going back to his story. "And I got my sights set on a full-bodied red with legs that'd make you cry."

Well now. This is *a good sign.* Manolo had been concerned that the only people Sam trusted anymore were the ones he'd served with. Covert assignments that ran a couple years over time tended to mess with a man's head like that. He slung an arm over his compatriot's shoulders. "Why, Samuel, you old rascal, you." Maybe Sam's invisible wounds were finally starting to heal.

Sam grinned, glued his eyes to his feet, and endured Manolo's brusque, one-armed squeeze.

"But I meant what I said earlier," he added earnestly. "Bad as we pissed Junie off today, we take care of our own around here. You two would never work. She's got enough aggravation."

"That big-brother act wouldn't have anything to do with old ninth-grade guilt, would it?"

"Maybe it does and maybe it doesn't. And, Lieutenant?"

At the look on Sam's face, Manolo's smile faded.

"That's an order."

Chapter Three

Junie tucked Manolo's bills into her metal cash box, pleased at the way they filled up the empty slots. Manolo Santos had presence. And Junie wasn't the only one who'd been affected. He'd had her guy friends eating out of his hand on his first day in town.

She tossed her head, hoping to shake him out, but all that did was register that he had really asked her out to dinner! And, genius that she was, she'd turned him down, pleading too many chores. Weeding and mowing? *At night?*

But getting involved with an admitted drifter was the last thing she needed.

She had just dived under the desk to retrieve her late notices when she heard the tasting room door open again. One of the guys must have left something behind.

"Junie?"

"Mom?" *What is she doing home already?* "I'm in here."

From the floor where she knelt, Junie saw a pair of Velcro-strapped Mary Janes coming toward her. Next, Mom's pink face came into view, the blood having rushed to her head when she bent over. "What are you doing under there?"

"I dropped something." She backed out on her hands and knees and slid the late notices to the bottom of the paper pile.

When Dad died, his life insurance had erased what was left of the mortgage, but his capital investment in the winery had left her with substantial debt. Storm had already moved to Colorado. Mom wanted to immediately put the house and vineyard on the market and pretend Dad's dream—Mom's nightmare—had never existed. But Junie, with the blind enthusiasm of a new college grad and no clue of the long, hard road ahead, had been adamant that she could make it on her own. If Mom found out she was now having money problems—

"A better question is what are *you* doing here?" Even when Mom was at home, she rarely ventured out to the big outbuilding containing the tasting room, press, and cellar.

"It's Friday, remember? I don't schedule appointments Friday afternoons."

"It doesn't usually work out that way, though, does it?" Even when Mom did manage to quit working at a decent hour, she usually stayed in the city with colleagues to take advantage of its superior restaurants.

"I made it a point to get home early today. I am tapped *out*." She looked around for a place to sit, but the only chair was the one behind the desk.

Junie studied her mother's face. If she had something important to talk about, why now, when they had all weekend?

Mom smiled cryptically. "How about you? When was the last time you ate anything? Something good for you."

Junie stuffed the late notices into a drawer. She tried to recall her last meal, but came up empty.

"That's what I thought. Want to go out and grab a quick bite before you have to get ready for work? There's nothing in the fridge. As usual."

Junie stiffened. Mom was always on her to eat better. Most nights, Junie mechanically wolfed down whatever was on special after her shift at Casey's Roadhouse. She knew she should make more of an effort. But food was way down on her list of priorities. Nothing ever seemed to really satisfy her hunger, anyway. Maybe working at mediocre restaurants for the past nine years had dulled her appetite.

"How about Poppy's?"

Poppy's, whose menu was stuffed full of the kind of sugary, highly glutenous confections that tempted even Junie's palate? Something was definitely up. Normally, Mom would have suggested a salad from Demeter or at least the Radish Rose, whose menu had lots of choices.

"Sure." As long as Mom was paying.

Chapter Four

"**P**oppy!"

Poppy Springer's looks were as startling today as they had been back when she and Junie were lifeguards at the Clarkston Community Pool. Junie jumped up from her booth to give Poppy a hug.

"What are you doing home?"

"Busman's holiday. Mom and Pop took the motor home up to Whistler for a few weeks. Lately my job situation is complicated, so I'm helping to hold down the fort. I left you a message."

"I know. . . ." Junie slid back onto her vinyl seat. "Sorry I haven't gotten back to you. It's just that I've been so busy with work. . . ."

Poppy set down their water glasses, eyes lowered.

"Join the club. She doesn't return her own mother's calls," Mom said.

Junie knew her excuses were getting old, but what could she do?

"How are you, Dr. Hart?"

"I'm fine, thank you very much. Nice to see you again so soon, Poppy."

Poppy turned to Junie with a patient smile. "Your mom and I ran into each other at the place in the city where I'm hostessing part time."

"Really?" Junie frowned. Mom hadn't mentioned that. "I'm not blowing you off, Poppy. I promise."

"Stop!" That was Poppy for you, swallowing her own disappointment so that Junie wouldn't feel bad. "I know you have your hands full out there. Now, what can I get you two? The sticky buns are hot out of the oven." She beamed at Junie. "Guaranteed to spike your blood sugar."

"I'll just have green tea. Decaf," said Mom.

Junie skimmed the menu for something her mother would approve of.

The bell above the door jangled, and two couples, the women in expensive linen and the men in cargo shorts, a camera with a telescopic lens swinging around one of their necks, entered the café.

"Do you need a few minutes?" To the untrained eye, Poppy appeared unaffected. But Junie knew she had alerted like a bloodhound on a kilo of heroin. In a town like Clarkston, catering to tourists was how restaurants survived.

Junie bit her lip. Those sticky buns sounded awfully good. . . . "Okay." Junie slapped her menu down on the Formica. "I'm in. A bun and coffee."

Poppy swept away their menus. "Coming right up."

"I'll be good tomorrow," Junie muttered.

"I'm not judging you. But it is worth remembering that excess sugar consumption causes diabetes."

Thank you, Doctor Mom.

Now that they'd ordered, Junie waited for her to come out with whatever it was she'd brought her here to talk about.

"Poppy's doing well," Mom remarked with mild surprise. "Did you hear about her new career path?"

"Yeah. I'm really happy for her."

Poppy had left Clarkston right out of school to stock wine in a dusty little shop on a Portland side street. When the manager quit three years later, the owner had tagged Poppy to replace him, even though she was still a month shy of being able to take her first legal drink. From there, she'd started hostessing. Recently she'd begun studying for her sommelier certificate.

"She's had luck on her side. Somehow she managed to find a great niche. Who knew female sommeliers would be the next big thing?"

"Or it could've been her strong work ethic and her natural way with people. Plus, she has a great memory. Have you noticed? She never writes down an order."

Mom folded her arms on the table. "If Poppy can make it in Portland, anyone can."

"Meaning?"

"Now, don't you get all defensive on me. You know as well as I do that nobody ever had any great expectations of Miss Poppy Springer. She's got good genes, I grant you that," she said, in an obvious reference to Poppy's classic good looks. "But she has the cranial bandwidth of an amoeba. And without a degree . . ."

"Newsflash, Mom. College isn't for everyone."

A graciously smiling Poppy approached the table. Mom sat back to make room for her to set down her steaming tea. When she left, Mom went on. "I'm not here to argue about Poppy or extoll the virtues of college. Junie, you're my only daughter. I love you very much. And it's about time you got a real job."

"Mom." Junie closed her eyes, struggling to remain calm. "We're not doing this again. I already *have* a real job. Do you still think enology is some passing fancy?"

At their table nearby, the tourists turned and stared.

"Keep it down," said Mom. "And you've got circles under your eyes. You look exhausted. Have you lost weight?"

"Haven't checked lately." She hadn't weighed herself in months. The workweek flashed through Junie's mind like clips from a movie. Monday, the concerned look on the face of the volunteer from the co-op after examining her financials. Tuesday and Wednesday, trudging miles through rows of vines to tweak the pruning, racing to tie cordons to the top wires to keep the flower buds off the ground in case of a late frost. Her jeans did feel looser, come to think of it. Trust Mom to notice.

"*And* your freckles are coming out already, and it's only April. Aren't you wearing sunscreen? Juniper, darling, I know how much you loved your father—we *all* did—but don't you think that vineyard has cost this family enough? It's been five long years. When I think of all the money sunk into this venture . . . and then losing Storm so he didn't have to see the disappointment in his father's face every time he looked at him—"

"Storm didn't *have* to move to Colorado."

"You saw what farming did to your father in the end." Mom knew how to angle the knife for maximum damage. "If he hadn't kept chasing that pipe dream, he would still be alive today."

Junie frowned. "I can't believe we're having this conversation again, after all the times I've tried to explain it to you. Weren't you even listening?"

Mom appraised her with a cool eye. She wasn't used to being told no. When she walked down the halls of the hospital the nurses snapped to, and in the ER she had absolute control over her staff. "You're a bright girl, Junie, a hardworking girl," she said in the detached tone used for stubborn patients. "I have connections. I could find you something Monday if you'd only let me. Stefon's partner is the people champion over at—"

"Who's Stefon?" Junie asked, exasperated. "And what's a 'people champion?'"

"*Stefon.* One of my surgical techs. People champion . . . what did they used to call them? Human resource managers? Whatever. Maybe you could even find something in the wine field that doesn't put your health at risk."

"Mom." Junie framed her words with her hands, homing in on her as if she were the parent and her mother, the child. "For the hundredth time. It's not Dad's dream anymore. It's mine. I'm the third generation of Harts to raise grapes. And it's only a matter of time before I start to break even." She took a meager salary, and she'd been doing all she could to keep up with her credit line and meet expenses. "All I need is a distributor. Sam says the market for Willamette pinot is growing so fast it can't keep up with the supply. It's just that I'm still new, I have a small yield, and my advertising budget's close to zilch."

"Tom Alexander gave me a call yesterday."

Junie cradled her forehead. "Why does he call you? Why doesn't he just call me? I'm twenty-eight years old. I don't need my mother to speak for me."

"Tom and I are colleagues as well as friends. We can communicate—unlike my own daughter and me."

Dr. Alexander probably owned tons of pretty coffee table books about grape growing and winemaking, but he'd never sifted the Willamette's ancient marine sediments through his long, elegant fingers. He hired other people to do the dirty work.

"Let me guess. He's worried about me."

"He asked how you were, that's all."

"He's trying to wheedle out of you whether he's going to be able get his hands on half my yield again this fall."

Last crush, Junie had had no choice but to sell some of her grapes to Dr. Alexander. Hand selling bottles out of her tasting room hadn't covered the payment on her line of credit, and coincidentally, Alexander had been scrounging for every bushel of grapes within a thousand acres of Clarkston.

Mom's eyes widened. "Honey. What's wrong with that? He's a shrewd businessman as well as an excellent physician."

Nothing was wrong with that. But Junie poured her heart and soul into her wine, while people like Tom Alexander used the interest off his investments to fund what was for him merely a prestigious hobby.

"He saved Storm's life."

Junie sighed. "That was a long time ago, and Storm's completely recovered."

"I'll never be able to repay him for that."

"None of us will, Mom. But that was then. Now, Tom Alexander just wants to buy up as many Clarkston area grapes as he can so his wine qualifies for the AVA stamp."

"AVA, XYZ. It's beyond me, the finer points of the wine business."

"Wine begins in the vineyard. You heard Dad say that a hundred times."

"About as many times as I heard him say, 'You can make a small fortune in the wine business, provided you start out with a large one.'"

"It's simply supply and demand. When the local vintners realized they were sitting on the mother lode of American pinot noir, they got together and lobbied for legal designation for six distinct viticultural areas. That changed everything. It painted a clear picture that wine from grapes grown on one side of the road tastes different from the other side, everything else being equal."

"You told me Tom's generosity was the only thing that got you by these past few months."

"Generosity? Hah. Yes, he bought some of my grapes. But now he's having them made into a wine that will compete directly against mine."

"You'll both benefit. What's wrong with that?"

How could Junie make Mom understand her grapes were her children? Selling to Tom Alexander had broken open old wounds. It had made her mourn Dad all over again. Shock, denial, anger—the whole cycle. She'd promised herself: *Never again.*

"I'm sorry I brought it up," her mother said.

"That's not what you left work early to talk to me about?"

Her mom looked genuinely puzzled. "No, not at all."

Good Lord. "Then what?"

"I bought myself a townhouse."

"What?" Junie blurted.

"If you'd listened to my messages, you would know. I have asked you and asked you to go house hunting with me. You never wanted to come. You know how bad traffic's getting, thanks to the tourists and all the new development. And that was a close call I had last winter on the ice during the cold snap. Besides, it doesn't make financial sense for me to waste two hours a day commuting when I could be operating."

Junie's head swam. *First Storm, then Dad.* Mom had been threatening to move to Portland ever since Dad died, but Junie hadn't wanted to believe she really would. "You're moving out of the farmhouse?" The house Dad had built for them with his own two hands? The only house Junie had ever lived in that wasn't on some military base?

"It's sweet that you're nostalgic about the house. But be practical. This starry-eyed vision of living off the land never came true for your grandfather. You saw how your dad lived growing up—practically in squalor. And, Junie, as I live and breathe, it's not going to work for you. I've tried to be patient. But you've been chasing your tail for five years, and where has it got you?"

"There's a saying: 'Do what you love and the money will follow.' Most small businesses don't show a profit in their early years. Wineries need even longer to get in the black."

Mom shook her head. "I wish I could convince you to get out now, while you're still young. Like Storm did."

Junie worked like a demon waiting tables and managing the vineyard without any real help. Now her deep-rooted anxiety bubbled up to the surface. Was she doomed, like Granddad and then Dad? Tears stung the back of her eyes. Was Mom right?

"The townhouse is in The Pearl. It's brand new, which means I can move in right away. It has three bedrooms, plus plenty of storage, and a cute balcony overlooking the shops and restaurants."

Junie envisioned The Pearl's crowded sidewalks, the cacophony of the late-night partiers when the bars let out.

Mom laid her hand on Junie's. There was a plea in her voice when she said, "Come to Portland with me. There're jobs, great food, culture, men. . . ."

"One thing about being a server, I'll never starve. And there are plenty of men in Clarkston. . . ."

The bell on the door signaled the arrival of a quartet of bearded lumbersexuals wearing colorful plaid shirts and skinny jeans. Bringing up the rear was an out-of-place, clean-shaven Hercules whose deltoids strained at the seams of his neatly pressed oxford shirt. He'd lost the navy blazer somewhere along the way, but Junie would have recognized him anywhere. When Manolo spotted her, he broke out in a spontaneous grin and scrubbed the top of his head, leaving his layered hair endearingly spiked. He angled his body in her direction.

Her heart stopped.

Then something spooked him, gave him pause. Maybe it was Sam and Heath's polite but guarded waves. The next thing she knew, Poppy had lassoed Manolo in with the others and led them toward a table on the other side of the café.

Only Keval peeled off from the group. But then, Keval had always been a maverick. In the words of Red McDonald, voted Clarkston's best therapist two years in a row, poor Keval had been "born without the ability to ascertain the emotional temperature of a room."

"Hello, ladies! Sam thought we could use some coffee—considering he got us all day drunk. Didn't expect to see you again so soon, Junie. And Dr. Hart! Don't you look precious? *Love* those glasses with your face shape."

"Hi, Kev." Junie sighed with a combination of relief and disappointment that he had been the one to come over instead of Manolo.

"Thank you, Keval. But now, if you'll excuse us, Junie and I are in the midst of an important discussion."

"Oops!" Keval's fingertips flew to his lips. "Sorry! Didn't mean to interrupt," he whispered loudly, tiptoeing backward. "Pretend I wasn't even here!"

"I meant *eligible* men," Mom said when Keval was out of hearing range.

Unlike Keval, Junie was apparently cursed with an *over*developed emotional barometer. The electricity that had been arcing between her and Manolo from the moment he'd entered her tasting room was stronger than ever, making the hair on her arms stand on end. It took all she had not to look over at him, to stay focused on the conversation at hand.

"Mom. I know what cities are like. When I was at college, I hung out in San Francisco more weekends than I can count."

"Even if we put the house and vineyard on the market right away, it will take a while to sell. But, Junie, the movers will be here first thing tomorrow morning for my things. I could ask them to take yours while they're there."

"*Mom!* I've moved seven times in my life—eleven, if you count each year of college! I'm sick of moving. I want Clarkston to be my forever home. Wait—*tomorrow?*"

Across the room, five heads jerked up in unison. Manolo caught her eye over the top of his menu. His face remained carefully blank.

Mom putting a date on her move somehow made it real. Junie felt her face threaten to crumble. She swallowed the hard lump in her throat. "I'm meeting a guy about the porch at noon. Besides, tomorrow's Saturday. A good day for tourists."

Her mom sank back in her chair with a pitying look. Then she drained her teacup and intoned, "There's something else."

Now what?

"I've met someone, Junie."

Another one?

Just then, Poppy brought the check. She glanced at Junie's gaping mouth and the half-eaten sticky bun, sitting forlornly on her plate. "Chin up, sweetie," she whispered, bending down to give her a tight squeeze. "I'll call you."

Chapter Five

"Touch-*y*!" Keval slid into the booth next to Manolo. "I *love* Dr. Hart. But watch out when she's in a mood."

Sam sipped his coffee without looking up. "Those two going at it again?"

"Who knows?" Keval picked up his menu. "Something about how the jobs and the food and the men are all better in Portland. Well, *duh*. Poor Junie looked like she was ready to burst into tears."

"It'll be interesting to see who gets the prize for most bullheaded in the end," said Sam.

"No one ever said making a living off the land was easy," said Rory, flexing his meaty hands. Manolo noted that they were already work-stiffened, the hands of a forty-year-old on a thirty-year-old's body.

"Preach it," Heath grunted in accord, ripping the top off a pack of sugar with his teeth and dumping it into his own cup o' joe. "My old man's been growing nursery stock all his life. Takes its toll on you."

The server they called Poppy appeared and took their orders. Before she scurried off again, Sam sent a subtle glance in the direction of Junie's booth. "What're you hearing over there?" he asked her under his breath.

That's a small town for you. Everyone up in everyone else's business. City neighborhoods were the same way. Manolo's folks knew everyone within ten blocks of the restaurant. He was glad he wasn't stuck in that cloistered life anymore.

"Oh, the usual. Junie's mom's talking about moving, Junie doesn't want to."

"Move? When?" Somehow, Manolo found himself sucked into the gossip mill.

"Tomorrow?" Junie's timely exclamation could be heard over the muted clatter of cutlery on china and the low buzz of conversation.

"That answer your question?" The waitress lifted a sardonic brow as she swooped their menus out of their hands. Manolo watched his new friends share a concerned look.

His phone vibrated.

"Hey, Amanda," he asked in a low voice, tucking his chin into his neck. "What'd you find out?"

"We don't have any volunteer opportunities for engineers in the Portland area this summer."

"Huh. Thanks for looking. Can't say I'm surprised."

"Your offer is much appreciated. Now, it's not too late to teach a summer course in 'Analyzing Earth-Friendly Design Technologies' outside of Mexico City. It's classified high-risk because of the current political situation, but I know that doesn't scare you."

"I might consider it if I weren't obliged to work in Oregon this summer."

"I thought as much, but it doesn't hurt to ask," she said with a smile in her voice. "On the other hand, I have some good news about Belize. Your biggest competition for the paid consultancy heard a rumor he's going to be redeployed. If that turns out to be true, the job is all but yours."

Manolo glanced over at Junie. Her heated conversation with her mother reminded him of the painful argument he'd had with his dad over joining the Army. He cursed the timing of this phone call. If not for that, he might've been able to pick up a word or two of what Junie was saying. But this was important.

"That is good news."

"Belize is a paradise, and you can still fly back once a month for your Reserves training. But keep in mind, Lieutenant, we'll need that six-month commitment."

Junie's worried face across the room made it hard for him to concentrate.

"Yep."

Amanda's laugh was cool and confident, exactly the way he remembered it. "Well, it sounds like you're preoccupied, so I'll let you go."

"Keep me posted."

"You know I will. It goes without saying, I'd love to have you."

"You mean for the consultancy."

"You know what I mean. If you do get the Belize job, I might have to pop down there once in a while, just to make sure you're behaving yourself."

Now communication between Junie and her mom seemed to have broken down completely. Junie was toying with her food, her mom looking around the room, tight-lipped.

"Manny?"

"Huh? Yeah. I'll look forward to that."

"Me too."

Chapter Six

A rectangular shaft of light poured into the farmhouse where the front door had sat propped open all morning. Dust motes danced eerily through the living room, recently emptied of the bulk of its furniture.

"Still time to change your mind, honey," Mom said, her caramel eyes peeping over the box she carried. "I think we could still squeeze in your bedroom suite." Her chic, short curls waved around her flowered headband. In her mid-fifties, she still had the body of the ballroom dancer she had been when Dad hauled some guy in handcuffs into the ER during her rotation at Fort Sam Houston.

Then again, thought Junie, *it's hard to get fat on fiddleheads and lamb's quarters.*

She tried to clear her head. If she was honest, it made perfect sense for Mom to move to Portland. What would her moving change for Junie, anyway? Mom didn't take any interest in the day-to-day workings of the vineyard. She didn't even get home in the evening until after Junie left for work at the Roadhouse.

Junie looked hard at her mother. Though she'd never in her life doubted that she was loved, her mom wasn't the cuddly, maternal kind. She had the precise, controlled movements of the competitive dancer she had once been combined with the self-assurance of the surgeon she was today.

It would always be a mystery to Junie how an effervescent San Antonio doctor had hooked up with a reticent farmer's son from the outskirts of Springfield, Missouri like Brendan Hart. But then, marrying Dad was only the first example of Mom's nearsightedness when it came to men. More than a year ago, to Junie's dismay, Mom had confided that she'd been fooling around on those dating apps.

Every time Mom "found someone," it ended up that he wasn't quite what he'd made himself out to be. One of them, it had turned out, was married. Another had pushed her out of his car in the parking lot of a restaurant when she'd turned down his advances.

It wasn't that she begrudged her mom male companionship. It was Mom's way of going about it that worried her. When she mentioned her concern to her therapist friend, Red had replied that there were entire books written about smart women who made dumb decisions when it came to love.

Junie sighed. It was going to be lonely in the house without Mom, even if they'd never been particularly close. She'd found comfort in knowing she wasn't alone at night, down that long country lane. Mom's simple wave good-bye out her car window in the light of a summer morning had been a sign that there was still some semblance of family left.

Now, under Mom's supervision, the men who'd come with the truck balanced the sofa half in and half out the door . . . that sofa that Dad had fallen asleep on watching the eleven o'clock news, back when Junie was in high school. The sofa she collapsed onto most nights after her shift at the restaurant, to scare herself silly watching *Worst-Case Scenario*. Where would she flop now, late at night? She could buy another couch, but it would never be the same.

Somehow the sofa had gotten stuck. "Bring it back in and turn it the other way," directed Mom from inside the house.

"Push!" said the older mover to his partner, contradicting her.

"I can't, goddam it! I gotta set 'er down a minute!" came the voice of the shorter, potbellied one, clutching the end that jutted out onto the front porch.

Then, as if by magic, a third pair of strong arms appeared from out of nowhere to tip the couch strategically by a few degrees. "Now," said a soft, deep voice. "Bring it through. Careful."

The couch slipped through the doorway like a greased pig. The opening filled with sunshine again, only to be darkened by the silhouette of a man so perfectly proportioned that the negative space was transformed into the cover of a romance novel.

"Morning!"

Junie squinted, suddenly horrified by her sweatpants and shapeless tee. "What are you doing here?"

"Junie!" her mother scolded. Deftly rearranging her face into a company smile, she sauntered over to the door. "Hello there! I don't believe we've met. I'm Jennifer Jepson-Hart."

Manolo nodded and took the hand she offered. "Manolo Santos, friend of Cap'n—er, Sam Owens. Pleased to meet you, ma'am."

"Well now. I just love a man with manners. Don't you, Junie?"

Junie's flip-flops slapped across the floor. "What are you doing here?" she repeated. She trusted him about as much as a nun doing squats in a cucumber field for exercise.

"I heard there were two ladies who might need a hand this fine morning."

"Where'd you hear that?"

Poppy's. If Manolo hadn't pieced it together himself, her gossipy friends would have gladly filled him in. One person's honesty was another's oversharing.

"Doesn't matter. That big Mayflower van sitting outside pretty much confirms it. Now"—he rubbed his hands together briskly, like there was nothing he relished more than a good moving day—"how can I be of assistance?"

"If you saw the van, then you must've seen the two rent-a-hulks that came with it. That's all we—"

"I have just the job for a big, strong man like you," Mom interjected. "Upstairs." She headed toward the steps and crooked a finger. "Follow me."

Behind Mom's back, Manolo gave Junie the V sign for victory.

How dare he show up uninvited, aggravating an already stressful day? She watched him ascend the steps to the part of the house that was reserved for family, close friends, and anonymous movers she'd never see again. Her heart stopped when she remembered that yesterday's panties were still on the floor where she'd dropped them and her bedroom door was open.

The sight of his rear end conjured up pure leashed energy. No doubt he'd have sprung up those steps three at a time if Mom wasn't in front of him, slowing him down. Manolo smelled like a honeyed blend of Middle Eastern spices and hot city sidewalks. If that scent were bottled, it'd be called Citizen of the World.

For the next hour or so, Manolo hoisted armload after armload of heavy objects out to the truck like they weighed nothing. A slipper chair, a sprawling schefflera in a terra-cotta pot. A large framed print in one hand and a box marked LINENS in the other.

What was it about Manolo Santos? Mom had known him ten seconds and she'd picked him over the bonded and insured movers to handle her most precious possessions. If that wasn't proof positive Manolo wasn't to be trusted, nothing was. How many sketchy characters from Matchup had Mom already taken a chance on, only to be disappointed? According to Red, lots of book-smart women got taken in by flashy smooth talkers. It was sheer luck that Dad, the man she'd married, had turned out to be the best of men.

For the next half hour, Junie stayed out of the way, rearranging the things left behind as Manolo lugged more of Junie's beloved childhood knickknacks out to the van to be wedged in between the larger pieces. There were the heavy, antique brass candlesticks and the box holding her paternal grandmother's crazy quilt and hand-embroidered tablecloth. Finally, she heard the heavy truck doors slam shut and the bolts screech into place, followed by footsteps coming back into the house.

"What else?" Manolo still seemed fresh as a daisy.

"Whew! That's it." Mom sighed. "Junie and I already packed up my car before you got here. I don't know where you came from, but I'm awfully glad you showed up when you did. How can I thank you?"

In the kitchen, where Junie stared into a wasteland of a cupboard containing only three mismatched mugs, she rolled her eyes at the way Mom sucked up to Mr. Hot and Handy.

"It was nothing. Just glad I could lend a hand. Sorry I didn't get here earlier."

"That's very kind of you," said Mom. "Now, I apologize, but I have to be going. I want to get to my new place before—er, the movers . . . Junie?"

Junie peeped out from behind the cupboard door.

"That's it. The movers are ready to go. I'm going ahead so I can get there first and unlock the door to the townhouse. Do you think you could fix Manolo a little breakfast, for all his trouble?" She turned to Manolo. "I'm afraid you caught us a little shorthanded, but I know there are some eggs in the fridge. Do you like eggs?"

Manolo appeared in the doorway, grinning like the Cheshire cat. "Love eggs. Eggs are my favorite."

Mom beamed. "Good! Junie, can you make Manolo some eggs, then, while I scoot?"

Junie faux-smiled and gave her mother a death glare. *"Suuuure!"*

"Great! I'll see you later then." Mom disappeared, only to reappear seconds later when she remembered to give Junie a parting hug and a peck. "Thanks for your help, sweetheart." She cupped Junie's chin and gave her a wistful parting glance. "I'll call you."

Junie trailed Mom out to the porch to find her already skipping down the front steps, her mind three steps ahead of her body.

"Mom, wait—who's this guy you started to tell me about?"

"Huh? Oh. A friend. Just a friend. I hope you'll come to like him, in time. He's very good for me," she replied, digging through her bag. "Now, where'd I put my keys? Heavens. Oh! There they are!"

Junie watched her mother's SUV, loaded to the gills, crunch down the gravel drive for her last time as a Clarkston resident. Then the movers fired up the van, fracturing the peaceful countryside.

The comforting warmth of an unseen hand settled on her shoulder. "You're going to miss her."

Junie whirled around. "If you knew that, why were you so eager to help her pack?"

He shrugged. "Not much I could've done to stop her."

Junie felt as though her guts had been ripped out without anesthesia and Manolo had assisted in the surgery.

She turned and shuffled back to the kitchen. Taking refuge behind the fridge door, she squeezed her eyes shut and pinched the bridge of her nose until later, when she could cry in private.

She came out holding the egg carton. "How do you like your eggs?" she asked in a lackluster voice.

Six feet, three inches of man planted in a wide-legged stance in the center of her kitchen made it seem suddenly smaller. All traces of mockery were now gone from his face. Junie shivered. They were all alone in this big old house, miles from anyone else. Anything could happen.

"You going to be okay?"

Damn, he was good. He had her almost believing he was sincere.

He walked over and rescued the cardboard carton from where it drooped precariously in her hand. "I'll do it."

"You?"

"I really screwed up yesterday. You won't let me take you to dinner, so . . ." He took over, opening and closing cupboards with a clatter. "Your mom must have left you a pan around here somewhere—"

She walked over and grasped the other end of the egg carton.

"You don't have to do that." She tugged. The carton fell to the floor, a few eggs cracking open on impact. She lifted a foot. *Ew.* A clear, viscous membrane stretched out between her toes and her flip-flop.

Before she knew it, Manolo was wiping up the mess with one hand and scraping out a chair leg with the other. "Sit while I rinse this dishtowel."

Mutely, she obeyed. Tramping around would only make a bigger mess.

He was back in a flash. "Pull your pant leg up."

The stretchy fabric folded up smoothly over her knee. Last night had been shaving night. Thank God for small favors.

"You're stubborn, you know that?" Chocolate-brown eyes smiled up at her.

Not stubborn. Just determined.

Manolo wrapped her calf with the steamy towel, drawing its warmth down over her ankle . . . her foot . . . her toes. Then he folded it over to the clean side and did it again.

She stared down at him, at a loss. She wasn't used to being taken care of. She didn't know how to react, what to do with her hands. Her fingers itched to reach out and ruffle his crown of thick hair. Her bird's-eye view of his shoulders made them appear even broader, his waist narrower. The movements of his biceps stretched the fine knit of his close-fitting sweater. Her lower belly tightened traitorously.

"Good news is, they're not all broken. Now, where were we? You got that pan?"

She got up and handed him a copper pan.

He twirled it expertly. "This looks barely used."

"That's because it is. When Mom's home—that is, when she *used to be* home—she practically subsisted on bean curd and kombucha tea."

"What tea?"

"Kombucha. You know. It's green and it looks like it has pond scum growing on the top."

Manolo was already drizzling the pan with olive oil. "That some kind of Left Coast thing?"

Junie shrugged. "One of those ew-tricious fad foods. I never traffic in the stuff, myself."

"A girl after my own heart. Can't go wrong sticking with the classics. You shouldn't keep your olive oil above the stove. It gets rancid when it's exposed to heat. Got any cheese? Any kind will do. It's the wrong time of the year for tomatoes, unless you got canned. Back east, I only buy fresh ones in season. They're only good in August and September. Ah, here's the salt. Same deal with your spices. You ought to move them away from the stove."

Junie watched, mesmerized. He had the moves of a professional chef. Both arms were in constant motion, one tipping the pan to swirl the oil, one rummaging around for ingredients. Standing on her tiptoes, she peered over his shoulder. His thick, muscular shoulder. With every movement came the ripple of biceps and his rugged yet sophisticated scent. She stood so close that if he weren't so into his task he'd probably have felt her breath on him. So close, she jumped when he whipped around unexpectedly.

"Cheese?" he repeated, like she didn't understand English.

She blinked. "I'll look, but don't get your hopes up. Mom doesn't do dairy, and I practically live on peanut butter and granola."

A moment later, she slapped a long-forgotten bar of cheddar into his outstretched left hand. His right was occupied with working the pan, tipping, swirling, letting it clatter onto the burner with a loud bang. "Use this at your own risk. I don't know how long it's been in there."

He ripped back the plastic and sniffed. "It'll do. Grater?"

"Huh?"

"Never mind." He pulled out a drawer and rummaged around impatiently, pulling out a knife, using his thumb to test its edge. "Cutting board?"

Junie remembered one in the tall, skinny cabinet next to the sink.

"Why just peanut butter?" he asked with his back to her, slicing the cheese into uniform slivers.

She shrugged. "It's a cheap source of quick energy."

"You need to get out and get a decent meal from time to time, if only for a mental break. Helps you come back to your work refreshed."

Yet another reference to a date? What was that—three? Not that she was counting.

"Just one more thing. Be right back." He flipped off the gas. "Get out a bowl for me?" Then he dashed out the front door.

From the kitchen window, Junie watched him jog out and grab a beat-up duffel bag off the front seat of a late-model black pickup.

Back inside, he pulled a jar and a plastic squeeze bottle from his bag.

"You carry your own condiments?" she asked in disbelief.

"I've learned to be prepared."

"There's prepared, and then there's obsessed."

He flashed her that chandelier grin. "It's in my blood. Italians love to eat. You don't know that?"

She picked up the jar and examined it. "I know other Italian people, and they don't carry around their own homemade seasonings."

He turned back to the range. "Ah. Maybe they've never been stranded in the desert where they had to survive on dried grass for a week. Maybe they don't know food like I do." With a flick of his wrist, the blue flame rekindled. Then, one-handed, he broke the remaining eggs into the Pyrex cup she'd found and began whisking them.

Junie sidled over to watch. "That's a nice pickup you've got out there."

"Sam offered me the use of his while I'm here. Said there was no use in renting one since he usually drives the van anyway, but I'd feel better having my own. Something about a man's truck. So I went over to the dealership and a guy hooked me up with this loaner for the summer."

By the time she got some cutlery and a couple of plates, the perfectly turned omelets, oozing cheese and topped with his spices and special sauce, were done.

Manolo scraped in his chair and arranged his napkin on his lap while Junie poured him some coffee.

"Mmmm," Junie mumbled the moment the rich fluffiness touched her tongue.

He grinned, digging in with his fork. "Yeah? You like that?"

The warm, delicious food served by a warm, delicious man thawed her usual reserve. "Okay." She swallowed, laughing in spite of herself. "No one just shows up at my house for the second day in a row, helps my mom lift heavy furniture, and cooks me a gourmet breakfast. Who are you, for real? Besides Sam's Army buddy?"

"Lieutenant Manolo Santos from Hoboken, New Jersey, ma'am." He pulled a card from his wallet and handed it to her. "At your service."

"Where'd you get the culinary skills?"

He took a slug of his coffee. "I grew up in my family's pizzeria. While all my friends were outside learning to ride bikes, I was learning the restaurant business. How to sling dough and make marinara."

"Your parents had their own restaurant?"

"My parents, their parents, and so on, all the way back to Naples. And I'm not talking Florida." His plate empty, he wiped his mouth and laid his napkin next to his plate. "All that was missing was some good bread. Maybe next time."

Next time?

He rose to clear the dishes, but not before she finished eating. That small, considerate gesture didn't go unnoticed by a seasoned waitress like Junie. It must have been one high-class pizza shop where Manolo learned the ropes. The dives she'd worked in rushed service to turn over tables as quickly as possible. But she forgot about that when she saw how he looked behind the big apron sink— as if all the pieces of a puzzle had suddenly fallen into place.

Back when the house was under construction, Mom had scolded Dad for going overboard on a kitchen designed for whipping up elaborate feasts and hosting large gatherings instead of something more suited to a small family in which the mother was at work more than she was at home. Admitting Mom was right felt disloyal to Dad's memory, but Junie had to admit, the microwave got used more than the stove.

"You didn't want to continue the tradition?"

He shook his head. "No way. Not for me, all work day in and day out, with no time for a life. And it wasn't just my father and me. My mother and my three sisters worked, too. Seven days a week, fifty-two weeks a year. Including Christmas."

"The restaurant is still there, then?"

"Still there," he said, retrieving the dishwashing liquid from under the sink. "Forty years. Opened the year my parents got married. My sisters have mostly taken over, but my parents still go in every day."

"You think you'll go back someday?"

He shrugged. "Plenty of time to think about that later."

"I used to be part of a family business. Now I'm a one-man band: vineyard manager, cellar rat, and winemaker. Not that I'm complaining. I'm the luckiest girl in the world to be doing what I've always wanted to do."

Hand cupped under the running water to gauge the temperature, he cocked his head and smiled. "To each his own. Better you than me, sweetheart."

Junie hopped up. "You cooked. I'll clean."

"I got it. Hand me that pan, will you?"

She tidied up around him while stealthily scrutinizing his body some more from behind.

He whirled around just as she was returning the dishcloth to the sink. "'Bout time I get back to town. Sam had a meeting, but it's probably over by now. We're getting together at the site of the new consortium this afternoon."

Feeling oddly disappointed, Junie thrust her hands into her pajama bottom pockets. "I have work to do, too."

"Got time to walk me out to the truck?"

"Let me slip on my boots."

Chapter Seven

Outside, Manolo pointed to the scaffolding surrounding the side of the house. "What's the story with that?"

"My dad designed a new side porch, but he died before he could finish it. I've been trying to finish it myself along with taking care of the vineyard and everything else, but things keep happening."

"What kind of things?"

"I've hired two different guys to do it, but they both disappeared after a couple of weeks. Then something else comes up that I need to throw money at. The winery's not turning a profit yet. The porch won't make me any money, but the vineyard will, so that takes priority."

He stood pondering the framed-out structure. "Have you bought the rest of the lumber and the other materials yet?"

She pointed with her chin to a metal roofed building. "They're over there, in the barn."

He walked over and tried an exposed floorboard. "Decks feel secure. It's just a matter of cutting the railings, attaching them to the posts, and adding the top caps." He tipped his head back to scrutinize the house as a whole. "Good, solid construction. Shame your family didn't get to live in it longer."

"I know. We moved from base to base my entire childhood. When people asked me where I was from, I didn't know what to say. Sometimes at Christmas we'd visit my dad's family in Missouri. I envied my cousins, growing up in the same place their whole life, having what I called 'old friends.' Granted, I had friends from all over, probably even more than they did, but no one who'd known me all my life. Then, when I was thirteen, my dad retired from the military and bought this land so he could grow grapes on it and make wine. I was so happy to finally have a home of our own."

Manolo sniffed at the irony. "You couldn't wait to find a home, and I couldn't wait to leave mine."

Lost in separate thoughts, they ambled out to Sam's truck, drawing out the short trip.

"Your dad was the one who got you interested in wine?"

"At first, it was a hobby passed down to him from my grandfather. Granddad was a tenant farmer. Growing up, his family didn't have much money, but they had fresh-grown vegetables . . . homemade wine . . . fish pulled from the Ozark Mountain streams, and venison Granddad hunted in the woods. Dad said it was the best life a kid could have. Then the landowner sold the ground to a developer. Dad and his family moved to an apartment in Springfield, and at the age of forty-one, Granddad got a job in shipping and receiving for one of those big-box stores."

She looked up. "Can you imagine the prospect of spending the rest of your life endlessly rotating stock inside a dark warehouse?"

Manolo didn't respond.

"The day Dad graduated from high school, Granddad drove him down to the nearest recruiter's office without telling him or my grandma where they were going until the papers were signed, rather than doom him to the same fate."

"Your mom like to cook? 'Cause that kitchen was made for someone who does."

"Honestly, she's too busy with her practice. But Dad didn't take shortcuts. He wanted to build us something solid and lasting."

"He did a commendable job. Beautiful brick chimney. I saw the fireplace in your bedroom when I was helping your mom."

Junie blushed. First her bills, now her dirty underwear. Could it get any more embarrassing?

"At least your dad left you with a comfortable foundation. You can even walk to work."

The late morning sun felt warm on her back, her stomach was pleasantly full, and a cute, smart builder was joking with her. A smile tugged at the corners of Junie's mouth.

"Speaking of work, how's the wine business?"

"I think my pinot could really go somewhere—if I could find a way to get more people back here to taste it, get the word out."

"Do you have a distributor?"

A burst of laughter escaped from her throat. "You're kidding, right? I'm still hand watering the vines myself from the world's longest hose that I pieced together. No. Sam's been using his connections to help me look, but he hasn't found anyone yet. It's tricky. Distributors are looking for businesses that are already established, but how are you supposed to get established without a distributor? I manage my own website and hire Keval to help out with occasional promo. During the crush time, I take on part-timers to do the picking and pressing."

"Tell you what," Manolo said as he opened the truck door and slung his condiment-filled duffel over onto the passenger seat. "I'll get a handle on Sam's project, then come back in a couple days and you can show me what you got in the barn. It won't take long to slap that porch together. Hell, I'd pay *you* to let me do it, do it just for the fun of it. Nice change of pace from supervising others. Then you can put that behind you and focus on your grapes. . . ."

Junie's work-weary heart swelled as she watched him climb into his truck. The door slammed shut, the engine roared, and the window slid down. Manolo draped his elbow out the window, looking as at home in his rented truck as a cowboy in a well-worn saddle.

"Not that I think you have a snowball's chance in hell of being successful at this."

Before she knew what she was doing, she hauled off and gave his truck a mighty kick.

"Hey!"

"You self-righteous . . . misogynistic . . . moron!" She should have known better than to let down her guard.

"You're lucky this is a rental!"

"For your information, I don't need your help, Mr. High and Mighty. I've got this. I've got another guy coming at noon."

With that, she turned and flounced away. There were no breaks in this life. Everything always came back to cold, hard reality: The only person she could depend on was herself.

Manolo yelled to her back, "Where'd you find this one?"

"None of your business!" she hollered without bothering to turn around. This next guy had better work out. The crush could start as soon as August, and if the porch was still unfinished during the high point of the tourist season, it wouldn't look good. Not good at all.

He called out over the engine. "Check his references, and this time don't pay anything up front. You change your mind, you got my cell."

Change her mind? She whipped around, hair flying, and jammed her fists on her hips. "That'll be the day! I wouldn't take your help if you were the last builder on earth. You hear me? No way are you laying so much as a finger on my porch!"

"Suit yourself." He grinned, lifting a paw-like hand in a wave.

The truck's suspension bounced audibly over the uneven ground before fading into the distance. Junie didn't look back again until she reached the front door, just in time to see taillights disappearing over the rise.

Her anger wilted almost as fast as it had sprung up. Now she was really, truly alone.

Still, being alone was better than putting your trust in someone only to be let down yet again.

Her toe started to throb.

Chapter Eight

All the next day, until twilight chased her indoors to the hush of the empty farmhouse, Junie kept an ear peeled for an approaching vehicle while she ran her gloved hand down every trunk of every vine to remove unwanted suckers.

But the porch guy never showed.

Saturday night, since her favorite couch was gone, she plodded upstairs to watch *Worst-Case Scenario* in bed.

She woke at dawn on Sunday morning with a swollen toe and a half-empty jar of peanut butter for company.

She limped through the clanging door of Poppy's Café as she did every Sunday morning, to find Poppy and Red already cradling mugs of coffee. The smell of Stumptown's Holler Mountain mingled with relief.

Once she was tucked into their favorite corner booth, Poppy and Red gave her their advice.

"No." Resolutely, Junie folded her arms. "I'm not going to do it."

Poppy reached across the Formica and squeezed Junie's hand. "Listen to Red. She wasn't voted Clarkston's best family therapist for nothing. Everyone knows she gives the best professional advice money can buy, and she gives it to you for free."

Junie studied the ceiling. "I know. I know you're right, but I can't take Manolo Santos up on his offer."

"Why not?" Poppy pleaded.

"So many reasons!" She massaged her temples.

"Let's take them apart, one by one," Red counseled.

"Why do always you have to be so logical?"

Red smiled evenly. "I call it being objective, and I can do it because I'm not emotionally attached to your issues. Not to say I'm not concerned about you. I consider you a dear friend, not a client." Red folded her hands and waited patiently for Junie to begin.

"Okay. Well, for starters, he's so freaking *cocky*! Strolling in like he owned the place, strutting around my tasting room like a rooster . . . you should have seen them. Manolo was all like, 'To the Beaver State!' And Sam and Heath and Rory are all like"—she lowered her voice several octaves—"'Yeah!' I'm telling you, in a single afternoon, Manolo Santos erased a million years of progress for the men around here. One minute they're sensitive, twenty-first-century human beings, the next they're bumping chests like Neanderthals."

Poppy giggled. "I would have loved to have seen that."

"No, you wouldn't have," replied Junie. "It wasn't pretty. Even Keval was caught in his spell!"

"Sounds like men being men to me," said Red. "Add a little alcohol, stir, and you've got a pissing contest. I wouldn't make too much of it."

"You're forgetting . . . I was stuck there in the middle of them."

"Things aren't always as they seem. Sometimes people act over-confident—show off—to compensate, when deep down inside, they're insecure."

"Insecure? Manolo Santos? Wait till you meet him. Then tell me he's insecure. He had the nerve to tell me that even if I did let him work on the porch—*for fun,* mind you—there was no way I could ever make my winery successful!"

"He came in here yesterday with Sam and the rest of them," Poppy told Red. "He reminds me of someone. I've been racking my brain, but I can't think of who it is."

Poppy even *scowled* prettily.

"Daryl Decaprio," Junie breathed, methodically shredding her napkin into confetti. "Manolo and Daryl look like twins. They even smile the same way, with that little curl of their upper lip."

"That's it!" Poppy pointed at Junie.

Practically every woman in Clarkston had had a thing for Daryl at one time or another.

Red tilted back her head and gave Junie a wise, Freudian look—if Freud had had freckles and strawberry-blond eyelashes. "Just because he looks like Daryl doesn't mean he's unreliable."

"If that's all it was, I wouldn't be so concerned. But he's also a huge flirt. I'm not sure how to take him."

"But Manolo is old friends with Sam. What better recommendation is there than that?"

"Says the one who's madly in love with Sam!" Junie shot back with a friendly grin. "Don't pretend you're not. Everyone saw how you 'accidentally' spilled your Riesling down Sam's shirt at his homecoming party."

"Bee Tee Dubs," Poppy added thoughtfully, "I've been meaning to give you props on that move. I may have to borrow that someday. . . ."

"Who says that wasn't an accident?" Pink splotches dotted Red's milky skin. "But this isn't about me. This Manolo must have *some* redeeming qualities."

"Well, Sam did say that he's done a lot of work on schools and hospitals and things."

"See? Somebody who devotes his time to improving the lives of others can't be all bad."

Junie sighed. "So what I'm hearing you say is, go back to him with my tail between my legs and tell him I need him to finish the porch, after I already turned him down."

"It depends. How important to you is the success of this fall's crush?"

"It's everything. You know that."

Red lifted her palms. "Well, then."

"But I barely know the guy! And what I do know, I don't like. It's embarrassing. Humiliating!"

"So you turned him down?" said Poppy. "That made perfect sense at the time. You already had another construction guy on his way over."

Beneath the table, Junie curled her toes. She'd kept that little detail about kicking Manolo's truck to herself, but the throbbing was a constant reminder. "Manolo knew that guy wouldn't show up, and even if he did, I could tell he didn't think it was a good idea, hiring yet another Joe Schmoe. Maybe I'm naïve, but I just can't afford a professional's rates right now."

"Junie." Crystal-blue eyes gazed out steadily from beneath pale brows.

Junie squirmed, wishing she'd never come into town today and run into Red MacDonald, certified wise woman. *Here it comes—the hard stuff.*

"How long have we known each other?"

Awash in a decade and a half of shared memories, the three exchanged faraway looks.

"Since that time we went up to Mr. Sullivan at the hardware store and asked him to show us his bird, and he turned beet red 'cause he didn't know we meant his pet parrot?" said Junie.

"And then when we realized why he was blushing, we started laughing so hard we could hardly stand up?" finished Poppy.

Peals of laughter echoed through the café. Across the room, Jed Smith, the president of Clarkston Savings Bank, glanced up over his Sunday paper and smiled complaisantly.

"No!" exclaimed Poppy. Her hand shot up and she bounced on her padded booth. "I know! I know! That Christmas when we snuck a bottle of your dad's eggnog and you got drunk and made up your own words to 'Grandma Got Run Over by a Reindeer' and then you peed your pants and there was a puddle on Red's bedroom carpet—"

Red's trademark loud, lusty laugh echoed through the café. "My mother never found out that wet spot wasn't from our golden retriever. Poor Zak was never allowed in my room again!"

Poppy had to hold on to the table edge to keep from falling out of her seat.

"Stop!" Junie crossed her legs. "You're making me do it again!"

"Don't!" Poppy thrust out her hands, suddenly sober. "Don't you dare pee in my booth!"

Jed Smith rattled his paper, signaling that a little merriment was fine, but he was trying to read over here.

"A day that will live in infamy. So," Red finally sputtered, "what I'm trying to say, Junie, is that I love you like a sister. And I would never put words in your mouth." She wiped a leftover tear from the corner of her eye. "But to boil a year's worth of counseling sessions down to one breakfast—hear me out. We know that a lot of good things have happened in your life. A lot of *great* things. You had loving parents. A secure childhood, even if you did move more than you would have liked. A terrific education. Wonderful friends."

Poppy waggled her fingers in a self-congratulatory wave while silently mouthing the word, *Me.*

"I know. You guys . . ." Words failed her. Her nostrils stung with unshed tears.

Red continued in a calm, professional manner. "And, also like everybody else, some not-so-great. Storm walked away from his promises. Then you lost your dad just when you two were getting started with the business."

"Don't forget, her mom left too," Poppy hiccupped cheerfully.

"Something about Manolo makes me...I can't describe it." Junie fidgeted. "I feel like . . . like I'm teetering on the brink of a big vat of honey."

Poppy slurped from her trademark flowered mug. "It's called lust," she stated matter-of-factly.

"Because although honey may be sweet, it's hard to swim in, and you might even drown?" asked Red.

"You tell me. You're the therapist."

"You're afraid he's going to let you down, like the others." Red sat back in her seat, satisfied with her diagnosis.

"Yeahhhhh..." Poppy nodded in wide-eyed revelation. "It's about trust. It's a trust thing!" She touched Red's arm with the reverence due a high priestess. "You give such. Good. Shoulder."

Junie gathered her bag and hoodie and slid out of her seat. "Spoken like a true Portlandian." She sighed.

The gauntlet had been thrown. As of today, this fall's harvest was still nothing but a gleam in Junie's eye. But once the vines flowered and the flowers developed into berries, they'd grow fatter with every passing sunrise until they were finally full term. When their time finally came, Junie would have to scramble to get her grapes picked and pressed at their peak of juicy ripeness. The crush was no time to be worrying about pimping her property. The time for that was now.

Junie knew what she had to do.

She called Keval.

Chapter Nine

"**Y**ou are such a coward," Keval spat when she'd filled him in. *Dear, sweet Keval.*

"Red has you pegged to a T."

"I know," Junie replied miserably. "But you're my very best friend, and I need you more than I've ever needed you before. You'll intercede for me, ask Manolo to finish my porch?" Junie winced, praying he'd say yes.

"I most certainly will not! You're going to ask him yourself. Hold on a sec. I'll put him on the phone."

"He's *there*? At the consortium?"

"Hold on to your tiara. I've got eyes on His Hotness, as we speak."

"Shhh! Don't talk so loud." Instinctively, she lowered her own voice. "He might hear you. What's he doing?"

"Talking with Peter Dubois. You know Peter, don't you? He's the winemaker over at Crimson Cellars. He's got the most amazing—"

"Keval! I'm going home now to think about this. I have to burn the cuttings from yesterday's pruning—"

"Uh-uh, no, siree, girlfriend. I don't think so. You're going to get your bony ass over here *tout de suite* and ask Mister Manolo Santos for his help in person, like a man. If you're not here in ten minutes I'm going to tell him you're madly in love with him and you want him to do you over a wine barrel. Ciao."

"Keval!"

Her phone's screen went dark.

The home that Sam operated his consortium out of was right around the corner from the café. Junie arrived to find cars wedged every which way in his driveway, with more lining the street. Good for Sam and the wine community. Bad for Junie. It would be hard enough to admit she needed Manolo's favor when they were alone, let alone beg him with a bunch of townspeople and fellow growers as witnesses.

Junie managed to squeeze her car into an opening along the curb half a block away and started walking back to Sam's. The closer she got to the house, the more anxious she grew. Only sheer determination kept her from turning around and sprinting back to her car. Pausing at the threshold, she took a steadying breath, lifted her chin, and walked in.

It was easy to see why Sam needed a new building. The entire downstairs of his settlement-era house had been taken over by the fast-growing consortium. Knots of industry people stood around talking shop. It was like stumbling into a cocktail party for hipster farmers, only instead of cocktails they were all clutching to-go cups of gourmet coffee. The ubiquitous Levis and Danner boots made it impossible to tell the smallest growers from the most renowned winemakers.

"Junie!" chirped a petite brunette. Holly Davis, one of Sam's sales reps.

Junie jerked her head toward the perimeter of the room. Maybe she could keep this whole thing on the down low.

Holly met her along the wall. "Long time no see!"

"You know how it is. You wouldn't happen to know where Sam's friend from out of town is, would you?"

"Manolo?" Holly faked a swoon. "Is he not the most gorgeous specimen you've ever laid eyes on?"

"That's the one. Did you see him here somewhere?"

"He went that way." She pointed toward the kitchen. "Good luck!"

Junie wove through the packed living room and into the kitchen, returning a wave here, a nod there. Along the way, her ears picked up fragments of market news.

"... spike in sales is a classical example of supply and demand ..."

"... forecast for warmer conditions, thanks to this El Niño we're having ..."

An evocative blend of spices, leather, and forest floor stopped her in her tracks. He was here, somewhere. She could smell him. Then, from over Peter Dubois's shoulder, she heard a thin, strained voice.

". . . you figure eight to ten tons of grapes per acre. I'm counting on acquiring at least fifty tons from Broken Hart Vineyards."

Junie's ears strained to hear what came next.

"Are you talking about Junie Hart's place?"

A callous laugh grated on Junie's ears. "Junie's had a run of bad luck. There's not a person in this room believes she's going to make it. She was forced to sell me half her yield last year to keep the wolf from her door."

The owner of that voice loved holding forth about wine. But try asking him if he'd ever spilled his own blood in the Jory soil like Dad had. Ever stayed up all night on frost watch. Or ever made a single one of the myriad decisions required to create a living, breathing work of art, which was what wine was, when it came right down to it.

Anger and humiliation froze Junie's feet to the floorboards.

"Hey, Junie! Come on over here." A hand weaved between two women deep in conversation and wrapped itself around Junie's bicep. "We were just talking about you."

The women gave way, and Junie found herself held captive against Manolo's side, face-to-face with her worst enemy. Suddenly all of her attention was focused on the parts of her body that were touching his, as if the rest of her had ceased to exist. Somehow, she managed a feeble smile.

Unaware of her dilemma, the man who'd insulted her took a sip from his to-go cup.

"Junie," said Manolo, "I was just telling—sorry, what was your name again?"

"Alexander. Tom."

"I was just about to tell Tom here how pumped I am that you're letting me intern this summer."

"Intern?" She looked up at him blankly.

"Can't wait to get started. Dividing my time between the consortium and one of the finest small vineyards in Oregon. Right?" His mighty squeeze forced the air from her lungs.

"Right!" she squeaked.

Tom's haughty smile shrank in a most satisfying way.

"Good to meet you, Tom." Manolo dismissed him with a single

pump of his hand. "But Junie and I have plans." He winked down at her, lifting her off her feet with another squeeze. "Ready?"

"Ready!"

"Let's jet."

Outside, Junie finally could breathe again. "Thank you."

"I should be the one thanking you, for giving me an excuse to get away from that guy. Who was he—other than a massive bore?"

"An investor who gets a rush out of being on the cutting edge of a trend," Junie said drily. "That's the only way for people like him to be a part of the mystique of winemaking—buying their way in. What I meant was, thanks for sticking up for my vineyard, saying you were going to be my intern."

"I'm in, aren't I?" With Junie still tucked under his arm, he peered down at her, eyes teasing yet genuinely hopeful. "Can't think of anyone better than you to give me the real dirt on pinot noir."

"I thought—"

"Sure, I'm here to lend Sam a hand. But I like a good bottle of wine almost as much as I appreciate a good New York strip steak . . . a tiramisu with perfectly whipped mascarpone. I've been hearing about Oregon pinot noir for a while. Thought it was high time I saw for myself what all the talk was about. All I need now's someone to teach me." He looked at her expectantly.

He was the most contradictory man she'd ever met. "Me, teach you about pinot noir?" She huffed a laugh. "Nothing could go wrong with that."

"I know. You're busy. But if you can take some time out of your schedule to show me the ropes, I'll pay you back by fixing your porch. Even Steven."

"Get Sam to teach you about wine."

"He will, some. But it's always good to get different perspectives."

She smirked. "I thought you said I was a lost cause."

"I know from experience it's hard enough to run a business when you got six people sharing the load. I can't imagine how one woman—one *person*, of either gender—could do it. The odds are stacked against you. But who am I to judge? I love a barter, though, and this is a perfect chance to barter services if I ever saw one. Straight up, now. I'm not kidding around."

Junie looked at him sideways. "No strings?"

"Tit for tat."

She smiled in spite of herself. "You better quit while you're ahead."

He stuck out his hand. "So we got a deal."

Deep as her reservations about Manolo Santos were, this just might work. At least she wouldn't be taking charity. She put her hand in his.

"What do you think? Sam and I are done for today. We could start right now—if that works for you."

He walked her to her battered, old Volvo and held her door. She climbed in and he slapped the roof. "These things were built like tanks."

"My dad got it for me, used, for college, nine years ago."

"Sounds like you and your Dad were pretty close."

"We were." But for the first time in a long time, Junie's dad wasn't at the forefront of her mind. She was thinking about Manolo's eyelashes. They were as long and dark as the lashes on a soft-eyed horse she'd once trusted to gallop on the trail off Meadowlake Road—before it threw her. "I guess you're close to your dad, too. I mean, he gave you all his recipes."

His response was another slap on the roof that made her jump in her jeans and that knockout grin that made her heart race like she'd just run a mile. "So. Where do we start?"

"If you really want to know about Oregon wine, there're a couple of good places on the way home. You can drive with me and I'll bring you back later."

The next thing she knew, he was sitting next to her, filling her car with his presence and smoky-sweet scent. What on earth was she doing? More than ever, she felt as if she were balancing on the edge of a precipice.

"Let's roll," he said, eagerly peering out the windshield.

This could not end well. Anyone who'd seen as many episodes of *Worst-Case Scenario* as she had knew that.

Chapter Ten

They headed north on the Tualatin Valley Highway. Manolo was as interested in Junie's lithe body as he was in the distant mountains ringing the valley. She was close enough to touch. It would be so easy. All he'd have to do was just—

"Want to listen to some music?" she interrupted his thoughts, turning on the radio.

"Sure."

A sweet, timeless love song came on.

"This song reminds me of my dad," she said. "I used to take it for granted that we'd dance to it at my wedding."

If there was one subject that never failed to throw cold water on steamy fantasies, it was weddings.

"That's the Coast Range," she said, humming along with the song. "They're a pretty cadet blue from here, don't you think? It looks different up close, where we go hiking."

He pictured her hill climbing in skimpy shorts and sturdy boots.

"Who do you hike with?"

"Someone's always hiking or waterskiing or floating down the river. You'll find out, once summer gets here."

Junie turned up a narrow lane until a long stucco edifice, sitting like an ocean liner in a sea of swaying orange flowers, came into view. Closer to the building, the wildflowers gave way to meticulous landscaping and a sign that read, ANNIE'S WINERY.

"Now, this looks like something you'd see in California."

"You've done Napa, then? Or was it Sonoma? We were stationed at the Presidio, just south of there, for a few years. That's when the wine bug really bit Dad hard. Annie's was one of the first vineyards to be planted in Clarkston. They've been growing old-vine Riesling here since the eighties."

Napa had nothing on Annie's, in Manolo's opinion. A dozen or so people were eating lunch under the market umbrellas dotting the spacious patio. "They have a restaurant! And look at that view! I bet you can see ten, fifteen miles." He headed off in the direction of the patio to explore.

"Oh no, you don't." Junie snagged his arm. "This is an educational field trip. Inside."

"You need to relax, you know that?" he replied, allowing her to steer him in the opposite direction.

"I'm here to teach you about wine."

"Someone needs to teach *you* how to have fun." But there were worse things than being led by the nose by a West Coast girl with eyes the color of blue spruce and muscles toned by honest, outdoor labor, not bought in some smelly city gym.

Inside, modern art hung on burgundy-colored walls between custom cabinetry designed to showcase bottles. The lighting was low, the atmosphere hushed, the bar stools upholstered in gray velvet.

"Whoever built this Shangri-la spared no expense," Manolo muttered, looking around at the top-notch construction.

A barista in braids who looked flexible enough to wrap her legs around her neck greeted Junie by name. Then she examined Manolo with open curiosity. Earthy, Pacific Northwest girls were miles apart from glossy New York women, but a come-on look was a come-on look, no matter where in the world you were.

"Who's your friend?" the barista asked Junie, her eyes glued to him.

Junie slid nonchalantly onto a bar stool. "This is Manolo. Manolo, Cerise."

"You look like you're not from around here," purred Cerise.

Whatever vibes Cerise was putting out, Junie either didn't notice or didn't care. Which only made her more intriguing to Manolo. Like a devil on his shoulder, Sam's hands-off warning came back to him.

Junie asked Cerise, "Can I try your Riesling? And Manolo will do a vertical of whatever pinot vintages you have available."

Cerise poured Junie's white and set down Manolo's two glasses of the same wine from sequential years, for him to compare.

"Cheers." Junie lifted her glass. "See?" she added playfully. "I'm relaxed. I'm drinking something purely for pleasure, not to compare it to the kind of wine that I make."

"You're not fooling me." He laughed. "You already know what these taste like." Dutifully, he tried what she'd selected for him. He waited until more patrons entered and parked themselves down the bar, diverting Cerise's attention, before telling Junie his opinion.

"This one smells like a scorched cherry pie. The other tastes like a day-old teabag."

Junie gave him a catlike smile and an almost imperceptible nod of approval.

Leaving their drinks unfinished, they went back out on the highway, passing a line of bicyclists in colors bright as jockeys' silks and a nineties-era Subaru with a bumper sticker that read, I CAN SEE YOUR TETONS.

"Where to next?" he asked.

"Annie's is one of the more impressive estates. Now I'm going to take you somewhere a little less fancy."

She drove him to a modest A-frame with no sign out front. Just like before, Junie did the ordering. "You see how transparent this red is?"

Manolo took a sip and licked his lips. "Is that fig? No, raisin, with a hint of wet leaves. Whatever, it's way better than the stuff at the last place we stopped."

"Fig. And congratulations. You've just learned your first lesson: You can't judge a wine by its tasting room."

"Point taken. But I keep thinking about the food back at Annie's. You saw how full the patio was, even though the wine wasn't that great. Offering food's a marketing thing, Junie. It's a no-brainer: The more people drink, the more they want to eat."

"No-brainer, huh? Where's the research?"

"I grew up in the restaurant business. I saw it with my own eyes."

"I thought you wanted to get serious about wine? Or was that just another one of your lines?"

"Lines?"

"I have a mirror. I know I'm no beauty."

Manolo studied Junie frankly, taking her apart with his eyes. Her hair was plain brown, her brows dark and thick like his sisters', not like the plucked and polished women he was typically drawn to. Her nails were short and bare, and she could use some flesh on her angular frame.

"Fair enough. You want my unvarnished take on beauty? I was brought up by four mothers—my mom and three older sisters—Paloma, Maria, and Isabel. I was the baby, and they spoiled me rotten. For eighteen years, not a day went by that someone didn't tell me how pretty I was. I survived being suffocated—barely—but my respect for 'pretty' didn't. Beautiful is boring, you ask me. All luck and no merit."

Junie snorted. "I guess I asked for that," she said, looking down at where she drew a tight circle on the bar with the foot of her glass.

He set the tips of his fingers on its base, stilling it to make his point. "There's way more to you than a pretty face. There's something substantial about you. Call it . . . integrity."

"How can you say that? You barely know me."

"I know it by the passion in your voice when you talk about your wines. Your devotion to living your dream." Not to mention, her earnestness, which threatened to break his heart. "Besides"—he took another sip of the good wine—"I've been getting an earful. You have a broad fan base."

"Not according to Tom Alexander."

"The exception that proves the rule."

"Too bad he's so obsessed with my grapes."

Manolo laughed. "I'm glad it's just your grapes he's interested in."

She smiled self-consciously, endearing herself to him even more.

"What about you? You already know something about wine. I can tell by the words you use to describe it."

He shrugged. "Who, me? Not so much."

"Figs? Wet leaves? Liar."

"I told you, I grew up in the restaurant business."

"You said it was a pizzeria."

"Pizza, spaghetti, ravioli . . ."

"I've been around, too, don't forget, and I know every state's laws are different, but I haven't seen many pizza shops that have a liquor license."

He shrugged. "One complements the other. With my parents, it started with the food. We got the liquor license to increase business. I don't know why it shouldn't go both ways."

"So, what do you like to drink?"

He considered. "Can't go wrong with a 2010 red Burgundy."

Junie lifted a brow. "You *do* know something about wine. Would you be surprised if I told you pinot noir grapes are what goes into most Burgundian wine?"

"See? I didn't know that."

"It'd take a lifetime to learn all there is to know. That's what's so fascinating about it."

Manolo's eyes swept the room restlessly. "All this drinking is making me hungry."

"Again with the food. Are you ready to go back to Sam's?"

"What about the porch? You were going to show me your dad's old specs and the materials left in the barn."

"I still haven't gotten to the market. There's nothing in the house to eat."

"We could grab some stuff for sandwiches. I need to pick up a couple things for the apartment, anyway."

"Does your place have a nice kitchen?"

"If you consider a hot plate and a mini fridge nice."

She pulled a sympathetic face. "That's too bad. You said you like to cook. . . ."

"It's still better than field rations. It'll have to do for the next few months."

Chapter Eleven

Standing at the market deli counter waiting for his order, Manolo was checking out Junie's narrow hips sashaying down the refrigerated aisle in search of milk when some hotshot in aviators and a leather bomber broken in at all the right places appeared from the canned-goods row and gathered her into his arms. Manolo immediately went on red alert as he watched him whisper something in her ear, then hold her at arm's length to observe her startled reaction.

"Daryl!" Junie reddened, to the guy's satisfied grin.

"How've you been?"

When he whipped off his shades, Manolo recognized him with a start. The guy who'd leased him his truck.

"You look fantastic. The winemaking agrees with you. I think about calling you all the time, and then something happens. You know how it is."

Flustered, Junie sputtered something unintelligible.

"Heard about your mom moving out."

Word sure gets around in a small town. Dr. Hart has barely been gone twenty-four hours.

"You gonna be all right over there all by yourself?"

HE KNOWS WHERE SHE LIVES.

"I'll be fine, thanks for asking."

"There's a new place over in Newberg I been wanting to try. Something Trattoria. You heard of it?"

"Yeah, no—"

"It just opened a couple weeks ago. Getting rave reviews. We oughta go."

"I don't know. Maybe."

The flood of testosterone pumping through Manolo's veins had his chest thudding.

"I mean it, Junie. We ought to."

Touching, this little reunion. Shame it has to end now. Casually, Manolo strode over and reached for Daryl's hand.

"I remember you." He applied more pressure to the salesman's hand than was necessary. They locked eyes, sizing each other up like two bull moose.

"Manolo, right?" said Daryl finally. "How's the twenty-five hundred running for you?"

"It'll do."

"Yo, buddy. Your prosciutto," called a tired voice from behind the deli counter. "Anything else?"

Manolo only half heard the summons. He and Daryl continued to glare at each other with their chests puffed out.

"Welllll . . ." came Junie's voice, her gaze darting like a bluebird's between Daryl and Manolo.

Eyes still glued to Manolo's face, Daryl answered Junie from the side of his mouth. "You have to go. So do I."

It wasn't Daryl's square jaw and resolute eyes that were so disconcerting. It was what Manolo sensed behind those eyes—a reflection of himself. Even more disturbing, he knew without a doubt that Daryl had seen right through him, too—straight into his soul.

Daryl blinked first. He leaned over and bussed Junie's cheek, a tad too close to her mouth for Manolo's comfort.

"Buddy! I don't got all day." The deli man slapped Manolo's prosciutto and provolone against the top of the meat case and walked off, leaving it there.

"I'll call you," Daryl told Junie, holding an imaginary phone to his ear while walking backward through the condiments aisle, past the checkout line and toward the exit. The bag in his other hand signaled he'd already paid.

Where was one of those West Coast earthquakes when you needed it? Manolo relished a vision of Daryl Decaprio buried beneath a mountain of pickle jars. He followed Junie up to the register, steaming like a freight train. "How do you know that guy?"

"Who?" she replied absentmindedly, checking her text messages.

Manolo jutted his chin toward his evil twin's back as it finally disappeared out the store's automatic door.

"Him?" she asked, glancing up. "Daryl?"

Who else? "What's he to you?" A friend? *A lover?*

"Just a sec. My mom's texting me."

Patience wasn't Manolo's strong suit. Jaw clenched, he paid the cashier for his food.

On their way out to the car, Junie finally stopped texting and slipped her phone back into her bag. "Now, you were asking me . . . ?"

"Daryl," Manolo growled, the name bitter on his tongue.

"We're old friends."

"I guaran-damn-tee you, he thinks you're more than just friends."

"How do you know?" She frowned, peering into the rearview as she backed out of the parking lot.

"I know exactly what guys like that are thinking. What they want—"

Manolo's arm shot to the dash when Junie slammed on the brakes. "*Jesus, Mary, and Joseph.*"

"Sorry. That old lady was backing up without looking."

"Look, screw the sandwiches. I'm starved. Let me buy you a real meal."

"Can't. I still have cuttings to burn before dark. I've goofed off long enough today."

"What about Daryl? You gonna find time to go out with him when he calls?"

Junie dismissed his concern. "Daryl says that every time he sees me. He never follows through."

"What if this time he does?"

"What if he does? You sound almost . . . *jealous.*"

Jealous? "I could no more be jealous of that"—he scrambled for a metaphor suitable for female civilian ears—"that *peacock* with his phony military jacket than . . ." He abandoned his attempt, scrubbing a hand through his hair in frustration.

Manolo had always had the most sophisticated women at his beck and call, without having to promise them anything. So why had he offered his construction skills, gratis, to a skinny girl in overalls with dirt caked under her fingernails? He was a total puss nut, that's why.

Once he gave his word, he was good for it. But when all was said and done, he had a built-in exit ramp.

"Forget Daryl," said Junie.

"So you won't go out with me, but you'll let me make you sandwiches."

"I thought you liked to cook." Her eyes taunted him; her teeth gleamed straight and white.

"Someone has to do it. Seems like the only time you eat is when someone feeds you." With the jumble of conflicting feelings she brought out in him—lust, protectiveness, and respect—Manolo didn't know whether to grin or grit his teeth.

He knew one thing, though. He didn't want to say good-bye to her yet.

Junie and Manolo watched the dull orange glow of the smoldering brush pile over at the vineyard's edge. Every now and then, she caught a whiff of wood smoke.

"That sandwich hit the spot," she said, wincing at her cliché. Yet somehow, tonight, every thought that came to mind sounded lame the moment she gave it voice. It made no sense. All any passerby would notice was the ordinary sight of two people perched on a porch step. They couldn't smell Manolo's provocative male scent, or feel how his mere presence caused the air to vibrate with expectation, despite her instinctive reservations.

"Everything's good when you're hungry," he said.

An awkward silence fell between them, as if he might be nervous, too. Then they both started talking at once.

"Go ahead," said Junie.

"Tell me about you and Daryl."

Her defenses immediately sprang up. Was her moth-eaten obsession with Daryl, which was so ancient it had lost all but a trace of its former power, that transparent? "Like I said, he's hardly worth talking about."

"How did you two meet?"

She treaded carefully. "In high school."

Manolo waited patiently, examining the curls in the vine fragment he fingered.

"Okay. You want to know? I had a massive crush on him for years. But then so did every other girl at Clarkston High. I mean, you've seen him. . . ." She halted. She was making a mess of this.

Manolo looked just like Daryl. She might as well be telling him how hot *he* was.

"Go on."

"He always used his looks to his advantage, flirting with everyone every chance he got. He had so many women on the burner, it was insane." Sam's words leaped to Junie's mind: *Last I knew, Lieutenant, you had women in, let's see—Fort Bliss, Fort Belvoir, New York City.* . . . She was digging herself deeper and deeper into a hole.

But if Manolo noticed, he didn't let on. "He never culled the pack, settled down?"

She shook her head. "I was never privy to his private life—I don't know anyone who was, especially after I left for college. But to this day, I never knew of him being with any one person for any length of time." It wasn't the first time it had occurred to her. She had to admit that was a little strange. But back in the old days, she had been invested in keeping Daryl atop his pedestal, and now it hardly mattered. Her fixation had lost its potency.

Or at least, most of it.

Chapter Twelve

On May Day, Junie awoke at dawn to the sweet sound of birdsong. She dressed and carried her coffee mug out to the vineyard.

The ground was awakening, subtly but surely. People could be unpredictable, but there was comfort in knowing that even the fiercest winter eventually gave way to the warmth of spring.

The land was her refuge. Out here, it was just the solid, reassuring earth supporting her weight, the soft air caressing her cheeks. Beneath her soil-caked rubber boots was a small miracle: her crop of wildflowers coming into bud. The flowers did double duty. They attracted the birds that ate the bad bugs, eliminating the need for pesticides. Then, later this summer when the flowers went to seed, the hatchlings would feed on the seed heads. She straightened from where she examined a Johnny jump-up to watch a pair of bluebirds carrying nesting materials into one of the little wooden houses she had erected around her property. Of all the places she'd lived, none was as beautiful as this. She was determined to fight for this vineyard with everything she had.

In the afternoon, she showered and put on her waitress uniform in preparation for work. While the restaurants along Clarkston's Main Street went after tourist dollars, Casey's catered mostly to senior citizens on a budget and families with rambunctious kids.

It was dark when she got home again. The sharp, resinous tang of freshly sawn wood filled her nostrils the moment she exited the car. *Manolo.* He had said he might come over after his work at the consortium was finished. The very thought of him out in the barn, bent over Dad's old table saw, made her wish she'd been here to watch his strong back, his coordinated movements while he worked.

Last night, he'd been in a pensive mood after she'd told him about her history with Daryl. He'd left shortly after. She wondered where things stood between them now.

She picked up the paper bag left on the stoop and read the label printed in a careful hand: MONDAY'S SPECIAL. SPAGHETTI WITH RED SAUCE. The bag sagged with the weight of its contents. She felt a tingle of anticipation imagining the sight of Manolo stirring a pot on a hot plate in his tiny kitchenette, rolled up shirtsleeves baring thick forearms.

There was a lot of food. After nibbling between customers at the diner, more food was the last thing on her mind, but she couldn't resist popping some of Manolo's spaghetti into the microwave. Her mouth watered at the aroma released by heating. One bite, standing up, was all it took. She fell into a chair and dedicated the next five minutes to savoring the food's nourishing goodness. Before she knew it, she had eaten the entire dish. She set down her fork for the last time and sat back, feeling whole and restored. Then she trudged upstairs, one hand on her satisfied stomach.

Saturday's jeans were lying on the top of the pile in the clothes hamper. Junie fished through the pockets until she found Manolo's card. Then she switched off the light and fell back onto her comforter.

"You made that on a hot plate?" she asked when Manolo answered her call.

"I've made Dad's spaghetti with goat meat over a campfire started with a bow and drill."

"I am so full I can hardly move."

"Good. I like knowing I satisfied you."

She flushed with illicit pleasure. But encouraging him would be insane. By his own admission, he was a drifter. Later, when he'd gone on his merry way, she'd be the one to get hurt. Safer to stick to the topic of food. "Seriously, where'd you learn to cook like that?"

"It's an old family concoction, passed down through the male line."

"Well, it's amazing. Thanks."

"Wait'll you taste what I make Tuesdays."

She chuckled. "You have a specialty for every day of the week?"

"When I don't eat out. And since you won't go out with me . . ."

"I told you, I waitress."

"Looks like I'll just have to keep cooking, then."

Lying across her bed in the dark, Junie's heart tightened. Was Manolo Santos a silver-tongued player, up to no good? Or a lamb in wolf's clothing? He had already more than made up for the ruckus he'd caused the day he came to town. Maybe he deserved a break.

"Tell you what. Feel free to use the kitchen here when you're working on the porch if you want."

He hesitated. "That's quite an offer. You sure?"

"The key's under the mat."

"No bad guy would ever find it there."

"Shut up," she teased.

"Ouch. And just when I was making headway."

"Good night." In the dark, empty house down the deserted dirt road, Junie indulged in a grin. She lay the phone aside, folded both hands across her stomach, and looked up at the shadows dancing across the ceiling. Manolo didn't just take on a task; he wrestled it into submission. She envisioned his long, powerful legs tracking and backtracking across her kitchen floor as he cooked, his expert hands chopping and stirring. A girl could get used to that. But as anyone who had memorized all the episodes of *Worst-Case Scenario* knew, the odds of a man like Manolo sticking around for any length of time were close to zero.

Chapter Thirteen

On Tuesday between customers, Junie wondered what she would find waiting when she got home. The moment she stepped inside her house, she knew that Manolo had been there by the fragrance of home cooking that enveloped her. On the table was a note in his now-familiar, precise lettering.

RISOTTO & SAUSAGE.

She opened the fridge and pulled out a covered dish, still warm to the touch. She grabbed a fork, bumping the drawer shut with her hip, and dug in before she even sat down.

Junie had never been one of those Portland foodies. Eating was just something that took time away from more important things. Besides, whenever she did cook, the salad was soggy by the time the meat was done and the vegetables were still crispy—not in a good way.

But Manolo's cooking was different. It seduced her into slowing down, to savor each bite with all her senses. She concentrated on identifying the separate components of the sausage and rice dish, the same way she evaluated wine. First, there was the delicate scent of sage filling her nostrils. Then the silky rich broth caressing her tongue. The rice, moist yet firm to the tooth. This wasn't mere sustenance. Manolo's gift filled some vague emptiness that she hadn't even known was there. Eating the product of his hands somehow made her feel connected to him. Between bites, she set down her plate and pulled out her phone. If she couldn't be with him, at least she could talk to him.

Wait, warned the part of her that was conditioned to expect the worst. Her index finger hovered above his name. Calling him a second night in a row was just asking for trouble. But she'd have to thank him eventually. Before her over-cautious side won out, she punched in his number. Her pulse thrummed and her ears roared like the sound of a seashell held to her ear as she waited for him to pick up.

"Santos."

"Your sausage is amazing." *Gaaa!* Her head went back and her eyes squeezed shut with embarrassment.

"No complaints so far," he shot back lightly.

Her face was on fire. Why did she even try? When it came to flirting, Manolo was a pro and she was bush league.

"Oh, you mean my risotto? For a second there, I thought you were talking about something else."

"You know what I mean," she replied miserably.

He laughed good-naturedly.

"Next time you're talking to your father, tell him his risotto changed my life."

At that, there was only silence on the other end.

"Manolo?"

"Yeah."

"Did you hear me?"

"I'm picturing you there in the kitchen," he said silkily, changing the subject. "Am I right? Is that where you are?"

She nodded though he couldn't see her. "Yeah." *Brilliant.*

"Someday I'm—" He cut himself off.

"Someday, what?"

Now he was the one who hesitated.

"Tell me." Her pulse thrilled simply to be on the phone with him.

"I was going to say someday I'm going to have a kitchen like yours. But that's not important."

"Then why would you go there in the first place?"

"I don't know. Forget it."

"What's wrong with admitting you want a nice kitchen? It's no secret you like to cook."

"Yeah, well, it's also no secret I don't plan on settling down any time soon. Any time at all, for that matter."

Her thudding heart sank. "You made that pretty clear the first day we met."

"I don't make any bones about it. I'm up-front like that. Got too many other things to do."

"You mean like building things?"

"That. And seeing the world. I started out with the goal to visit every continent and there're only two left, Australia and Antarctica. I stay in one place too long, I start getting antsy. That's why I joined the service in the first place. But now that my tour is up, I still like being a vagabond."

"I'm just the opposite. I never lived in one place more than three years when I was growing up."

"Sounds like heaven to me."

"Maybe for you, but it made me feel like I didn't know where I belonged."

"Who needs roots?"

"I do, I guess. I was always envious of my Missouri cousins who'd grown up in the same town and had friends they'd known all their lives."

"Don't tell me you didn't have friends. A girl like you?"

"Oh, I had friends. But never what you'd call *old* friends, not back then. Everyone I knew was just like me—a military brat from somewhere else. It wasn't until I was thirteen that I realized my cousins were the rule and I was the exception, that not everyone in the world moved every three years."

"Staying in one place your whole life isn't all it's cracked up to be. People expect things out of you. They know everything there is to know about you, your parents, everyone. They've been witness to every little misstep you ever made."

"I never thought of it that way."

"Hmph. You know what they say. Grass is always greener."

"But where's all your stuff? You must have a home base somewhere."

"I have a couple of storage sheds back east, near my folks' place. Does that count?"

"A storage shed is hardly the same thing as a home. How does that work? I'm still not sure I understand exactly what it is you do to make a living."

"I look for contract jobs in project management. There's plenty to choose from, long as you're not picky about location—which I'm not. And when there's nothing that lights me up, I squeeze in some volunteer work."

"Is that what you're doing for Sam? Volunteering?"

"No. Supervising Sam's project is a real, paying job. The non-profit I consult for is called Engineers With Compassion."

"What do they do?"

"Whatever they can to help meet basic human needs. On my first assignment, floods washed out the only road leading to this remote village in El Salvador. We went in with heavy equipment and hauled boulders as big as cars out of a ravine so the kids could get back to school and their mothers could get to town to buy food. The mission after that, we installed a solar power plant in a children's home in India. Then, last year, I was project manager on a school reconstruction right here in the States, in a poor part of Arizona."

"I'm impressed."

"People need help everywhere you look. The little I do barely scratches the surface. Why shouldn't I lend a hand? I got nothing tying me down. And I like it that way."

There it was again, that warning flag.

Chapter Fourteen

Warning flag or not, Wednesday night after work, Junie was torn between which to do first: devour Manolo's steak Florentine or call him up just to hear his soft, deep voice.

She called him while she ate.

After he greeted her, he said, "Sam was tied up with growers all day. We had some contracts to go over after I left your place. I'm just now headed home."

"How long have you and Sam known each other?"

"He was a year ahead of me in Officer's Candidate School. Our advanced training took us in different directions, but we stayed in touch."

"What did Sam do in the service, exactly?"

"Well, ah . . . not sure if you heard me say that we ran into each other a couple times overseas."

"Rory says Sam was a spy."

"You'll have to ask Sam about that."

"I did. He said he wasn't."

"Then, there's your answer."

"He would say that whether he was or not."

"So you were trying to get it out of me? You can't manipulate me. Don't forget, I was raised surrounded by women. I know all their tricks."

"You're so lucky to have three sisters."

"I'm willing to rent them out for a nominal fee."

She chuckled. "Seriously, sometimes I feel like my family's disintegrating. I never saw much of my aunts and uncles and cousins, then Storm left and Dad died and now Mom. All I have left is my legacy. And I'm hanging on to that for all it's worth."

For the first time since she'd met him, Manolo didn't seem to know what to say.

"Are you there?"

"I'm here."

"What are you thinking?"

"I hope that works out for you." There was a distinct tone of resignation in his voice.

That night, Junie took advantage of the early spell of warm weather to sleep with her window open. Long past midnight, she was still gazing out at the stars, listening to the lonely howl of a coyote in the distant hills. Maybe she was overtired, maybe she'd been hypnotized by the movement of the gauzy curtains in the night air, but she couldn't stop reliving every moment since Manolo Santos had shown up in Oregon, starting with the day he'd exasperated her while charming all her friends in her tasting room. From his economy of motion when he'd cleaned up the spilled wine and broken glass, to the warm insistence of his hands on hers behind the bar, ending with his voice over the phone, the profound impact of their respective families on them.

Whenever she was near him, she couldn't think straight. He was irritating and impossible and cocky and egotistical. But underneath all that swagger, she sensed he was protecting something fragile. Something wholesome and good. As much as he joked about his sisters, it was clear that he adored them, and vice versa. And his life's work was doing things for people, things as simple as cooking risotto and as risky as building a hospital in a war zone.

When Manolo hung up with Junie, he was already calculating the time on the East Coast. The last customers in his father's restaurant would be shuffling out the door. The back of the house would be deafening with the clang of metal against metal as the staff scurried to sanitize every surface so they could punch out, yelling to each other over the mechanized whoosh of the dishwashers. He saw them all as if it were yesterday, wiping down the range, mopping the floors, emptying the trash. Out front, Isabel would be counting the till. He punched in Izzy's number before he thought better of it.

"Hello?"

"Izzy."

"Who's this?"

"Don't play games. You know who."

"My brother? I thought that was your voice, but it's been so long, I wasn't sure."

"Ha. Phone works both ways."

"Where are you?"

He thought for a moment. "Crunchy granola country. Land of the human Birkenstocks."

"Translation?"

"Oregon's Willamette Valley. How's Mom?"

"Mom's fine. The what valley?"

"How's her knee?"

"Still limping. Still fighting getting it replaced."

"If she'd listen to the doctor and get off it . . ."

"Like that's going to happen."

"How's everyone else?" he asked, turning the key to his modest apartment, stepping inside the quiet rooms, closing out the world behind him.

"Michael's good, kids are good, everybody's fine. We'd be better if we heard from you more than once in a blue moon. How come you don't call Polly and Maria sometimes?"

"I call Mom every Sunday." That, plus sixteen years of Mom lighting candles for him at Our Lady of Grace, would be the only thing to keep him out of eternal hellfire.

"That's not what I asked."

This was where Manolo would normally make a stab at humor. But tonight he had no patience for funny stuff. "'Cause you don't judge." That was why he and Izzy were tighter than the rest. "Do me a favor. Dad around?"

There was a tense silence on the other end of the phone. "He's here. Outside, talking to Donnie." The family's restaurant had once been a thriving business. All the movers and shakers had their favorite tables. But more and more, Manolo got the sense its patrons were aging along with his father. Donnie Minelli was one of Dad's oldest cronies and still, apparently, a smoker. Some things never changed.

"Go tell him I want to talk to him."

Isabel drew in a long breath. "How long's it been, Manny?" she asked in a voice tinged with sadness.

"Just go get him."

Manolo paced the floor of the apartment while he waited, picturing Dad out on the sidewalk with his hands thrust into his coat pockets against the damp New Jersey night, rocking on his heels and talking while Donnie finished one last cigarette.

A minute dragged by like an hour before Izzy spoke again.

"He won't take the phone."

"Ask him again."

She sighed. "He won't—"

"Is he still there?" Manolo interrupted. Without waiting for her to answer, he said, "Put him on."

"No."

"What'd he say?"

She hesitated again. "Manny, why do you do this to me? Torture yourself and put me in the middle of it like this?"

Why? Because he was cast adrift by his own hand and he was lonely. He missed having family in his life. He may be a grown man, but deep down inside there was still a boy who missed his father. His anchor. But a guy didn't confess things like that to his sister.

"Tell me."

"I told him Manny was on the phone."

"And then?"

"And then Donnie said, 'Manny, your son?'"

"Yeah? Then what?"

"Don't make me tell you, Manny," she choked thickly.

"Tell me, dammit!"

"He said, 'I don't got no son.'"

Manolo imagined Dad's angry mouth spitting out those words.

"Manny?" asked Izzy with sisterly concern.

His stomach roiled, his nostrils stung with tears. He uttered some inane closing, then tossed his phone onto the counter, this latest barb piling onto the heap he carried inside him.

He opened the fridge and started pulling out salad fixings by rote. Lettuce. Garlic. Lemons.

Then began the comforting, mindless ritual of chopping, pressing, and whisking. He dipped a fingertip into the vinaigrette, tasting and refining until its acidity was perfectly balanced.

When the salad was dressed, he warmed up his father's steak Florentine, which he'd prepared that afternoon in Junie's kitchen. Then he set a place for one, carefully aligning the cheap flatware that came with the furnished apartment. He flipped a bottle of wine high into the air, end over end, caught it one-handed behind his back with a flourish, swaddled it in white linen and presented it, label facing outward, to his empty chair.

"Here you are, sir. Excellent choice. A supple, harmonious pinot from Brendan Hart Vineyards."

He altered his voice, pretending to be his own customer. "Just so, my good man."

Expertly, Manolo withdrew the cork, the soft pop echoing through the quiet apartment. The kitchenette was dimly lit, but he could have poured the standard five-ounce serving in the dark. Finally he scooted in his chair, arranged his napkin in his lap and toasted to the tiny room. *"Buon appetito."*

He tried to focus on the classic Mediterranean blend of bell peppers and onions, parsley and basil. But every bite conjured smiling faces and boisterous voices of meals past, before he had put his selfish desires before family and struck out to see if the world held something more exciting for a brash, reckless young man than Hoboken, New Jersey. Missed birthdays, anniversaries, and other key rites of passage too numerous to count numbed his palate, and loneliness gnawed at his gut. After only a few forkfuls, Manolo shoved his plate away. His head fell into his hands.

Chapter Fifteen

Driving down the lane after work on Thursday, Junie's headlights picked out more two-by-fours added onto the porch frame. The linguini with anchovy and walnuts she found in the fridge gave her the perfect excuse to call up Manolo before she considered the wisdom of it.

She nibbled a nail, counting the rings until he picked up.

"Santos."

Every time she heard him say that in his deep voice, she melted a little bit more.

"I have a problem," she teased, surprising herself with her unaccustomed brashness. "I don't do anchovies."

"You won't even notice them. They're just there to add a layer of depth."

"Promise?"

His silence lasted a beat too long. Junie's foolish smile faded. When would she learn? Men like Daryl and Manolo didn't do promises.

"What if I told you I used artisan ranched, milk-fed, organic anchovies?"

"Oh, well, in that case . . ." She laughed, relief coursing through her body.

"I noticed you started adding on to the porch."

"Finally got all the boards cut to size."

"Have I told you how much I appreciate your help? Especially after you put in a full day at Sam's?"

"It's been nothing but 'stand by to stand by,' waiting for the consortium approvals to trickle in before we can start digging the foundation. I'd rather saw lumber out in your dad's barn any day than sweet-talk zoning officers. I like to keep my hands busy."

Junie felt again the illicit thrill she'd felt on the day they'd met with her hand sheltered in his, beneath the bar where no one saw.

"While we're on the subject of the porch, I'm going to pick up some more lag screws, then I'll be over again tomorrow afternoon. Then I have an early flight to Dulles Saturday."

"Excuse me?"

"I have Reserves one weekend a month. These past few months, it's been in Virginia."

"Oh." All the wind whooshed out of her sails. "I was hoping to show you some more wineries this weekend."

"Won't work."

After all his flirting, his abrupt one-eighty felt like a slap in the face.

"Now that all the lumber's cut, I only need nineteen more man hours to finish the porch."

"Nineteen? That's an odd number. Not twenty?"

"This is what I do. The consortium comes first, so depending on what's going on there, your porch should be done by the end of next week."

"Oh." That meant he wouldn't be hanging out at her place much longer. "Great," she said weakly.

"Right."

"Okay."

"Okay. Well, enjoy the linguini."

"I will."

Junie slowly lowered her phone to her side. At least he could have told her when he'd be back.

She recalled yet again what Sam had said that first day, before she'd even opened the tasting room door to Manolo: *"Last I knew, Lieutenant, you had women in, let's see—Fort Bliss, Fort Belvoir, New York City . . ."*

She started. Was Fort Belvoir in Virginia? Jealousy seeped into her veins. But other than a couple of phone calls, what sign had Junie given him to indicate she wanted more than just someone to fix her porch and share his father's recipes? Come to think of it, she'd done just the opposite, turned down his offer of dinner not once, not even twice, but several times.

Then, a lightbulb went off. What if she surprised him tonight? Showed up to sit down together to whatever wonderful meal he'd cooked up, instead of sharing it over the phone? Maybe she was only setting herself up for deeper disappointment, but the idea took hold. What did she have to lose?

All Friday morning long, while Junie suckered vines and pulled weeds, she tried to picture what Manolo would be doing at the exact moment that she pulled in tonight, an hour earlier than he expected her to. Would she find him outside, perched high on a ladder, nail gun in hand? Inside, at the stove, sampling a steaming pot of soup for just the right spices?

Around three, while she showered for work at Casey's, she thought of picking some wildflowers and putting them in a vase. Pulling out the real cloth napkins. She would change out of her server's uniform, too, put on something nice.

· A couple of hours later, while her hands were busy schlepping platters of meatloaf and instant mashed potatoes to her regulars, she was conducting a mental sweep of her drawers and closet, in search of something not made of flannel or denim.

As six-forty-five approached she started getting really nervous. Lying didn't come easy to Junie. Sure her guilt was written all over her face, she went to her boss and told him she had a splitting headache and had to go home early.

People told little white lies to get out of work all the time. But not Junie. She was a business owner. She couldn't help but put herself in Casey's shoes. Casey was a considerate boss, a kind man, and a friend to her late father. He let her choose the early dinner shift to fit around her winery schedule. Plus, he let her work on a seasonal basis so that her waitress job wouldn't interfere with the fall crush. By walking out in the middle of this evening's dinner business, she was forcing him to don an apron to pick up the slack, to keep patrons from complaining that they didn't get their food fast enough.

She found herself scurrying to her car, then caught herself and, with great effort, slowed her steps. Sick people didn't hurry.

But, as she drove to the farmhouse, anticipation overcame remorse. She was so charged up, her teeth felt like they were floating in her gums. She couldn't wait to see the surprise on Manolo's face when she showed up unexpectedly!

There was his truck, parked in its usual place. More two-by-fours had been nailed up on the side porch. But Manolo was nowhere in sight. She imagined him inside, looking adorably ridiculous in one of her grandmother's frilly aprons that Mom had left behind.

Junie bounded up the steps to the front door, mouth watering, wondering which Santos family specialty Manolo was whipping up tonight.

"Watch out!"

She almost ran into him as he walked out the door with a large covered container in one hand and her extra house key in the other.

"Manolo!" She eyed him up and down. He didn't have on an apron. As a matter of fact, he was looking pretty spiffy for someone who'd been doing construction all day, in his Italian leather loafers and navy blazer. "Are you leaving?"

His normally smooth smile wobbled. "Er, yeah."

Her eyes fell to the container in his hand. "What's that?" she asked, dreading the answer.

"Pizza." He tossed his head over his shoulder. "I left you a good-sized portion," he said with the same consoling voice Mom used to use when she'd thrown something together last minute to tide Junie and Storm over, before she and Dad went out to a fancy restaurant. That voice had never fooled her then, and it didn't fool her now.

"Did you eat already?"

"No. Not yet."

She tried to give him the benefit of the doubt. Didn't it make perfect sense, Manolo taking food back to his apartment to eat? Especially if he'd eaten already and what he held in his hand was leftovers?

"Did you see the side porch?" he asked, too brightly.

"Uh, yeah." Junie didn't care about the porch right now. All her energy was focused on figuring out this puzzle. "So . . . I got off a little early today," she said, in case he hadn't noticed.

"Ah." He nodded. "Good for you."

"You could stick around if you want." She eyed his container meaningfully. "We could eat together."

"We could . . ."

She braced herself for what she knew was coming.

". . . but I, um, made plans."

After twenty-eight years of perfect reliability, Junie's knees picked that moment to threaten to collapse.

Manolo gestured with the container in his hand. "I'm taking this somewhere else tonight."

Junie had put no restrictions on Manolo's use of her kitchen. Then again, she'd never dreamed he would cook for someone else. The concern in his face—or was that pity?—only made it worse.

"Sorry, Junie. If I had known—"

Too late, she saw that those dark eyes held secrets and motivations she would never be privy to.

"No, no, don't worry about it!"

His hands full, he lifted his elbows in an apology as he and Junie circled in an awkward *pas de deux*. "I asked you to go out with me, like five times. . . ."

And she'd turned him down every time.

Now he was facing the front door. He edged backward toward the front porch steps. "I'll be back next week to finish the side porch."

"Sure!" she replied with a grin that felt as fake as a rhinestone engagement ring. "See you then."

Edging farther away, he said, "It's going to be great. Even better than you thought."

"Sure it will. Have a good time!"

"You okay?" he asked, pausing before descending the stairs with a concerned look on his face.

"Fine, fine!" She laughed shakily. "Don't let me hold you up."

There was uncertainty in his step as he retreated, leaving her standing there, a balmy spring evening stretching before her with nothing to do and no one to do it with.

He held up a hand in farewell as he strode to his truck, and she waggled her fingers back at him, feeling like a gawky adolescent.

Junie closed the front door softly and wilted against the other side.

She had eaten next to nothing that day both out of nerves and to save room for this special night, but now the thought of putting Manolo's pizza in her mouth made her want to retch. Dry-eyed, she shoved off from the door, changed back into the jeans she'd had on this morning, and went out and ripped suckers off grapevines until it got so dark she was doing it by feel and not by sight.

Chapter Sixteen

Saturday morning, Junie heard a car. When she saw her mom's SUV pulling down the drive, she was disappointed that it wasn't tourists, until she realized how much she had missed her.

"I see the new porch guy is working out," called Mom, retrieving a cardboard carton from her back seat.

Junie crossed the grass to meet her. "It should be finished some-time next week." She'd just as soon keep the builder's identity out of it. She still felt like a gullible fool after last night.

"Finally finishing the house will make it much more salable."

Figures that would be Mom's first reaction.

Mom thrust the box toward her.

"What's this?"

"I'm returning some things."

Junie peered inside. "Grandma Hart's crazy quilt?"

"You're the only one who would want that faded old thing."

"Her brass candlesticks?"

"None of those antiques look right in my new place. They should stay here. They'll be good for staging. For homebuyers who are into that whole country thing. You know. Baskets and dried baby's breath and all that crap—I mean, stuff." Mom left Junie holding the box and headed toward the house. "I'm thirsty," she called over her shoulder. "Do you have time for a cup of tea?"

Junie struggled to keep up under the weight of the box. "You took all the tea. Remember?"

"There must be something in here."

Mom poured herself some water from the dispenser on the fridge door, then opened it and ducked her head inside. "Are you hungry?"

Before Junie could answer, she came out dangling a clear plastic bag. "Where did this come from?"

The irregularly shaped pizza was obviously homemade. But Mom knew Junie was a klutz in the kitchen. She wasn't merely *bad* at cooking—she seemed to be afflicted with some inherent disability.

Mom peeled it open and sniffed. "What is this? Mind if I take a bite?"

"It's pizza," said Junie flatly, stating the obvious. "Go ahead."

"Mmm! This is scrummy! Want me to warm you up the other piece for your lunch?"

Junie swallowed the lump in her throat. "I'd rather go out." Without waiting for a response, she headed for the living room. "I'll go change quick." She scurried up the stairs in an attempt to put distance between herself and Manolo's handiwork. Because that wasn't just plain old pizza. That dish was like her wine. Created with thought and care, infused with the essence of the maker.

"Wait!" her mother called, her mouth full of pizza. "Where'd you get this?"

Upstairs in the bathroom, Junie turned on the water full force to drown out Mom's voice. She took her time splashing her face with cold water, changing her shirt, hoping all evidence of the pizza would be disposed of by the time she got back to the kitchen.

Crossing the living room, she grabbed her bag and called, "Where should we go?"

But Mom didn't answer.

Junie came to an abrupt halt when she saw her cramming the second slice into her mouth, her cheeks pouching out like a squirrel's.

"You don't even *like* pizza."

"I know."

"That's covered with cheese, you know."

"I know!"

"And that looks like meat."

"I *know!*" Mom exclaimed, gulping. "But this—this is the best pizza I've ever had." She folded up what was left and crammed it into her mouth. When she'd swallowed that, she said, between licking her surgeon's fingers, "I'm serious, Junie. Where'd you get that?"

"A friend made it."

"Well," she said, wiping sauce from her mouth, "I could eat an entire pie." She rinsed her hands and only then noticed Junie had changed her top. "I'm sorry. You wanted to go out. I won't be able to eat another thing all day."

Junie sighed. "It's okay." She'd lost her appetite. She sank into a kitchen chair. "How was your first week in your new townhouse?"

"Lovely! It's very spare and modern. Here, look at these. . . ." She pulled photos up on her phone, handed it to Junie, and leaned over her shoulder to run commentary.

"Spare, indeed," said Junie, scrolling through Mom's pictures. "White walls, white rugs . . . is everything white?"

"I like white."

Sterile was more like it. Operating-room white.

"Speaking of friends, who's this latest man you started telling me about?"

Behind Junie, Mom stood up to her full height. "What did you hear?" she asked suspiciously.

"Nothing. Did you meet him online like the other ones?"

"Noooo?" Her reply rose in a question. Mom's astronomically high IQ went down the tubes when it came to men.

"Am I supposed to keep guessing?"

She smiled coquettishly. "It's too early to talk about it."

Fine. Junie didn't want to talk about Manolo, either. Not that Manolo was Junie's man. Not in any way, shape, or form.

Mom sat down catty-corner to her and drummed her fingers. "Have you thought any more about Portland?"

Junie slid her mother's phone across the table and took a drink of cold coffee, wincing at its bitterness. "Mom, can we drop the whole Portland thing? You know how I feel."

Mom folded her hands. "If you're absolutely sure, I won't try to persuade you to move any longer."

"I'm sure."

"Then, I have another proposition."

Now what?

"First, tell me. Do you truly believe this will be the year you finally start turning a profit?"

Junie nodded enthusiastically. "Sam says the valley's getting more recognition by the day. All I need to do is get the right people here during the crush to create enough buzz to get a distributor. That's what everything hinges on."

"I'm trying my best to be supportive. How many years have I heard that? But if I can't get you to change your mind, then how would you like to buy me out of my interest?"

Junie blinked. Dad's will had divided the property among Mom, Storm, and Junie. No doubt it had seemed like a good idea, back when everyone presumed both kids would someday make the winery their living. And then Storm had walked away. Since then, Junie had lain awake countless nights after watching *Worst-Case Scenario*, fearing that Storm would show up out of the blue someday and meddle, make some crazy decision reversing all her hard work.

But if she owned her own third plus Mom's, that would give her controlling interest. No one could touch her.

"It would also help me with my mortgage on the townhouse."

She should have known there was more to it. "Why would you buy a townhouse if you couldn't afford it?"

"I opted for higher monthly payments and a shorter term. That means I'll have it paid off sooner, but in the meantime, I'm feeling the pinch." She lowered her head and folded her hands on the table. For a long moment, the only sound in the farmhouse was the ticking of the mantel clock in the living room. "I might have overextended myself a bit. But I just want to move on, Junie." There was desperation in her eyes, raw yearning in her voice. "I want to dance again. As much as you need to hang on to the past, I need to let go of it so that I can live again, even if I have to cut back on my lifestyle a little. Can't you find it in yourself to understand? I've tried to be compassionate with you all this time. Now, I need you to show me some empathy."

Junie met her mother's earnest gaze. The computer dating, now the townhouse. Suddenly, Junie saw the woman across from her in a different light—not as her mother, but a vibrant yet lonely young widow, stuck in a backwater town with people she had nothing in common with.

"Where am I going to get the money for that?"

"I've heard that Clarkston Bank is friendly to local vintners. If you're right about the Willamette's potential, wouldn't Jed Smith be willing to take a chance on you?"

Mom didn't understand how to run a vineyard and a winery. She didn't know how hard it was already to pay down her line of credit each month.

"You don't have any college debt, and Dad's insurance paid off the land and buildings. You've only got the expenses associated with the vineyard and winemaking."

Even for a one-man show, packaging, bottling, the wages Junie paid her pickers and Keval, and other fixed costs added up to a substantial sum. Still, relief from that nagging anxiety about Storm returning, throwing a monkey wrench into the business she'd built up might be worth going a little deeper into debt. Maybe, just maybe, she could make Jed Smith see things her way.

Chapter Seventeen

Junie stepped out of Clarkston Savings Bank into the wet sidewalk. She flipped the hood of her jacket up against the farmer's rain and started walking, but in no time, water was dripping from the rim of her hood and onto her face. So she yanked it farther over her forehead and pinched it closed under her chin, blocking her peripheral vision, and tucked her head till all she saw was the steady forward progress of her boots.

"Junie, is that you?"

She peered out from her hooded cocoon at the blue pickup that had slowed to a stop. For a moment, she thought it was Manolo's. It was the same body style. Only the color was different.

"Daryl!"

"Where're you going in this rain?"

She didn't know where she was going. All she cared about was putting as much distance between her and the bank as possible. "Home, I guess."

Jed Smith had turned down her request to up her line of credit. But the prospect of sitting in her lonely office figuring out a new plan to buy Mom's share of the vineyard made her head hurt, and it was too wet to work outside today.

"You guess? Where you been?" He eyed her up and down from the cab of his truck, brown eyes sparkling.

Oh, that smile.

She bit her lip. If she told Daryl that Jed Smith had just turned down her loan request, it would be all over town by dinnertime. "At the bank."

She needn't have worried. Daryl was more interested in what he was doing. "I'm headed over to The Gorge for lunch. It's been ten years since I got the most receptions in a game at Carlton High, and my record still stands. To celebrate, they named a sandwich after me. Want to know what's in it?"

Junie brushed a raindrop from her cheek. "Sure."

"Turkey, applewood-smoked bacon, and havarti on grilled—"

She envied Daryl his warm, dry interior. "That's nice. Look, Daryl." She took a step. "I'm getting soaked out here."

"Don't you even want to know what it's called?"

She halted, sighing. "Yeah, sure."

"The Catcher in the Rye. Get it?"

She smiled. "I get it. Good for you. Now I gotta go."

"See you," he said, accelerating. "Don't forget—that Trattoria. I'm going to call you and set something up." He took off, spraying a plume of water onto Junie's pant legs.

Forget the Trattoria—couldn't Daryl have at least offered her a lift, to get out of the rain?

She continued slogging in the direction of where her car was parked, wondering what Keval was up to. His snarky wisecracks had a way of taking her mind off whatever was getting her down.

She could stop over at the consortium—but what if Manolo was there? He hadn't mentioned exactly which day he was coming back from the Reserves. Running into him would only make this day worse.

She got in her car and drove slowly around Sam's block. The vacant lot next to the consortium looked different. It had been cleared and leveled, and a trench had been dug around it. Various pieces of heavy equipment sat around, shut down by the rain, she supposed. But there was no sign of Manolo's truck.

In a corner of the consortium, a couple of growers argued politics. When Sam saw Junie, he finished his call and tossed his phone onto the counter.

"How's your porch coming along?"

"Manolo says he's almost done."

"Speak of the devil. That was the Lieutenant on the phone. He's on the way here from the airport. We broke ground while he was gone—did you notice? He said he's going to stop by and check out the site before he even unpacks."

"Here? Now?"

"Hey, girl." Keval waved from where he sat working on his laptop.

She would have a quick word with Keval and hightail it out of there before Manolo showed up.

But she'd only gone a couple of steps when Holly of the Perpetual Smile fluttered into her path, animated as a little brown sparrow.

"Hi, Junie!"

"You look bubbly." Even bubblier than usual.

"You won't believe it." From her scant five-foot-two, she slipped an elbow through Junie's and dragged her out of the growers' hearing. "Guess who brought me dinner Friday night?" she chirped. "Manolo Santos!" She squeezed Junie's arm in her excitement. "Nothing fancy, he just brought a pizza and a bottle of your pinot over here to the consortium and we ate in the kitchen. But it was homemade pizza. He made it himself. Did you know he's an incredible cook?"

Junie stared at Holly, speechless.

Keval zipped around his desk, tugging at Junie's opposite elbow. "Sorry to interrupt, ladies, but business first. Junie, can you come here? I need to talk to you. About . . . your promo campaign."

Holly frowned in disappointment. "Right now?"

"Yes, now."

"Holly!" called Sam from across the room, muffling the current in his unending string of phone calls against his chest. "Can you come here a sec?"

Holly edged away. "We'll talk later."

When she was gone, Keval whispered, "Are we okay?"

"We're—that is, *I'm* fine," replied Junie in a monotone.

"Are you sure? You look kind of anemic, all of a sudden." He brightened with sudden realization. "It's because Manolo's on his way, isn't it? Tell me the truth, because I feel like love is in the air." He pulled her farther away from listening ears and hissed, "Are you and Manolo—"

She pulled back. "What? No! No way! You're getting us all wrong."

"Because I know I tease a lot, but the day Sam brought us all to your tasting room, I thought I felt something between you two."

"Me and Manolo? I am not into him! No way. Never. He is not my type."

Keval scowled. "But I could have sworn—"

"Nothing is going on between us, okay? Manolo is not into me, and I am not into him. He works on my porch, that's all. Other than that, all we do is talk on the phone."

She turned toward the exit.

"That's all?"

"That's it. I'll call you later. I just stopped to say hi."

Keval propped a hand on his hip and cocked his head. "What do you talk about?"

She glanced around impatiently. She really had to get going.

"Food, mostly."

"Food? You've got this freakin' smoke show working on your house and all you talk about is about food?"

"Shh. Do we have to tell the whole world? You heard Holly. Cooking's his thing."

"Could he *be* more perfect?" Keval moaned.

Junie ignored that. "Look, I have to go."

"Where's our Lieutenant coming from? I left Friday to spend the weekend in the city and just got back this morning."

"Reserves," she muttered, walking backward. "Assembly. Virginia."

"Junie, darling. You're babbling."

"He could be back any time—"

The hinges creaked on the old consortium door. Every conversation in the room trailed off midsentence. All eyes flew to the tall, uniformed officer with a patch that said Santos in all caps sewn onto his broad chest.

Sam and Manolo saluted each other.

Keval covered his eyes. "Tell me he's wearing camo. I die!"

"Reel it in," hissed Junie. But she couldn't tear her eyes off him, either.

Peeking through his fingers, he muttered under his breath, "Girlfriend, is that your boo thang or not? Because if it's not, I'm about to Stake. My. Claim."

"Manny! Welcome back!" exclaimed Holly. While Junie watched, frozen, Holly flung herself at Manolo like there was way more between them than just an evening of wine and pizza.

Perky, fun-loving Holly. She was everything a lonely man, new in town, could want. Everything Junie wasn't.

Holly's headlock forced Manolo's lanky torso almost horizontal. One broad hand still gripped his sagging duffel bag while the other awkwardly answered her embrace. His eyes widened when he saw Junie standing across the room, taking in the whole scene.

Chapter Eighteen

Manolo gave Holly a token pat in exchange for her strangulating hug, then wasted no time making a beeline across the room.

"Hey, Buttercup! Saw an idea for your tasting room when I was in Virginia."

He had an urge to scoop her up in the same sort of tight grip he'd just escaped. But there was something about her expression that had him thrusting his hands into his camos in an attempt to keep them from reaching for her body. The fabric inside his pockets scratched against his skin. No wonder—it was like new. An officer was trained to stand erect, not with his fists jammed impotently into his pants.

He'd think about that later. Now, he plunged headlong into what he'd been looking forward to telling her during the entire, long flight west. "I was at this winery near Spotsylvania—"

"Our armed forces train at wineries? Why did no one tell me this before, and where do I sign up?" Keval interjected.

"Ah, this weekend was an exception." But that was sensitive information.

He turned back to Junie. "I saw this live-edge wooden bar, and right away I thought of that slab of white oak you have out in your barn."

Junie had yet to say so much as hello—not that she'd had much of a chance. She opened her mouth to reply, but before she did, something over Manolo's shoulder caught her eye.

He spun around to see that Sam had lost interest in whatever it was that his client was saying, and Holly was glaring at him with her arms folded. Both of them were wearing scowls. *Aw, Geez. Now what?* Manolo returned his attention to Junie. Whatever was eating

Sam and Holly could wait. She was the one he'd been thinking of all weekend, on the other side of the country.

"I've been on a plane the past seven hours. I need to get out of these boots and back into my civvies. Think about what I said. I could replace that old countertop with the oak for you if you want."

Abruptly, Manolo left for his apartment. After he changed, he went to one of the restaurants on Main Street. While he waited for his grilled cheese, he pulled out the sketches that he had drawn on the plane back from Virginia. He'd never worked on a tasting room before, but the idea had taken hold of him and wouldn't let go. There wasn't a doubt in his mind that he could talk Junie into letting him use her humble bar as practice. He couldn't wait to get started.

When Manolo returned to the consortium, Sam was the only one there.

"Buttercup?"

Manolo's grin came out as a grimace. Not even he knew what hat he'd pulled that endearment out of. Maybe it was because Junie looked as pure as milk, staring at him with his chin mashed into Holly's shoulder. He'd just opened his mouth and *Buttercup* had tumbled out. But he didn't owe anyone an explanation. "You got a problem with that?"

"*I* don't."

Manolo spread his arms. "I was only gone three days. Did I miss something?"

"All last week, you're cozying up to Junie, then come Friday you're putting the moves on Holly."

"Whoa. Look, man. You're the one who filled me in on how Junie's place is in such bad shape, remember? I'm just trying to help her out a little. That porch is a cake job. It's all but done."

"What was that about a bar back east?"

"The top brass were tied up in high-level meetings half the weekend. More trouble in the global war on terror, surprise, surprise. My task force got a pass Saturday night, so we snuck out to a couple wineries."

"Wait—let me guess. A certain blonde research assistant who works at the Pentagon just happened to be at one of them."

Manolo cursed his penchant for boasting. If he'd learn to keep his mouth shut about his conquests, they wouldn't come back to bite him in the butt. To ease his conscience, he tried to make light of the couple of steamy, yet meaningless hours he's spent in the blonde's bed. "Now, what kind of a feminist would I be if I kissed and told?"

"What's her name again? Heidi or something?"

Manolo's mood changed abruptly. Friend or not, a man could only take so much. He faced Sam straight on. "What are you, my mother? Quit pissin' in my ear and just say what you're thinking."

Sam squared his shoulders. "Holly can take care of herself. But I gave you heads-up where Junie's concerned."

"Are you trying to manage me again?"

"I'm just saying. No one wants to see her get hurt."

Anger and another unexpected, disturbing emotion seized Manolo: *guilt.* He closed the distance between himself and Sam. *"You think I'd hurt her?"*

"No. Not intentionally—"

Manolo raised his chin and peered down his nose at his friend. "Let's get something clear, Captain. We're back in the real world now. Out here, you don't outrank me. You don't get to tell me what to do."

"Stand down, man. No one's accusing you of anything."

"Then why does it feel like it?"

"I saw you. The way you looked at Junie today when you saw her standing there. You could barely hold back."

Sam might be able to read body language like a road map, and granted, he might have done a little more time outside the wire than was good for his mental health, but all of this overprotectiveness was getting on Manolo's nerves.

"Mission accomplished. Buzz killed. It's high time you ditched the trench coat, Spidey. We ain't in goat country anymore, and I'm not the enemy. We're on the same side, remember?"

Sam blinked. Then his shoulders relaxed. He sucked in a cleansing breath. "Doc's been telling me the same thing. Maybe I came on too strong. As long as all you're hammering is Junie's porch, there won't be any problems."

Manolo slapped him on the back, breaking the tension. "I've got my arms around this. I'm in the business of solving problems, not making more of them. Remember that and we'll be cool."

Manolo walked out the back door to gaze unseeing at the plot of land that had been cleared in his absence. Groundbreaking was a pivotal stage of any construction project. He should be excited. This time, it barely registered.

He lost track of how long he stood there, stewing. Sam's accusations were way off base.

But warning Manolo away from Junie had inadvertently pointed out her vulnerability. And though she bristled at any hint of a handout, Manolo was uniquely qualified to help her, whether Sam liked it or not. He could whip that tasting room into shape. Hell, he could make it the talk of this valley. Nobody would call it Broken Hart Vineyards when he was through with it! And he didn't need to make a profit at Junie's expense. Some men golfed, and some collected cars and other toys. Building things . . . helping people were both Manolo's vocation and his avocation. The only other hobby he had was eating out and an occasional good bottle of wine. Aside from that, what else did he have to spend his money on? With no home of his own, no plans for one, and no dependents, the modest amount he set aside out of each paycheck had added up over the years. He had a tidy sum socked away. More than enough to let him to spend a part of each year volunteering.

The EWC might not have been able to find any opportunities for him this summer, but ironically, Junie's tasting room had fallen into his lap like a ripe Roma tomato. And if Sam didn't like it, he'd prove to him when he left in the fall that the whole time he'd been here, his actions where Junie was concerned had been nothing but honorable.

Chapter Nineteen

When Junie gave her mom the news about the bank turning her down, she responded by suggesting Junie drive up to Portland on her next day off to have dinner and see her new place.

At the moment the snow-covered peak of Mount St. Helens came into view through the Volvo's windshield, Manolo called Junie's cell phone.

"I'm coming over to look at that oak slab in your barn. Did you get a chance to think about what I said?"

"I'm not there right now."

"I thought this was your day off."

"It is. I'm on my way to my mom's new place."

There was a pause. "Is she getting to you?"

"What do you mean?"

"It's no secret she'd love you to move to Portland with her. I was there when she offered to put your bedroom suite in the moving van, remember?"

"Then you heard me tell her no way."

"I hate to join the naysayers, but maybe your mom has a point."

"Whose side are you on?"

"Yours. Definitely yours. I just hate to see you banging your head against the wall. Now that the porch is done, it'll up the market value of the farmhouse."

"I'm not selling the house. Don't worry about me. I'll be fine."

"If you say so. Then how about that new bar?"

"Don't we need permits or something?"

"I know the local zoning officer from working on Sam's project. I have her eating out of my hand."

"I'll bet you do."

"Here's something I bet you didn't know. The town officials can't praise your dad enough. Besides, those laws exist in case some big developer comes along. Clarkston's not interested in slapping down their vintners. You're the ones who draw in the tax dollars. I've never seen a place where politicians and businesses shared the same agenda more than they do here. What's good for the wine is good for everyone. Wine is sexy."

But Manolo's provocative talk couldn't sway her.

"It was never part of the plan to redo the tasting room this year."

It was enough that he'd finished her porch. At least now it wouldn't look like she couldn't afford even the basic maintenance of her place.

"Now, here's what I'm thinking. We replace the current bar with the live-edge slab, boom. Done. Then I install a drop ceiling, put in a cork floor, knock out the south-facing wall, and build a covered patio."

"Did you not hear what I just said?" She had to admit his grandiose ideas were tempting.

"We'll install a patio with some high-tops so people can take their drinks outside when the weather's nice. Get some container plants, maybe put in some climbing roses. Take out one of the tables to make room for a guitarist in the summer evenings, for atmosphere."

She could see it all now, exactly as Manolo described it. Tourists mingling with locals under tiny white lights, the heady fragrance of roses in the twilight, the tinkle of crystal, and best of all, her bottles flying off the shelves.

"It sounds amazing," she admitted wistfully. "But it's way out of my reach."

"It's not just about the ambience. Think of it as a long-term investment that will bring in business."

"That's crazy, Manolo. You're talking thousands in materials alone."

"I know all the tricks of the trade. It'll cost less than you think. You'll see."

The highway dipped under an overpass. When it rose again, the rolling green countryside was gone, replaced by the Portland cityscape.

If she had extra funds, she'd spend it buying out Mom's interest, not on some gigolo's pie-in-the-sky ideas. She hadn't forgotten the Holly incident.

"I have to go now. There's traffic."

"Think it over, but don't take too long. I'll be tied up for the next few days with the sewer work and watching them pour concrete, but I'll stop by next week. We have to get on it quick to get done by the time your big tourist season starts."

If Junie got lucky and landed a distributor this fall, she could pay some bills and then maybe think about renovations to the tasting room next year. But what if Jed Smith had been right when he'd advised her not to gamble? What if she only ended up deeper in debt?

Junie parked her car in The Pearl and strolled past chic stores, thriving ice cream parlors, and funky bars to the restaurant where Mom said to meet her.

Once she was inside, it took a moment for her pupils to adjust to the dimness. Tables crowded up against a long, mahogany bar lined with businesspeople dressed in somber tones of navy and gray.

Mom was already seated. She saw Junie and waved.

"I feel a little underdressed," worried Junie, in her jeans, as she sat down opposite her mother.

"Glory Days caters to a professional crowd. But don't worry, you're fine," she replied, sipping her cocktail.

"What's that you're drinking?"

"A rosemary lemon martini. It's lovely."

"What?" Junie mused wryly. "Nothing with kale in it? No cucumber?"

Mom made a face. "Now, Junie, don't start. I thought you might like to try one too since you're staying with me instead of driving back tonight, so I ordered you one."

It had been a long time since Junie had drunk anything stronger than wine. When her own cocktail arrived, it tasted tart and bracing. While she sipped, she half listened to Mom prattle on about patients and coworkers she had never met. Before long, the vodka started to work its magic and she felt herself unwinding.

Mom ordered another round. "So, tell me what happened at the bank."

Once Junie opened up, it was like a dam bursting. She didn't stop at the fact that Jed didn't think she could swing an increase in her line. She even hinted she'd been having trouble meeting her expenses.

Then an unassuming man who'd been sitting with his back to them got up from the bar and walked the few steps to their table.

Junie looked up into Tom Alexander's face, then down at her mother. "What's going on?"

"I asked Tom to give us a few minutes to catch up before joining us for dinner."

"You don't mind, do you?" Without waiting for an answer, Tom pulled out a chair.

Junie gritted her teeth. "I thought we were having a private conversation. Just my mother and me."

"I won't insult your intelligence by saying I didn't know you were coming here. Why are you so resentful of me, Juniper? You knew when you sold me your grapes that I was going to make wine with them. That's no crime, last I heard. By your own admission, if not for me, you would have defaulted on your line of credit."

"Why do I resent you? Let me think. Maybe because not one week ago, at the consortium, I plainly heard you refer to me as a failure."

"Now, Junie. If you're going to be a businesswoman, you're going to have to grow a thicker skin. I wasn't saying anything every other vintner in the Willamette isn't thinking." He examined his manicure. "There's plenty of opportunity to go around. I want every vintner to do well, to continue to raise the reputation of the Valley. The success of every one of us feeds off the others."

Junie lifted her chin, eyeing him askance. "Again. Why are you here?"

"Merely to offer a struggling winemaker—and the daughter of a dear friend—a hand up. Tell me, Juniper. What's your formal, long-range business plan? What is it that you want most?"

Junie's brow furrowed. What did she want? What was the real motivation behind getting a distributor for her wine? "I want to bring my grandfather's dream to fruition. And I want to help my widowed mother reclaim her life."

"Very well. To reach those lofty goals, you're going to need to partner with someone who has a record of achievement. I'm willing to give you a personal loan to buy out half of your mother's ownership in the vineyard and winery."

Junie sniffed. "Half won't do me much good—not that I'd even consider taking money from you. Where am I supposed to get the rest of it?"

Mom said, "Actually, honey, a bit of good news. Storm agreed to buy half my share, so you only have to come up with the money to buy the other half."

Fury seized Junie. *"You went to Storm?"*

"After you told me Jed wouldn't give you the money, I got a little desperate—" Flustered, Mom appealed to Tom for help.

"Look at it this way. . . ." Tom's calm, patronizing demeanor was maddening. This was Junie's life, her future they were discussing! "Imagine the winery is a pie cut into three pieces. A third of the pie for you, one for your brother, and one for your mother. Storm is willing to buy half your mother's interest, or one sixth of the total. I'll lend you the money to buy the other sixth. If the crush pans out the way you hope it will, you can pay me back at the end of the year—with interest, of course—and then you and your brother will be left with equal shares. If your sales exceed expectations, Storm will probably even sell you his portion, and then you'll own everything. Winner take all."

"And if the season doesn't work out, you'll take my sixth as your collateral and Storm will still own half—more than me. He'll be the controlling partner!"

Tom lifted an arrogant brow. "If you've misjudged the market, or if the weather turns against you, or your wine goes sour or any number of other things—yes." He shrugged. "That, my dear, is business."

Mom tried to reason with her. "I know Storm's changed jobs a lot, but he's found his calling. His medical marijuana business is doing very well—"

Junie huffed. "Medical marijuana? Is that what he told you? And last I heard, he was a manager, not an owner."

Mom ignored that. "He bought a house in Boulder and he has a live-in girlfriend. I don't see him coming back to Clarkston. But if worst comes to worst with this year's grape crop and Storm would happen get controlling interest and agree to let Tom be his local man on the ground, remember, my door is always open. You can always move in with me and take a job in Portland."

Tom Alexander manager of Brendan Hart Vineyards?

In a flash, Junie recalled in graphic detail an April dawn, five years past.

Dad's bloodless face looked up at her from the ground where he lay. "Don't give up, Junebug." He panted with the effort of those four little words—a father's last behest to the child who was most like him.

She'd called 911 the moment she'd seen him lying there. "Dad!" Junie pleaded against the faraway refrain of sirens. "No! Stay awake! Open your eyes!" She knelt close, cradling his head in her hands. "Daddy." It came out as a choked sob. A teardrop splashed onto his cheek and rolled off.

Two EMTs jogged up with medical bags and a backboard in tow. "How long's he been unresponsive?"

She recounted the past twelve hours, her shaky words tumbling out in a rush. "My mom stayed in Portland all night on a difficult case. . . . She's a doctor. The rest of us—my brother, visiting from Colorado, Dad, and I—had a late supper, then Dad went back out to do grafting and Storm and I went up to our rooms and didn't come back down." Nobody had known Dad had been lying outside all night, fighting for his life, until that morning when he hadn't come downstairs for coffee.

Storm came running barefoot down the row of winter-bare vines, clad only in his pajama bottoms. "What's going on? Why is there an ambulance—?"

The medic poised for action. Without looking up, he asked Storm in a monotone, "Can you get her out of here?"

Storm looped both arms through Junie's and yanked. Dad's head lolled off her lap onto the frost-hard ground with a sickening jolt. She found herself being dragged backward several feet before she jerked free of Storm's grasp. From there, brother and sister stared, transfixed, at the surreal scene.

"Clear!" snapped the medic, and Dad's already lifeless body convulsed in a way that would haunt Junie for the rest of her days.

"Junie."

She blinked at the sound of her name on her mother's lips.

"What are you thinking?"

She turned to her mother in a daze. She couldn't give up on the winery. Not yet. Five years might seem like a long time to Mom, but she'd learned in college that five years in the red was not unusual for a fledgling winemaking business. That wasn't opinion. That was fact.

But Junie believed deep down in her soul that this could finally be her year. Sam believed it, too. The property already looked a far sight better because of the work Manolo was doing.

Junie met Alexander's green gaze. Greed emanated from every pore of his body. How could Mom not see it?

"At what rate?" she heard herself ask.

"Twenty-five."

Junie twitched as if slapped. Twenty-five percent interest was highway robbery. But if the bank wouldn't take a chance on her, where else could she go to preserve her father's legacy . . . to see to it that her mom danced again?

Her heart raced at the risk she was about to take.

Then she remembered: *Do what you love, the money will follow.*

"Twenty."

"Twenty-two point five. Take it or leave it."

She gritted her teeth. "I'll take it."

God help her, she would pay back every cent if it killed her—plus settle up with Manolo for his time and materials. She was no man's charity case.

A smug smile spread across Tom Alexander's face. "I'll have the papers drawn up." He picked up the wine list. "Now. A little sparkling wine, to celebrate?"

Chapter Twenty

Manolo stood with his arms folded, watching the little orange Kubota putter up one row of vines and down the next. The tractor's operator was disguised from head to toe in wrinkled white coveralls, an Oregon Ducks baseball cap perched comically atop her hooded head. One hand rested on the steering wheel, the other sprayed something onto the new, pale leaves.

He had been working on Junie's tasting room for two weeks. The new bar was in, the drop ceiling installed, and the cork floor tiles on order. While he came and went, Manolo had gotten a front-row seat on how a vineyard operated. Junie worked hard, every bit as hard as his mother and his sisters worked at his family restaurant. He hated to interrupt her just now. But he needed some answers.

When Junie realized she was being watched, she stopped, shut off the engine, and held up a gloved hand.

He cupped his mouth and shouted, "What about a display area?"

She pulled down her face mask. "What?"

"Shelves."

Yelling across the vineyard was ridiculous. He headed out to meet her, despite not knowing what toxic contents that spray bottle held.

"That stuff looks like antifreeze."

"Copper fungicide."

He sneezed loudly. "Smells rank—like vinegar."

"Once the leaves are out, you can't get by without spraying once a week for mildew. Especially with these cool nights and warm days we've been having."

"I had you pegged as one-hundred-fifty-percent organic."

"It's called biodynamic. I use organic plus holistic farming methods to conserve the health of the land and the ecosystem."

With gloved fingers, she picked what looked to him like a common weed. "This hyssop wards off pests. And those roses at the end of each row aren't just for decoration. They're my canary in the coal mine. Mildew shows up first on them." Junie scraped up a handful of rich, dark soil and crumbled it. "See this? Chemically treated soil looks pale and hard. But treat it right and the system self-regulates."

Manolo reached over and cupped a bunch of hard, green berries. "You sure these are grapes? They look like peas to me."

She laughed. "The fruit's just starting to set. Just wait a couple of months and you'll see."

"Before I go any further with the new tasting room wall, I need to know if you want some kind of display shelving."

She shook her head. "I told you. Just the bare bones."

"Display shelves are pretty basic. And built-in looks classier than free standing. If it's the former it can wait, but if you want built-in, now's the time to speak up."

She sighed. "Write up an estimate and I'll look at it."

Estimate? Manolo didn't have patience for estimates. He'd just go ahead and order the lumber. It wouldn't take him much over the round figure he had in mind for the bottom line. To save time arguing, he simply nodded.

"Sounds like things are on track at Sam's place."

"The walls should be up by this time next week. Everything's right on schedule."

Junie's eyes probed his. "You mean, for the crush."

He felt transparent under her gaze. *Tread carefully, Santos.* He always kept his exit strategy close to the vest. If a woman knew your plans, it weakened your hand.

"Yeah. The crush."

"That's why you wouldn't sign a lease over six months."

He never should have blurted out the details of that lease on the very day he'd met Junie. But how could he have imagined that little more than a month later, he'd be remodeling her tasting room and making her dinner a couple times a week? Not that that *meant* anything.

"Where are you going after that? Do you have a new contracting job lined up? A volunteer mission?"

"Nothing yet. But I've always got my ear to the ground." The Belize job was still up in the air. Sam was the only one outside of the EWC who knew about that prospect. "The only thing that's carved in stone is that I've got to be at Sam's first thing in the morning to supervise the framing crew. In the afternoon, I'm headed back to the Reserves."

Her eyes widened. "I can't believe it's that time again already!"

"Time flies when you're working your ass off."

"Other than a few extra tourists, I barely noticed it was Memorial Day last weekend."

"The consortium was hopping. Sam must've taken out a dozen vanloads of them on tours."

"When you're in the service industry, you work holidays. It's the same with me and most of my friends. Poppy, Rory, Heath. . . . By the way, did Sam tell you about the hike Monday?"

"He did say something. You going?" *Say yes.*

"It's my day off, thank goodness. I'd hate to miss it. Usually we all bring something to eat. But you're excused, since you'll just be getting off a plane."

"Me, pass up a chance to cook for a crowd? Not likely." He cocked his head. "If I'm not mistaken, this'll be the first break you've taken since I've known you."

"I never miss our post–Memorial Day hike! That, and the Clarkston Splash in July. A bunch of us get together and rent out the community pool at night. Poppy and I used to lifeguard there when we were kids. You're welcome to come."

Junie in a swimsuit? "I'll try to make it." Wild horses couldn't drag him away.

"All I can think about is keeping things moving along here and at the consortium. Do me a favor?"

"After all you're doing for me? How can I say no?" Eyes full of gratitude shone up at him. Her lips puckered into a fat, juicy strawberry as they fought a smile. She should have looked ridiculous with her face peeking out of that white hood like a nun's wimple. But instead she looked for all the world like a wood nymph from the nearby forest.

Manolo swallowed, his mouth suddenly dry. "Stay out of the tasting room until I get back. It's not safe with the floor ripped up." There was no reason she had to go in there until he was finished. He'd already transferred all her stuff over to her mother's old bedroom so she could use it as an office temporarily during the renovation.

She shrugged. "It's already off-limits to customers during the rehab—assuming I have any."

In the weeks he'd been hanging around Brendan Hart Vineyards, the only visitors he'd seen had been bussed in by Sam.

A pang of empathy hit him. "Don't worry, Buttercup." He crooked a knuckle under her chin. "Just wait till I get finished with this place. . . ."

That one square inch of skin fused them together like a magnet. His feet stepped closer of their own accord until the toes of his boots bumped hers.

Her lips relaxed and parted. He scrutinized every inch of her face, seeking fault . . . justification to quell his growing desire. It was true. Junie wasn't a conventional beauty. Her features were a tad too strong, and freckles from working outside sprinkled her nose. But with no makeup diverting attention from them, her irises shone like sapphires. Even under the glaring summer sun, her naked skin was poreless, her cheeks downy as peach fuzz. She was like an organic fruit, imperfect on the surface but better for you in the ways that counted.

His body stiffened with lust. But this was no run-of-the-mill attraction. An undercurrent of danger ran through it. His heart pounded like it did the moment his CO announced, "Operation mobile" unexpectedly and he knew all of his skills were about to be tested to the limit. At moments like that—when a man was never closer to death—he never felt more alive.

His fingers spread to cup her jaw possessively. He tipped her head back, sending her Ducks cap tumbling backward onto to the ground. Slowly, slowly his head descended until only inches separated their lips. His own jaw tightened with the effort of restraint. It took every ounce of self-control he had not to throw caution to the wind, rip that baggy white suit right off, and lay her down in the middle of the vineyard in broad daylight. *If she were any other woman . . .*

Abruptly, Manolo dropped Junie's chin, whirled around, and strode down the row of vines with their clusters of tiny green berries, sucking in a steadying breath. She *wasn't* any other woman. Sam was right—Juniper Hart wasn't just hook-up material. When it came to her, his past seemed like a dress rehearsal for something much grander, much more meaningful.

Finally, he did a one-eighty and walked back, massaging the knots out of his neck.

"You were saying?" she asked coolly.

He cleared his throat. "Like I said, it's only going to be a matter of time until you're beating them off with a stick."

"Customers, you mean?"

Customers. Men. He wasn't sure anymore what he meant. Just being around Junie made him too crazy to think straight.

"A month ago, you said I'd never make it. What changed your mind?"

What had *changed?* The economy was the same. Sam had always contended that Junie's product had the potential to catch fire. Was it just Manolo's big ego, banking on the notion that merely sprucing up her tasting room would be the magic bullet that would put Junie's winery on the map—and ultimately attract a distributor for her wines? Manolo was no more of a retailer than Junie was. But somehow every passing week found him more and more invested in her property. Hell, even more than the consortium.

Suddenly Manolo's collar felt like a leash around his neck, staking him to a single spot like a dog on a chain. He ran a finger between his shirt and skin. There was so much ground left to cover, so many places yet to see: the Sydney Harbour Bridge. The Falkland Islands. And if he ever did succumb to one woman, one place—when he was old and gray, that is—he'd never imagined it would be a struggling farm woman in a state that prided itself on its weirdness.

He stooped to retrieve Junie's ball cap and handed it to her with his old, lighthearted veneer. "What changed? Easy. Now you got *me* on the job."

Chapter Twenty-one

From the outset of the hike, Junie pushed herself to keep up with the guys, waiting for a chance to get Sam alone so they could talk without being overheard. She decided to hasten the process along by instigating Rory and Heath's favorite debate.

"Hey, you guys, I forget. Is it cider that's gluten free, or is it beer?" she asked innocently.

"Cider," Rory declared with a smug look at Heath.

"But beer has more protein and vitamin B," countered Heath.

"Studies show hard cider has as many antioxidants as wine."

"Big deal! Hops have flavonoids."

"Well, whoop dee freakin' do! Cider has polyphenols!"

And so on. Their gestures grew more emphatic as they compared benefit after benefit, and their pace was sacrificed to their argument. They didn't seem to notice that they were falling behind Sam and Junie.

Sam glanced behind him when he heard Junie's footsteps catching up with him. "Why'd you have to get them started?" he chastised. "Now they'll be at it all day."

"Don't worry about them. They love it."

"You're up to something."

Junie scrambled to keep up with Sam's long strides. "Who? Me?"

"Who do you think? Might as well tell me what it is."

"It's nothing, really. I was just wondering about something I heard you say that first day you brought Manolo to my place."

"What's that?"

She detected a tinge of wariness in Sam's voice. Stumbling over a root, she said, "Before I opened the tasting room door that day, I heard you say Manolo had women in several different places."

"I did?" He was stalling.

"Don't pretend you don't remember. Is that true?"

"That's not a question for me."

"Sam . . . just tell me."

"Let it go, Junie. You know how guys talk."

"That's just it," she said, panting. "I don't know if you were busting on him or repeating his shaggy-dog story or . . . or he's really that kind of guy."

Sam's boots chewed up ground while he thought about it. Finally he said, "Exactly what is it you want to know?"

She was tired of beating around the bush. "Does Manolo have a girlfriend? Girlfriends, with an S?"

"Today? I couldn't tell you."

"Does he really . . . is he . . . ?"

"Is he what?"

"Straight up, Sam—do you trust him?"

They trampled over the mossy forest floor, snapping twigs and skirting snags, until Junie wondered if Sam had heard her.

Finally, he said, "On the battlefield? There's no one I'd rather have as my wingman. But when it comes to matters of the heart, isn't there something you ladies call women's intuition?"

And then he left Junie standing there, as confused as ever, looking at his retreating back.

When she was almost back to the beginning of the trail, she heard Keval's voice. "Juniper! Hold up!"

She turned and waited for him to catch up. Together, they walked out of the pines to the designated picnic area.

A black truck was headed their way.

Keval clutched the stitch in his side. "Well, look who it is. Clarkston's newest lady-killer."

"You don't like Manolo."

"If by 'don't like him,' you mean I don't trust him, then no, I don't."

Clearly, Keval hadn't forgiven Manolo for taking food to Holly.

"I appreciate your loyalty. But are you forgetting all the work he's done for me for nothing?"

He stopped and cocked an eyebrow. "Really, Juniper? *Really?* Haven't you heard? There's no such thing as a free tasting room."

A dark cloud crossed the sun. "Thanks for reminding me."

"No problemo, *amiga*. That's what friends are for."

But neither her confusion nor Keval's lack of trust could stop the pounding of her heart as she watched his truck bounce over the grass toward the picnic grounds.

"I see you made it," said Junie coolly.

"Flight got delayed. Knew I wouldn't make the hike, but I didn't want to miss the party." He yanked back the tarp covering his truck bed and pulled out his camo duffel. "You didn't eat yet, did you?"

"Nope." She nodded toward the trail. "The others aren't even back yet."

"Hey, Keval." Manolo reached out his hand in greeting.

"What's new and exciting on the East Coast?" Keval asked, as if he hadn't just dissed him behind his back.

"Not a damn thing, unless you're into wall-to-wall traffic and bumper-to-bumper people." He tipped back his head, looked up at the sky and sucked in a breath. "Aaahhh. This is more like it. I kept wishing Lewis and Clark could have seen that view from the plane. The Columbia Plateau, then the Cascades. Mount Hood, still covered in snow in June. . . ."

He scoped the picnic area. "Good. I took a chance there'd be grills and brought burgers."

"Everyone should be getting here soon. We all brought something to share."

"Bring some of your pinot?"

"Better than risking poisoning you all with my cooking. Sam said he brought some bottles too, so we can do a little taste comparison if you want. Or if you'd rather have a beer, Heath brought some of his."

"Either one sounds great."

Not long after Manolo started unpacking his bag full of goodies, Rory and Heath appeared, still arguing the merits of cider versus beer, followed by Poppy and a few others.

Sam walked up from his van, carrying a cardboard box full of wine.

Manolo reached into his bag and pulled a large wooden paddle.

"Have peel, will travel," he said, giving it a twirl.

"You're going to make pizza—on that grill?"

"Gonna give it my best shot."

While the others scattered to their cars for their coolers, Manolo pulled out his spices and other ingredients.

He turned to Rory. "Any good, aromatic wood around these parts? Oak? Maple? I'd like to find some twigs to throw on top of this charcoal for extra flavor."

After they'd shared their food and wine, Poppy followed Junie to her car to get their hoodies while someone lit a campfire. "Manolo is really nice, and such a Renaissance man!" said Poppy. "Is there anything he can't do?"

"He definitely has his talents."

Sam left, while the rest sat around the campfire sipping coffee.

"I really like tasting wine with food," said Heath.

"Helping diners pick a wine to pair with their meal is a big part of what a somm does," added Poppy.

"Food and ale pairings are getting popular, too. As a matter of fact, I'm planning to do that for the crush. I've started experimenting already. Hoppy beers go well with game birds, like duck. And I can do roasted root veggies with a darker stout. I'm hoping it'll bring in a different sort of customer."

Firelight sparkled in Manolo's eyes as he shot Junie a look.

She could practically see his grandiose thoughts racing ahead, like always. She shook her head in advance of what he was about to propose.

"Imagine this," he said, raising his arms to the night sky like some charismatic preacher at an old-fashioned revival. "Stone benches around the perimeter of the patio at bench height for you to sit on. Lanterns hang overhead from a knotty pine pergola, hung thick with one of those climbing vines. What's that called? The purple one?"

"Wisteria!" exclaimed Poppy.

Manolo snapped his fingers. "Wisteria. The vines allow some light in, but block the harshest rays. At night, you can look up and see the stars. The entrance is at one end, with a big square fireplace opposite for heat and atmosphere, flanked by twin pizza ovens."

The faces around the campfire were rapt.

"Embedded into the longer sides are a few regular grills or warming ovens, sinks, and coolers. Then, in the center, four, maybe six round tables on matching stone bases shaded with market umbrellas in colors to match the current season. But the real highlight is the killer view all the way out to the Coast Range."

"You're killing me!" moaned Junie.

"Why not, Junie? Sounds amazing," said Rory.

"If I could afford it. But . . ." Junie hesitated.

"But what?" Poppy pressed.

"But I already have a loan with Tom Alexander, and if I can't pay it back by the end of the year, I'll have to hand over a portion of my vineyards."

"Why didn't you go to Jed, over at the bank?" asked Rory.

"I did," said Junie. "Jed wouldn't play ball."

Rory worked the kinks out of his neck, and Poppy and Heath exchanged glances.

"My back was against the wall. My mom wanted to make a clean break. She was sick of waiting for me to give up on what she sees as a hopeless cause. The farm kept reminding her of Dad, and she wanted a fresh beginning. She hinted that she even has a new man. I agreed to buy her out so she could start a new life."

The only sound was the mournful call of an owl.

Poppy leapt up from her camp stool. "Well! Like Red always says, no sense dwelling on the past. You've got to focus on the future, getting that loan paid off. What can I do to help? I know! I'll work the bar for you on the first day of the crush."

Rory nodded. "I'll pour for you too, as soon as my shift at the Cider Garden is done."

"The brewery has a stand downtown, but I'll be happy to send all the wineaux your way," said Heath.

"And I know Sam will keep working on finding a distributor," said Keval.

"Thanks, you guys."

A short time later, Manolo walked Junie to her car. He slung an arm around her shoulders. "Don't worry," he said. "It'll all work out."

Chapter Twenty-two

Manolo fell into a pattern in the following weeks. He went to Junie's place extra early to work on the tasting room before she woke up, spent the main part of the workday at the consortium, and returned to Junie's again in the late afternoons, after she'd gone to work at the diner.

The hours he spent designing, measuring, sawing, and nailing were what he enjoyed most. And then, one day, without him noticing when it happened, he realized that the prospect of Junie's pleased expression when he showed her the end result had started to eclipse even the satisfaction of working with his hands.

On June twenty-first, the new room was finished. He stood back and let his eye travel critically over the welcoming, sun-filled space. He'd never been prouder of anything than he was of the tasting room he'd built for Junie.

Through the picture window he saw her slight figure in the very center of the vineyard, bent over a spade. He watched her for a moment, trying to puzzle out what she was doing, then swiped away streak on the glass with his shirtsleeve and adjusted a bar stool half an inch.

The time was two-fifteen. He was meeting Sam at three to go over the rough carpentry at his place, and Junie had to get ready soon for Casey's, but he couldn't wait another day to show her his handiwork.

He jogged down through the herb garden surrounded with chicken wire to keep out the rabbits, past the built-up beds lined with lengths of fallen logs and the half barrels planted with nasturtiums and blueberries, into the vineyard.

He reached her as she crouched next to a newly dug hole in the ground.

"Hey, Junie," he said, breathlessly.

She peered up at him from under her ball cap and blew a stray lock of hair off her cheek.

Since the picnic, the connection between them was electric.

He reached out to fondle a nearby cluster of fruit. It felt heavy for its size. "You were right about the 'peas.'" The grapes had now doubled in size. While half were still lime green, the other half were turning purple.

Only then did he notice the cattle horns filled with sparkly stones and a bottle of Junie's best wine lying on the ground beside the freshly dug hole.

She inserted a horn into the hole, point up.

He squatted down beside her. "What are you doing?"

"Today's the summer solstice," she replied nonchalantly. "Time to bury the horns."

Manolo picked up a horn filled with sparkly gravel and examined it skeptically. "That some kind of voodoo?"

"Biodynamic principle. At the winter solstice, I'll unearth these, take out the quartz, grind it into powder, and put it in a glass jar in a sunny window until spring."

"Then what?"

"Then I'll mix it with rainwater and spray it on the grapevines."

"Excuse a city boy's ignorance, but what exactly is that supposed to do?"

"Improves the ripening action of the sun, of course," she said, placing another horn carefully into the ground.

"Of course. And you're going to get enough quartz powder out of these horns to spray the entire vineyard?"

She smiled patiently. "It's like homeopathic medicine. It only takes a minuscule amount."

"Can I help? Or do I have to be initiated in some weird rite first?"

"Don't be silly." She giggled.

He picked up the wine with one hand and tossed it into the other. "What's this for? Wait—let me guess: an offering to the fertility gods?"

"In the old days, people used to bury wine so it could ferment at a constant temperature, away from light and where it might get jolted around. Now, in the age of climate-controlled cellars, it's just symbolic. When we dig up the horns in December, we'll drink the wine in appreciation of the earth's bounty." Her eyes flew to his. "Oh, that's right. You won't be here in December."

They exchanged a look laden with meaning.

She averted her gaze, looking down again at where she scooped handfuls of dirt onto her buried treasure. "What brought you running out here?"

He sat back on his heels and brushed the dirt from his hands. "It's done."

She rose and let out a little moan when her thigh muscles cramped from squatting. He reached out and put a supportive hand on her arm, the skin inside her elbow petal-soft.

"C'mon," he said, his earlier eagerness returning. "Let me show you."

In his eagerness to show her the finished room, he had to force himself to slacken his pace to match hers until she regained her legs. Slowing down made him mindful of the buzzing of green and ruby-throated hummingbirds in the pear trees, and the heavy, almost cloying scent of honeysuckle that enveloped them like a cloud. He realized that more and more, he was becoming seduced by Junie's world.

When they got to the door, he made her close her eyes until he steered her exactly where he wanted her.

"Open them."

Junie gasped and stepped into the room. Just as he'd known they would, her eyes gravitated toward its showpiece—the floor-to-ceiling picture window.

Behind her, Manolo glowed with pride as he watched her absorb the seamless view of the vineyards spreading out to the greater valley, bordered by the distant hills.

"What do you think?" He approached her hesitantly, milking the magic of the moment. Compared with the buzzing of the gardens, the tasting room was so quiet he could hear his own heart beating.

"Oh . . ." she managed to get out. When she looked over her shoulder at him, her awestruck expression was something he knew he would cherish. "This is better than anything I ever dreamed of. . . ."

He wasn't prepared for what happened next. Junie pirouetted on her toes like a ballerina to face him. Her face crumpled, her wrists floated upward to encircle his neck, and she buried her head in his chest.

For Manolo—soldier, problem-solver, professional horndog— profound fulfillment conflicted with terror. He took her slim body into his arms as gingerly as if someone had just handed him a price- less object of art.

When he felt her melt into him, he relaxed a little, too. He held her in stillness, allowing the moment to soak in, to become part of him.

Junie's hands skimmed up his neck, cupping the base of his skull. Her fingers combed through his hair. She tipped her head up until the bridge of her nose found the sculpted hollow beneath his chin.

Manolo's fingers teased lightly across her T-shirt. Her warmth ra- diated through the featherweight fabric. Lust overcame caution, and his hands slipped beneath her shirt, straying no higher than her waist.

After all the exotic locales he'd explored in the last fifteen years, all the women he had known, his world contracted to the center of that one room he had built for this one woman. Her skin was like a warm beach in winter, the expanse of her back a fertile plain. The contours of her shoulders were ridges, cloaked in velvet. He closed his eyes and sniffed her hair. Her hippie dippy blend of patchouli and wildflowers swept him away to mysterious opium dens and sun- dappled meadows.

Wrapped in her embrace, the sun and the planets and the stars seemed to revolve around them.

His heart swelled. Tenderly, he pulled back, intending to take her in a kiss. Junie gazed up at him with soft eyes.

If she hadn't suddenly blinked—flinched—Manolo wouldn't even have noticed the bleating car horn.

Not now. Anytime but now.

Her fathomless blue eyes peered into his. "Thank you so much for this," she breathed. "I'll pay you back someday, I promise."

He was confused. Her thank you sounded ominously final.

Then the self-imposed blinders that had limited him to tunnel vi- sion for so long fell away, and he saw what he hadn't allowed him- self to see until this moment: a full range of thrilling possibilities.

The end of this project didn't have to be the end of everything.

This could be the start of something brand new. Something he'd never dreamed possible.

But before he could find the right words to tell Junie, she stepped out of his embrace and held up a halting hand.

"I have guests." Reluctantly she slipped away, leaving him with empty arms and an aching need.

Walking backward, she gestured at the room around her and said, in a wistful voice, "After all, that's the point of this, isn't it?"

As he watched her walk away, his phone rang. In a daze, he pulled it out of his pocket and looked at the screen. AMANDA, ENGINEERS WITH COMPASSION.

"Pack your Speedo. You're going to Belize."

In his enthusiasm to finish the tasting room, he'd almost forgotten about Belize.

"Manolo?"

"Here." Through the window, the swaying of Junie's rear end as she went out to meet her visitors wouldn't let him think.

"This isn't the reaction I expected. Did you hear what I said? You got the consultancy! I'll be emailing you the contract for your signature as soon as we hang up."

For a moment he'd been seduced by the potent blend of an arcane solstice ceremony, the buzz of honeybees, the essences of green herbs, and the arms of a captivating homesteader.

But Manolo knew better than to believe in magic. If he let himself fall under the spell of this place he would be trapped, just like generations of Santos men before him.

Chapter Twenty-three

The final week of June brought more clouds than sun. Junie was trying not to panic about the weather. But just to be on the safe side, she'd spent extra time in the vineyard the past three days, thinning leaves to let in more light on her grape clusters.

Every morning, when she went outside, she looked for little signs that Manolo had been there while she was at work. The leftovers were a thing of the past. He hadn't cooked in her kitchen for weeks. The signs Junie looked for were more subtle. Fresh splinters of yellow wood on the ground, boot prints in the soft earth.

She'd become attached to his presence. Even when she didn't actually see him there, evidence of him made her feel less alone. But now that the tasting room was finished, there were no more signs. He was probably devoting all his time to the consortium, as he should. No doubt he felt relieved to get back to doing just one job instead of two.

She'd been blown away when he showed her the tasting room. She'd never planned to throw herself into his arms. Planned or not, it'd been a mistake. He'd handled her like she was made of spun glass . . . almost as if he was afraid of her. She couldn't figure him out. How could someone as confident and self-assured as Manolo be afraid of *her*?

Manolo Santos was an enigma.

There was his infuriating habit of keeping her guessing about his plans, such as when he was returning from Reserves. Usually he came back on a Monday, but this year Independence Day fell today, a Tuesday. Maybe he'd stayed on the East Coast to celebrate with his fellow officers, or even gone home to see his family? Maybe, at this very minute, he was with one of those other women Sam had joked about when he didn't know Junie could hear.

She'd asked him if he was going to the Splash, but he hadn't said anything definitive. Even with something as minor as a party, he refused to be pinned down.

As for the more important things, such as where he was going when he left Oregon . . . what kind of work he'd be doing, he hadn't dropped so much as a hint.

Clearly, he was keeping her at arm's length.

There'd been a trickle of customers over the holiday. More than last year, for sure. But nothing like the flood she'd hoped for when word of the new tasting room got out.

She chastised herself to be patient.

But that loan from Tom Alexander was a heavy weight around her neck.

She looked up at the sound of an approaching vehicle. Her heart leapt when she saw the outline of a truck coming over the rise. But when she saw that the truck was blue, not black, she dropped her pruning shears, lifted her chin, and headed down the row to greet her visitors.

She should count her blessings. At least she had some customers, a brand-new tasting room, and a boss understanding enough to let her work around her own business.

Then she saw the approaching man's rangy gait, perfectly groomed hair, and shining brown eyes.

"Daryl! What are you doing here?" she asked, confused. "Do you want to try some pinot?"

"Pinot?" He frowned, dismissing the very idea with a wave of his hand. "No. I want to ask you to come to the Clarkston Splash with me."

She would have been less taken aback if he'd asked her to go skydiving. "You do?"

"Why do you look so surprised?"

"Um, maybe because you've been promising to ask me out on a real date since we were seventeen?"

"My mistake." He grinned fetchingly, his dimples still affecting her, though not nearly as much as they had before. "I'm getting wiser in my old age."

How many times had she fantasized about this very moment?

"What do you say? Pick you up at seven?"

Now it was happening, and something made her hesitate. "You could have just called instead of coming out here." That would have given her time to mull it over.

He shrugged. "I knew I'd have a better chance if I came in person. So I'll take that as a yes?"

"Well, it's just that . . . I mean . . ." Was she going to keep turning down dates for the rest of her life if they didn't meet her perfect conditions? If there was the slimmest chance of getting hurt?

It wasn't like Manolo was going to ask her to the Splash party. She'd all but asked *him*, in so many words, and all he'd said was he'd think about it.

She shrugged. "Okay."

"Great." His business done, he turned and walked back toward his truck. "See you tomorrow."

Chapter Twenty-four

Manolo expertly fondled a tomato at the Clarkston market. It had been one week and three days since he'd last set foot in Brendan Hart Vineyards. It had taken a lot of willpower to stay away since he'd arrived back in Clarkston yesterday. But he told himself he'd run into Junie later today, at the pool party.

He rejected the tomato and squeezed a different one. Only the best would do to top the burgers he was going to grill at the party. The summer vegetable crop was starting to come in. He could afford to be choosy.

He bagged the rest of his produce and went up to the check out. While he cooled his heels in the long line of holiday food shoppers, he tried to sort out the troubling past few days in Virginia.

Heidi had sought him out, knowing it was his Reserves weekend. Heidi was a babe, she had a kick-ass job in the nation's capital, and she was willing to take him on his terms—translation: whenever it suited him.

The tasting room job was done, and so was his tenure at Brendan Hart Vineyards. In two months, he'd be in Belize. Junie would be nothing but a memory.

That was as it should be. There was no place in a footloose man's heart for a grounded woman like Juniper Hart.

He would cherish this summer's detour in wine country. But soon it would be time to gather speed again, ramp onto the fast lane and all that went with that. If the past was any indication, he'd be back on the prowl, or at least open to whatever fruit fell into his lap.

Manolo had always loved the thrill of moving on.

So why did he suddenly feel indifferent?

His ardor for Heidi had evaporated. He bought a round of drinks, sat down next to her in a quiet corner of the bar, and told her gently but firmly that they were over and he wished her all the best.

The person in line behind him cleared her throat.

How long had he been standing there like a statue?

"Sorry," he said, and started unloading his basket onto the belt.

"Got big plans for tonight?" The attractive cashier, who didn't happen to be wearing a ring, gave him a saucy smile.

"Nope," he said, helping to bag his supplies. "Going to a pool party tomorrow. Tonight I'm staying home by myself."

"Good luck with that," she said with a hint of disappointment in her voice. "Tomorrow looks like rain."

July fifth dawned cloudy but thankfully dry.

After checking out the plumbers' progress on the consortium, Manolo returned to his apartment to slice lettuce, tomatoes, and onions and pat ground chuck into burgers. When everything was organized, he sat down on his rented couch and looked at his hands, mulling over an idea he'd been thinking about ever since he heard that Junie needed a wine distributor. It was a notion that had started as a glimmer and grown until, no matter how hard he tried, he couldn't get it out of his head. He glanced again at his watch. Back in Hoboken, the restaurant would be slowing down. This was as good a time as ever to catch his father when he wasn't too busy. Swallowing his trepidation, he punched in the number.

Izzy answered.

"How's it going?" He strained to hear the familiar clatter and chatter in the background. It all came back to him with a rush, each time he called home. The smiles on the faces of guests as they enjoyed their pastas, the tall pizza stands crowding the center of the tables. His mother, a permanent fixture at the entrance, greeting every customer, then later ensuring that everyone left happy. But lately, when he called, the visual memories were becoming less clear. Manolo was unsure whether forgetting was a blessing or a curse.

Izzy sighed. "Not bad."

"What's that supposed to mean?"

"I said not bad. Not good, but not bad, either."

Manolo didn't miss the subtle distinction in Izzy's standard reply. Without fail, she always said that things were fine.

"What's wrong?"

"Nothing's wrong."

"Something's wrong. Tell me what it is."

"Business is a little off, that's all."

A wave of foreboding restored his memory. In a flash, he was *there*, in the restaurant that was more the family home than the brownstone they slept in. Its murals and wood paneling had gone out of style in the eighties, but that hadn't stopped the steady stream of faithful who flocked to Santos's for his dad's famous sauce and steak and risotto.

"What's 'a little off'? Ten percent from last year?"

Izzy didn't answer.

"Fifteen percent?"

"Twenty-five."

Manolo rose from the couch and stared blindly out the window. This was all his fault. If he'd stayed, like a good son, he would have seen trouble coming. He would have known what to do. Revitalized it. Changed the decor, changed the menu . . . something. Anything.

"Where's Dad?"

"Please, Manny. Not again."

Frustration and guilt seeped into his voice. "I need to talk to him. Maybe I can help."

"You want to help?" asked Izzy angrily. *Izzy, the calm one.* "Why don't you come back here and do it then, instead of calling me?"

Manolo caught himself. "Never mind."

He thought he'd found common ground with his dad—trying to hook Junie up with Santos and Son's liquor distributor. He'd been planning to ask his dad to put in a good word for Junie. If it'd worked out like he'd planned, Dad would have been flattered. After all, Manolo had gotten his big ego from someone.

"Sorry I yelled," Izzy said.

"Forget about it. Give my love to Mom."

He hung up and stood there, processing what had just happened. It had never occurred to him—that Santos's wouldn't always be there to fall back on if he got tired of pushing back against the earth's spin.

Manolo thought he had carved out the perfect life, free of responsibility to anyone or anything. For sixteen years it had suited him fine.

Then he'd met Junie Hart. And for the first time in his adult life, he was plagued with uncertainty.

The Belize contract was still on his laptop. Why hadn't he printed it out and signed it? The prospect of yet another new job in a new location used to energize him. But this time it almost seemed like a chore.

He blinked into focus the horizon beyond the Clarkston Savings Bank that sat across the street from his apartment. Something about the Willamette defied the quiet, pastoral quality of an ordinary agricultural zone. He felt it wherever he walked, an energy humming just beneath the surface.

At first, he'd dismissed it as the shock of the new. Every unexplored place gave Manolo a rush. But then weeks had passed. He'd learned his way around the valley, started recognizing landmarks. Maybe he was getting sentimental, at the ripe old age of thirty-four, but this time the sensation didn't go away.

Analyzing topography was his specialty. He noticed things other people didn't. For instance, the ridgelines and valleys back east were packed together tighter than prom night. Here, the landscape rolled out gently, past Douglas fir, feathering softly out from a point like Christmas trees in a children's book, to the horizon of snow-capped peaks.

So he did some research. The Appalachians are old—four hundred eighty million years old. The Coastal Range is much younger—only forty million. *Twelve times younger.* Was that what gave the Willamette Valley its youthful feeling . . . a sense of untapped potential, as if anything could happen, and the best was yet to come?

Then there were the unique layers of Willamette soil, basalt on top of lava on top of ancient ocean floor. Junie said that and the maritime climate were the secrets to her wine. It went against logic, but he couldn't shake the sense that *anything* rooted in that soil could produce miracles.

Chapter Twenty-five

An hour into the Clarkston Splash, a casual observer would have thought Manolo Santos was having the time of his life . . . quaffing beers with the guys, competing to see whose cannonballs could make the women scream the loudest, run the farthest. No one would have guessed he was paying more attention to the area outside the chain-link fence than inside it.

Dusk was falling. Manolo estimated the crowd at fifty, give or take. Keval and Poppy, Junie's closest friends, were there. Sophia, the therapist who was nicknamed Red and whom Sam had a thing for, was poised poolside holding her plastic wineglass. *Whew*, Manolo whistled admiringly under his breath. *Legs for days, just like Sam said.*

So where was Junie? Asking would only start tongues wagging. He'd just have to wait.

Manolo's volleyball team was up by two when his ears detected an approaching vehicle. It was his turn to serve. He spiked it, then glanced toward the sight of the flame-blue pickup roaring toward the pool area.

When it reached the entrance, its driver stomped on the brakes. The rear end fishtailed around as the truck came to a screeching halt across two spaces.

Conversation stopped. The volleyball rolled out of bounds, unnoticed, while the truck bounced on its struts and the dust settled. Over on the board above the churning water, a swimmer poised to swan dive changed her mind at the last second, teetering precariously on one foot.

The alpha driver jumped down out of the cab and paraded around the hood. He was tall and undeniably handsome in his aviators and leather jacket, worn in all the right places.

"I'd love to take that bad boy for a spin," Keval breathed over the pop song playing in the background.

"The truck?" asked Poppy, eyes glued to the spectacle.

Daryl held open the passenger door, strategically positioned to showcase the emergence of its occupant like a butterfly from a cocoon.

The crowd held its collective breath as a pointed and polished toe laced into a strappy sandal dipped out.

"Who's that?" Heath drawled, craning his neck.

Daryl had timed their arrival for that moment when the sun's long rays lent a golden glow to everything in its path. A tanned leg was followed by a yellow sundress, fitted to a waist the span of a man's hands, and a head of glossy seal-brown hair.

"There's something you thought you'd never see," murmured Rory.

"What?" Keval asked. "Junie Hart with Daryl Decaprio? Or Junie, all decked out for a *Vogue* cover shoot?"

"Either," Poppy said, wide-eyed.

Manolo's jaw clenched. She was killing him in that dress. For once, he couldn't fake his usual careless smile. He didn't even try.

With her weighty canvas bag in one hand and Junie's arm in the other, Daryl led his queen toward them, and the crowd parted as if a bridal couple was marching down the aisle.

Her lips glistened with a hint of color, her lashes had been curled and lengthened until they almost brushed her freshly groomed brows. Even the most polished New York diva had nothing on her. Yet her expression was as inscrutable as the Sphinx.

Manolo sent her a silent plea. *What the hell are you doing?*

Daryl broke the silence with a loud slap to Heath's back. "Hope you saved me some brewskis." He found a bench to deposit the bag on. Then he abandoned Junie without a word to stroll over to the clutch of people standing at the opposite end of the pool and pop open the dripping cold growler someone handed him.

Manolo's muscles bunched in anticipation of springing toward Junie, but Keval, Red, and Poppy beat him to it. They closed ranks around her, shutting him out of their inner circle.

He felt the vein in his neck throbbing. Thank god his burgers needed attention. That gave him something to do with his hands, instead of marching over there and waterboarding Daryl Decaprio for no reason except for that jacket and the fact that Daryl had had the unmitigated audacity to lay his hand on Junie Hart's arm.

While he kept one eye on the degree of pinkness in his burgers, he kept the other on Junie. Before long, her crew shrank back from peppering her with questions, and she pulled her wine bottles from her bag and placed them on the picnic table.

Her hair, which used to be plain brown, shone with golden highlights in the sunset. And what was with that skirt? He didn't recall ever seeing her in anything but jeans. No better proof that her mama was a dancer.

Meanwhile, on the far side of the pool, Daryl had joined in a rowdy game of beanbag toss.

Something smelled like it was burning. Manolo tended to the grill. When he looked up again, Junie was surrounded by a clutch of brand-new admirers. He recognized them from the job. Daniel owned the roofing company. Carlos was an estimator. Sharp as a tack. He couldn't recall the electrician's name.

Sam walked up and thrust a fresh beer at Manolo. "How's it going over here? Can I give you a hand with anything?"

"You can get over there and do what it is you do," Manolo growled between his teeth. "Guard the henhouse."

Sam rocked back and forth on his heels as if they were discussing nothing more volatile than the weather. "Why should I?"

"You didn't waste a minute telling me to back off when you thought there was a *ghost* of a chance I'd be moving in on Clarkston's icon of womanhood," he growled.

"Big difference between you and them," Sam said, calmly swigging his beer.

Manolo brandished his spatula in the air and copped a challenging pose. "What's that?"

"Not one of those homegrown boys is going to love her and leave her."

Manolo tried to digest Sam's blunt words as he plated the burgers. They were hard to swallow, but Sam was right. Junie would be better off paired with someone who wouldn't destroy what was left of her tattered heart.

Chapter Twenty-six

The following week, Junie and Keval were at Sam's place for a class in promotion for small wineries. Junie was restless. She kept fidgeting, thinking about all the unfinished work waiting for her back home.

"Can't you be still?" Keval hissed, giving her bouncing foot the evil eye.

She drew her foot up and sat on it to anchor it.

A minute later, she looked longingly out at blue sky and white clouds. Clear days were scarce this summer. She pointed her nose in the direction of a faint breeze.

"You look like a Labrador with her head out the car window."

She switched her feet out from beneath her. "Right now I should be positioning shoots and spraying for mildew, or be down in my barrel room, racking last year's wine. Instead I'm sitting on my butt in this stuffy house."

She'd gotten a glimpse of Manolo in his hard hat on her way to class. How could she concentrate, knowing he was working mere feet away?

The instructor's monotone droned on.

Junie replayed the pool party yet again in her mind. After arriving an hour late to pick her up and then choreographing their entrance, Daryl had pretty much ignored her for the rest of the evening. That night had shown her what Daryl really was: a lightweight, plain and simple. She'd lost so many nights of sleep over the years, pining for him! But now she felt nothing. Daryl was out of her system, once and for all.

She'd lined up with the others for one of Manolo's burgers, getting more and more nervous as the line dwindled, knowing that any minute she'd be standing right there next to His Bare-chested High-ness. He had been clad only in board shorts and a souvenir apron em-blazoned with KEEP PORTLAND WEIRD. Not staring at his body as she inched closer and closer had been nearly impossible. Other than Daryl, he'd been the only man within miles not sporting facial hair. His upper body had been as smooth as his chin. Inked across one bicep was a compass rose. If more proof of his footloose philosophy was needed, the globe on his other arm left no doubt. Junie had to clench her fist to stop her finger from reaching out to trace the lati-tude and longitude lines encircling it. Once she started, she wouldn't stop there.

But when she was standing before him, paper plate in hand, he'd treated her the same as everybody else, with his usual irreverence. He hadn't even seemed to notice that she had arrived on Daryl's arm. There'd been no hint of the jealousy he'd displayed the first time they'd run into Daryl at the market.

After everyone was fed, Manolo had played lawn darts and swam and acted like he didn't have a care in the world, while Junie wished she'd worn her swimsuit and cut-offs instead of a stodgy dress.

Now, in Sam's house, the cross-breeze gained strength. "I smell rain," she whispered.

"Pay attention," Keval scolded without moving his lips. "It'll help you understand what I do online for you better."

She tried. Sam had said staying abreast of trends would give her points with distributors.

She skimmed over the bullet points in the handout and leaned against Keval. "Who can afford a flashy new website or buy tons of doodads stamped with their name to give away?"

"You want my opinion?" Keval asked.

"Is there a question back there?" the teacher snapped, craning her head to glare at Junie and Keval.

"No question," Keval answered meekly.

When the teacher looked away Keval tapped his pen on the words, *Food Service*. Next to it he wrote, *Munchies = ka-ching*.

In fact, more than one visitor to the new tasting room had in-quired where they could get something to eat. She was starting to feel like a broken record, repeating the directions to Main Street. Also, she didn't like seeing the disappointment on their faces when the vis-itors realized how scarce food was on the wine trail.

They had a point. But even if she had had the money to spend on a kitchen, the very idea made her head hurt.

It's not about Cheez Whiz and crackers, she wrote back, illustrating her point with a sketch of a face with its tongue sticking out sideways and Xs for eyes.

Keval rolled his eyes at her stubbornness.

Hardly any wineries serve food, she wrote.

Exactly, he scribbled back with a flourish, dropping the pen and folding his arms in a victory pose.

Chapter Twenty-seven

S am sheltered his eyes as he peered up through the fine drizzle at the roofers. "I don't know, Lieutenant. Laying shingles in the rain doesn't seem like a good idea to me."

"I made sure they kept the decking covered whenever they weren't working on it. If we were laying a new roof on an old building, that could be a problem. Once the siding's installed, everything'll dry out."

"If you say so."

"I have interior paint samples to go over with you. But first I could use a cup of Poppy's coffee. Want me to grab one for you while I'm over there?"

"That'd be great. Now I'm getting in out of this damp." Sam shoved his hands into his jeans pockets and hustled back to his house.

Manolo took his time strolling over to the café. With Junie's tasting room finished, he should be relieved to be doing only one job instead of two. But the truth was, he missed it. He'd loved everything about that project. Aside from the obvious, the actual construction, he'd found satisfaction in donating his time and expertise. Maybe EWC hadn't found him a volunteer opportunity this summer, but he'd found one himself, right under his nose. The invoice Junie was expecting would never be sent.

He looked left and right as he traversed Clarkston's main thoroughfare, admiring its clean streets, its red brick buildings and dark green awnings. It was easy to pick out the tourists from the locals. They were the ones in rain ponchos craning their necks at the architecture, peering into shop windows, reading menus posted in the windows of the few restaurants. There wasn't a tour bus in sight, though. Clarkston was still unknown to the hordes who flocked to Napa and Sonoma. The town was still a charming slice of Americana, largely undiscovered. If people like Sam had any say, Clarkston would stay quaint, no matter how popular its pinot became.

As he reached Poppy's Café, he thought yet again about Junie.

Red looked up from her corner booth when she heard the door's bell jingle. Manolo envied how dry and cozy she looked, hunkered down with a steaming cup of tea, reading on an electronic tablet. They exchanged greetings as he headed for the lunch counter.

"Hey, Poppy. I'll take two black coffees, to go."

"Coming right up."

"Your parents still up in The Great White North?"

"Huh?"

"Canada. Little country above Washington state."

"Oh! I get it. We talked about that at the hike, didn't we?" she recalled as she rang up his order.

"You told me you were just filling in."

She pulled two cups from the sleeve. "It's a little more complicated than that. I got a call from Portland. The wine shop I manage there is being sold, but there are still a million details to be worked out." She secured the lids on the cups. "I'm juggling all that plus keeping an eye on the staff here and hostessing at a restaurant known for its extensive wine cellar."

"Word is, you're going to be a lady somm."

"Just a somm," she corrected him good-naturedly. "We take the same test they give the guys."

"I grew up in the restaurant business, a long time ago. We used to call them wine stewards."

"I passed my introductory test. The next step is becoming certified. I sit for my exam later in the year."

He raised his to-go cup in a toast. "Well, here's to you. I hope you pass the test with flying colors. By the time you take it, I'll be long gone."

"Oh? Where are you going?"

"Not sure yet." Some place far, far away, where he could learn to forget about a certain brown-haired girl.

A photo of gooey-looking rolls on the stack of menus on the counter caught Manolo's eye. *Poppy's Famous Buns*, read the caption. He bet Sam, Keval, and Holly wouldn't hate him if he brought back a plate to share. "Hey, you got any of these sticky buns?"

"Coming right up."

The shop phone rang and Poppy answered.

"Dr. Hart! How are you? Junie? No, I haven't seen her."

Manolo froze at the mention of Junie.

"I wouldn't worry too much. Junie never listens to her messages." There was a pause. "Yeah, sure. Hold on. Red," she called, "have you seen Junie lately?"

Manolo swung his head around to where Red sat curled up, reading. Red shook her head. "Sorry."

"Red hasn't seen her either. She's probably just swamped. You know how it is this time of year in the wine business. You need to get last year's wine in the bottle, and this year's crop picked. When those two jobs overlap, things can get really hairy."

Manolo's mind raced. He hadn't been out at the winery since he'd finished the tasting room. Hadn't seen Junie in town, either. He'd figured she just had her hand to the plough.

But for her mom to be worried didn't bode well. Jen and Junie weren't as close as some mothers and daughters, but they kept in touch.

Was Junie in trouble? Farm work was hazardous. Anything could happen. His imagination flooded with all the things that could go wrong. A roll of the tractor, a nasty slice from her pruning shears, or simply a bad fall, out of reach of her phone.

Poppy was speaking again. "Don't do that, Dr. Hart. Don't drive all the way down here if you don't have to. I'll go over for you and see if she's there."

He wanted to jump in his truck, speed out to Brendan Hart Vineyards and make sure that Junie was safe.

But wasn't that exactly what he'd done when he'd gotten involved in her tasting room? Run off half-cocked before thinking about the consequences? Even when he had toiled there during the hours when she was at Casey's, her scent of wildflowers and sandalwood lingered, disturbing his peace. It was enough to drive a man insane.

He'd promised himself he wasn't going to interfere in her life anymore. But now his thoughts went back to the pool party . . . Junie wearing that sundress, local men buzzing around her like bees to honey. Salt-of-the-earth men, every one of them. *That* was the kind of man she should be with. Not a drifter. Not him.

Red came up to the counter. "I'm coming with you," she told Poppy. "Should we take her something?"

"Good idea." To a wide-eyed server, Poppy said, "Take care of business till I get back?"

Poppy thrust Manolo's bag of buns into his hand, and then, with the jangle of the doorbell, she and Red were gone.

Manolo would be worthless until he saw for himself that Junie was all right.

He grabbed his coffees and headed out the door at a trot.

He made it back to the consortium in record time. "Ow! Dammit," he exclaimed, setting the cups down on the first available surface and waving his burning hands.

Sam raised an eyebrow.

"Take my advice, don't ever run carrying hot coffee," said Manolo.

"You didn't have to hurry on my acc—"

"You talked to Junie lately?"

Sam's amused grin turned upside down. "Not since the pool party." He swiveled his head and yelled in the direction of a back room. "Keval, you seen Junie?"

Keval appeared in the doorway, looking concerned. "Not lately."

Manolo said, "Her mom can't find her. She was getting ready to drive down here from Portland to look for her."

Sam rose slowly. "No reason to panic," he said, his words contrasting with his body language. "Junie's probably just got her hands full. Lot of pressure this time of year, especially for a grower *and* a vintner. You've got a bunch of things happening all at once."

"Hold on," Keval said, disappearing again. Moments later, he called out, "The last time she checked in on social media was early last week."

Ten days ago. "How often does she normally get online?" yelled Manolo.

Keval walked back out from his geek lair. "Most everyday."

"I'm going out there," he said, grabbing his keys.

"Give us the lowdown when you get there," called Sam to his back.

Keval and Sam were still standing in the consortium doorway wearing somber expressions when Manolo roared by Sam's house in his truck.

Chapter Twenty-eight

Junie smiled to herself when she saw the Mini Cooper bopping toward her house, forgetting her anxiety over the forecast for yet more rain. From the far end of the vineyard, the car looked like a child's toy.

But her smile was fleeting. *What is Poppy doing here at this time of day? Shouldn't she be manning the café?*

Her next reaction—that she didn't have time for a social call—was immediately followed by guilt. It was already three, and she still had to mop the tasting room floor before she got ready for her other job.

But she couldn't ignore her friend. She stopped spraying and turned the tractor back toward the house. Given that her Amish Ferrari only went about five miles per hour, just getting there was going to eat precious minutes out of her day.

When she reached the barn, she climbed off the tractor and strode across the grass at a determined clip, pushing back her hood as she skipped up the porch stairs where Poppy and Red sheltered themselves from the rain.

Poppy greeted her with, "You look awful."

"We all can't look like a Nordic goddess," Junie snapped.

"Poppy didn't mean that, did you?" Red gave Poppy a pointed look.

"What? What'd I say?"

"Never mind," said Red. "Listen to me, Junie. Your mom called. She asked us to come check on you."

"She's freaking out! Wondering why you won't—"

Red cut off Poppy's hysterics with a quelling hand.

Junie said, "I was planning on calling her—" *When?* She shook her head, trying to recall the myriad items on her to-do list, when the drink in Poppy's hand caught her eye. Her stomach growled. She was thirsty—and ravenous. "What's that?"

Poppy thrust the bottle toward her. "One of those good-for-you drinks. I know how you sometimes forget to eat. By the looks of you, you've been forgetting a lot. What are you doing, Junie? I've been trying to get through to you, too. You don't answer your phone. You won't respond to anyone's texts."

"What does it look like I'm doing?!" Junie screeched, holding out her arms in their protective suiting. "I'm working! You have no idea of the work that needs done around here! Speaking of which, if you don't mind—" She whirled around to go back to her spraying.

Red caught her before she reached the first step. "Calm down. We're just worried you might be pushing yourself a little too hard. It's not healthy to shut out the people who care for you."

Poppy narrowed her eyes. "You're pale as death."

"Did you happen to see that fat orange ball in the sky lately?" Junie screamed, pointing skyward. "Me neither! Maybe if the frickin' sun would come out, the grapes would start maturing and—"

"Shhhh," cooed Red consolingly. "I know you're dedicated to making the winery a success, Junie. It'll happen, in time. But you have to balance work with rest and seeing your family and friends and—"

"Stop telling me what to do! I'm fine! If I don't do all this work, who will? Don't you get it? I need to get last year's vintage bottled before the crush and the barrels rinsed, and my quarterly taxes are due and—"

Poppy and Red went wavy all of a sudden, as if she were seeing them through antique glass. She felt weak...so weak. She was faintly aware of the unopened drink slipping from her grasp, falling onto the porch as her knees collapsed beneath her.

When Manolo saw Red and Poppy bent over a body on Junie's front porch, he broke into a run, reaching her within seconds.

He knelt beside her. "Junie."

Her eyes were closed, her lips white. Frantically, he searched Red's and Poppy's faces.

"What happened?"

"She passed out. I would have called 911, but I only have two bars on my phone and I'm saving them for—"

"She just overdid it," Red interrupted. "She's exhausted. Or it could be her blood sugar. Who knows when she ate last. Poppy, see if you can get her to drink some of that juice."

While Poppy unscrewed the bottle's lid, Manolo lifted Junie's head and shoulders onto his thighs. She was as limp as a rag doll. He held her head steady while Poppy said, "Here, drink this."

Junie's forehead furrowed and she coughed as Poppy poured a bit of the liquid down her throat.

"That's better," Red soothed.

"Now, what actually happened?" Manolo repeated.

"She was on her tractor. She didn't seem too thrilled to see us," said Poppy.

He studied her face more carefully. Her pallor made his heart clutch. New hollows carved out her cheeks. She needed a good meal in her. And then another one. And another, until her strength was built up again.

Poppy prodded her to drink again.

Manolo lowered his face to within inches of hers. "Junie. Can you hear me?"

At the sound of his voice, her lips curled upward in a faint, yet unmistakable, smile.

Manolo exhaled for what felt like the first time since he arrived.

"It looks like the drink is helping," Poppy said.

"For now. But if she keeps up this lifestyle, she's going to have a *real* collapse," said Red.

"Let's get her inside." He gathered Junie up into his arms. "Someone get the door."

Manolo deposited Junie in a kitchen chair.

After they'd assured themselves that she was steady enough to sit by herself, Poppy promised she'd call Junie's mom, and Red said she would update Sam and Keval. Then they left Junie in Manolo's care.

Manolo rooted around in her cabinets.

"Where's the peanut butter? You always have peanut butter."

"I'm out of peanut butter."

"What else do you have that might have protein in it?"

Behind the fridge door, Manolo grinned, releasing the strain of weeks of self-denial. A soldier sacrificed feelings to duty. He'd been sacrificing his desire to avoid hurting her. But it had taken its toll. Seeing her again, even under these dire circumstances, buoyed his whole being.

Of course, admitting that to her was out of the question.

He slammed the fridge door, planted his hands on his hips, and strode over to where she sat. "Why don't you get out of that OSHA suit and we'll go get something to eat? Something that'll stick to your ribs."

It must have been the mention of dining out. This time she *leapt* to her feet.

"What time is it? I have to be at Casey's!"

"You won't be much good to them today. Can't you take a day off for once?"

She sighed. "I suppose it wouldn't hurt, just this once. I'll go upstairs and call while I'm changing."

The moment she was out of his sight, he couldn't wait till she was back. He hoped she didn't take her time getting ready. "No sundress required," he called after her.

Chapter Twenty-nine

Junie marveled at the pleasant sensation of a full stomach. She'd come to disassociate that gnawing feeling from its meaning, that she needed to stop her infernal striving and eat. At some point in the past few years, she had come to accept that empty feeling as normal.

Instead of cramming the second slab of buttered bread Manolo handed her into her mouth like she had the first, she took a breath, savoring the sweetness of the butter, the fragrant, fresh-baked goodness.

"You're staring."

"I like watching you eat."

Her eyes crinkled at the corners. "You're just a tease."

"Not always." He seemed intent on one thing and one thing only—filling her up.

"I was thinking of the day I made you eggs."

"And I didn't have any bread."

"It took awhile. But I always knew there'd be a next time. Want what's left of my pasta carbonara?" His hand was already poised to slide it across the table.

"Thanks." She squelched a burp. "I'm good. Now, will you take me back to my place? Now that I don't have to go in to Casey's, I'd like to finish spraying."

"Not yet."

Whenever she was around Manolo, the air throbbed with his energy. She wasn't the only one who felt it. He could work a room better than anyone she'd ever met. But there was something else. Something personal that only she felt. During the day, she could stuff it into some hidden recess of her mind. But that only forced it to seep out later, when she let her guard down. More than once since she'd met him, she'd sat up gasping for air, blushing in the dark from the explicit dream she'd been having about him.

Still. His ego was already big enough.

Besides, having a crush on someone and taking orders from him were two distinct things. "I'm perfectly capable of making my own decisions. I don't need to be babysat."

"I'm not into babies. I prefer big girls who can take care of themselves."

She rejected the notion that he could be interested in her as anything other than another conquest.

No. She'd be safer keeping her feelings locked up inside where he couldn't use them against her. Take advantage. And then disappear, like all the others.

"Dessert?" asked the server, offering two menus.

Junie gently pushed the menu away. "No, thanks."

Manolo cracked his menu open to point to the picture of a decadent chocolate cake.

"We'll have the *No Really, Though* cake and two forks."

Junie raised her index finger. "One fork."

When the server was gone, he looked at her approvingly. "Strong. That's what I'm talking about."

Oh, he was good. He knew just what she wanted to hear.

"How about a compromise? I'll finish the spraying. You kick back the rest of the day."

"And what about tomorrow, and the next day, and the day after that? I could hand over all my chores to you. That still wouldn't accomplish what needs done. Bottom line, it's not working. Don't get me wrong, the tasting room's beyond gorgeous. The few tastings I've taken you to don't begin to compare with what you've done for me. But I still don't have enough customers." She sighed and ran her hands through her hair. When they met with resistance, she tore out the elastic band that held her top knot and stretched it taut between her fingers. "I've got to think of something else by the crush. I don't intend to lose a single vine to Tom Alexander."

Manolo let his usual careless mask fall and softened his voice a notch. "I wish to hell you had told me you were going to that guy. I'm not made of money, but I'd have found it somehow." He leaned in, resting his forearms on the table until their hands were almost touching. He looked down at where she fiddled with her elastic band and caught one edge of it with the first knuckle of his middle finger.

She tried not to notice their micro version of tug of war. But her traitorous finger parried with him against her will. "Aren't you the one who told me my idea would never fly?"

"That was before I got to know you. Before I saw your grit. Found out how loyal your friends are. If you knew how many people in this town have your back . . ."

The band stretched more. "If I'd borrowed from you, I'd be in the same position, handing my property over to you if I default."

"I never would have taken your vineyard as collateral. There are other ways to go about it. I could have invested in it as a silent partner. That way, you would still make all the important decisions."

Junie's eyes dipped down to the band, stretched to its limit between their fingers. "Well, it's too late now."

"It doesn't have to be."

Damn him, tempting her to hope.

"Have you noticed that out of all the wineries you've taken me to, the most crowded were the ones that had food?"

All at once, she made a face and folded her arms in open defiance. The elastic band sprang across the table.

The waiter set down a slab of the richest looking chocolate cake Junie had ever seen. "Here you are. One *No, Really Though*, one fork."

Manolo took a giant bite. He swallowed and asked, "You want to be a point of destination for people? Feed 'em." He dug in and held up another bite to illustrate his point, and then happily devoured it.

"If you recall from our tastings, it's a rare winery that offers food. Maybe a little cheese and crackers, but that's it."

Manolo sat back on his chair. "I noticed that. And I don't get it."

"If people want food, they can bring their own."

He nudged the cake plate aside and locked eyes with her. "Now, see, that rubs me wrong in so many ways. For example, how is someone who's never been to a winery supposed to know that it's acceptable—even expected—that they bring their own food?"

"The wineries usually mention it somewhere on their websites."

He threw up his hands. "Who has time to read the fine print? Maybe it's my restaurant background talking, but in my humble opinion, there's something strange about toting food into a watering hole. When you go to a bar, do you take your own peanuts?"

"I guess if you come from a place that doesn't have wineries, you might find it a bit unusual."

"I noticed it the first day Sam brought us into your place. We'd been drinking all morning. We were already lit. No news there."

She opened her mouth to speak.

"I know what you're going to say. 'It's okay to spit when you're tasting wine.' Encouraged, even. But to the average Joe, that sounds like industry speak. In case you didn't know it, wine tasting can be pretty intimidating. All my life I'm told, spitting's rude, spitting's bad—unless, of course, you happen to grow up and play for the Yankees. Now all of a sudden I come out here and you're telling me spitting's good? How many of your customers actually use that spit bucket you keep at the bar?"

Not wanting to admit he had a point, she made a wry face. "Not many."

"Exactly. Know why? Because men have been given the subconscious message that if you can't hold your liquor, you're not a real man, and women are conditioned that spitting's not ladylike."

Junie couldn't help chuckling. He'd hit a bull's eye with his observation.

"That day we showed up at your place half tanked, we needed food. But there wasn't so much as a bowl of popcorn. I thought it was because you were operating on a shoestring."

"Why are you telling me this now? You can't expect me to open a restaurant. I'm already in hock up to my neck."

"Remember the outdoor kitchen I was talking about at the lake?"

She'd been trying to erase that picture of tasting room porn in her head ever since. "Noooo . . ." She shook her head adamantly. "I don't want to serve food."

"Hear me out."

"I've been schlepping food since college."

"You don't have to be open year-round, you know. You can be seasonal. And I'm not talking about a full menu. You just need something tasty and simple that can be tweaked to pair with your different wines, and you will have people talking, coming back for more. How about this? I'll be your pizza man for this year's crush."

"Haven't you done enough? I know that tasting room set you

back more than you're willing to admit, even without charging me for the labor."

"That project rocked! I loved that there was no blueprint. Nobody telling me what I could and couldn't do."

Hard as she resisted, the idea was tempting. "Is there even time to do something as complicated as an outdoor kitchen before the crush gets here?"

"It'd take, let's see . . . build the frame, set the mortar, shape the stones, veneer, install fixtures . . . twenty-one man hours."

"Twenty-one?" She couldn't help laughing. "Not twenty, or twenty-two?"

"What will take the longest is getting the permits and waiting for the appliances to arrive. We need to get them ordered right away."

By the way he talked, it was already a done deal.

"You'll have zero budget," she warned him.

"Limitations free up creativity. In redoing your tasting room, the challenge was to utilize as much as possible of what was already there, scrounge for bargains, and throw in one really unique piece like that wood slab. Usually I'm trying to please someone else with my work. Here, the only ones I had to please were you and me."

"That all sounds great. But you're missing the whole point. It's about the wine."

"No." He scooped up more cake with his fork and jabbed it toward her. "*You're* missing the point. This is not about furthering your dad's legacy or setting your mom free to find a new life. It's not even about the wine."

She frowned, watching the cake disappear into his mouth.

He swallowed the last bite and dropped the fork to the empty plate with a clatter. "This is about you holding on to the only home you ever had."

Junie felt her face blaze with anger. How could a rambling man understand her need for permanence? His values were the exact opposite of hers!

"I can make that property of yours the talk of the Willamette. Then those wines you work so hard on will finally get the attention they deserve, and you'll start turning a profit and finally have some financial security. If you want to make it all official, I'll have something drawn up in writing, the same way that maggot Alexander did."

Junie struggled with her competing desires.

Finally, she said, "You must really love building things."

He shrugged. "It's fun coming up with something in my head then watching it take shape. Might be a hospital today, a big plate of lasagna tomorrow. Even better when it makes someone's life better."

"Enough to do it for free?"

"You've heard that saying, 'Do what you love, and the money will follow'?"

Her eyes lit up. "Ask my mom—I tell her that all the time." Then the light went out. "She doesn't get it."

"The saying isn't 'Do what you love, and everyone will understand.' I'm living proof of that. Following your heart means taking chances, trusting that things will work out." He reached across the table and laid his hand atop hers. "Don't worry. It's gonna be great."

Chapter Thirty

By the end of the first week in August, the oven and grills as well as a half-size fridge were on order. Junie watched the glowering sky as Manolo poured the concrete for the patio.

"What if it rains before the concrete sets?"

"It might even look better with the aggregate exposed. But to be safe, I'm going to use a prophylactic." He winked.

"'Scuse me?"

"Cover it with plastic."

While Manolo drove off to town to oversee the interior work on the consortium, Junie went down to the cellar to taste last year's vintage. It had to be bottled soon if she wanted to prevent the worst-case scenario—bottling last year's wine at the same time she was crushing this year's harvest. There wasn't enough room at her boutique winery for pickers and bottlers to be there at the same time. It would mean mass confusion, just when she was getting ready for the year's biggest festival. But you couldn't rush the wine. It was like a baby inside the womb, a living, growing thing. It told you when it was ready for the next step in the process; you didn't tell it.

Junie pulled up her spreadsheet. She slipped her wine thief into a barrel, withdrew a sample, and deposited it into a glass. The routine was always the same. First, note the color: light cherry red. Then the nose: mild and restrained, with hints of red fruit. Next came tasting. She was looking for balance across the tongue. She entered, *Flavors of mild red fruits; sweet cherries*. Last, a strong peppery finish.

She tasted again, still not satisfied.

There was nothing to do but try again later.

* * *

Sam and Manolo clapped on their yellow hard hats and entered the consortium.

"Aaah." Manolo sniffed audibly. "I love the smell of sawdust in the morning."

"How's Junie?" asked Sam, inspecting the trim on a doorframe.

"Still pretty wired. That woman's a machine. She's trying to do the work of six men."

"Vintage Junie," Sam replied, as they continued down the hallway. "Her pinot's unmatched. Unfortunately, there's more to it. A potential distributor wants to know how a brand is going to improve their portfolio. They're looking for professional producers that already have a solid customer base."

"It's more than the lack of visitors that's got her in a tizzy. It's the lack of sunshine. Thought you told me Oregon has dry summers?"

"We usually do. Haven't you noticed? Weather's crazy all over this year. Junie's not the only one who's worried. I'm hearing it from all the members. The grapes need sun to ripen. If this keeps up, every AVA in the valley could be facing a bad vintage."

"None of the wine will turn out good? That can't happen," he pronounced, shaking his head, as if he could control the climate.

"Do you think you could bring a couple distributors out to Junie's place to see the changes we've made?"

"Hart Vineyards is on my crush itinerary. Be nice if the place wasn't empty when they showed up."

"I got an idea."

"You always do."

"We're going to lure our prey in with food."

They had circled back to the new consortium's public tasting room. Sam stood with hands on hips, admiring his clean, new venue. "I have to hand it to you, Lieutenant. This is going to be amazing."

"All that's left to do are the floors, painting, and landscaping."

The crush was a mere two and a half weeks away. A hundred things could still go wrong. Manolo crossed his fingers behind his back that nothing would.

Sam turned to him. "Now what's this about food?"

"I convinced Junie to let me put in an outdoor kitchen with a pizza oven. There aren't many wineries that serve food, and those that do only have measly snacks. She'll be the only game in town."

"Hold on," Sam said. "How far have you gotten with this hare-brained scheme?"

"Applied for the building permit, ordered the appliances, and poured the patio. What's the matter? Are you scared that building a bistro for Junie will take me away from your project? 'Cause you should know by now—"

"It's not that."

"You're not going to slap my wrist again for being too involved with Juniper. Because if that's where you're going—"

"Man, did you ask yourself *why* none of the other wineries around here offer food?"

He paused. "I'm not going to like this, am I?"

"It's because it's against the law!"

"It can't be. Junie already has Keval advertising it all over the valley and on the internet: *Come one, come all! Brendan Hart Vineyards will have pizza for the crush!* Once that's out there, it can't be undone."

Manolo had promised this to Junie. He couldn't renege.

"You of all people should know that food service is regulated—"

"—and every state has different rules, no matter how archaic," Manolo finished for Sam. He snatched at the first solution that came to mind. "You've got connections. Is there anything you can do? Anyone you can talk to?"

"I've just built up my collective of wine growers and vintners. I'm their voice. Everything I do, every move I make, represents them. They're counting on me to be a straight arrow. You don't expect me to jeopardize that with so much as a whiff of controversy."

Manolo scraped his hand through his hair. "Of course I don't. Forget it. I wasn't thinking. Like when I made this gallant gesture to Junie without researching it."

"Man." Sam shook his head. "You're in deep."

Manolo ducked his chin, though he knew trying to hide his twisted grin from Sam was futile.

"Red saw it, too."

"Red? I don't recall sharing anything with her more profound than our opinions on the best burger toppings."

"Hypothetically, Red might have mentioned you looked a little green when Junie waltzed into the pool party on Daryl Decaprio's arm."

"Whatever happened to doctor-patient confidentiality?"

"I said *hypothetically*. But it doesn't take a therapist. You'd have had to be blind not to see it."

"Junie's a nice girl."

"Who's caught you, hook, line, and sinker."

He threw out his arms in surrender. "I like her. What's not to like?"

"She's not going to appreciate being embarrassed in front of the whole world."

That was an understatement. "I'll figure it out."

"No."

"No, what?"

"I owe you."

"You don't owe me a damn thing."

"Yeah. I do. She came to me and asked me to vouch for you, and I didn't step up to the plate."

"She did? Junie?"

"The day of the hike. She wanted to know if you could be trusted."

Manolo's heart started thudding. There were a million things Sam could have said in response to that question, only a few of which were positive. "What'd you tell her?"

"I told her to listen to her gut."

"That's it?" He exhaled. "You went easy on me."

"I could have done better by you. I should've told her about the time you risked your own skin to step in the middle of that kerfuffle involving the AK, over in the sandbox."

"Aw, cut it out."

"How, when I was trapped between a rock and a hard place, you got me out."

"Standard procedure," said Manolo, flicking a wall switch, pretending to check the power. "You'd have done the same thing."

"If Red had come sniffing around for intel, you'd have had my back."

Manolo huffed. "All I'd have done was tell the truth. *My* record isn't exactly spotless where women are concerned."

"About that law. Let me see what I can do. I know a certain soft-bellied, cake-eating politician who owes me a favor."

"I'm not asking you to pull any strings. I just want to know where we stand before those appliances get here and I need to tell Junie we have to turn around and ship them back."

"Mind telling me one thing first? What's going to happen after all this is over?"

"You already know the answer to that. I'm out of here."

"The Belize job?"

He'd stared at that contract for an hour, deciding whether to sign it. He tried to fool himself, telling himself his main interest in Brendan Hart Vineyards was in the property, not its owner, despite the fact that Junie's mere presence sent every nerve in his body on edge. That his growing obsession with pleasing Junie was nothing more than the satisfaction he got from helping any person who needed a hand.

But the truth was, he was scared.

Did he want to bed Junie Hart? More than he cared to admit, even to himself. But that wasn't what scared him. What got to him was knowing in his gut that, unlike with all the others, once he turned that corner with Junie . . . once he held her slender body in his arms . . . devoured every, captivating inch of her, no one else would ever compare. From that moment onward, he would spend more and more time with her in that sweet farmhouse her dad built for her on that fertile hillside overlooking the valley, until the day came when he'd wake up feeling like he had his leg caught in a trap.

No. *That* wasn't even what got to him. What scared him, finally, was imagining the pain it would cause both himself and Junie when he had to chew *off* that leg in order to free himself.

Unless, of course, he had an obligation to fulfill, somewhere far, far away.

That employment contract was his exit strategy. His insurance policy.

"I'm committed. The contract's signed, sealed, and delivered."

Hell yeah, he wanted Junie, though he was going to keep trying his damnedest not to cave to temptation. But just in case he did, now he had an excuse not to stick around.

Sam tsked. "Things are about to get interesting."

Chapter Thirty-one

On a warm, overcast afternoon in mid-August, Junie was potting roses in planters while Manolo was hard at work on the bistro.

Whenever he was there, Junie had fallen into the habit of looking for random chores to do near the tasting room.

When she heard a rapid-fire *pop-pop-pop*, she looked up to see him discarding his snap-front denim shirt, slinging it across a tree branch.

She spent the next couple of hours sneaking glimpses of his upper body in its full range of motion as he applied mortar to the stones and set them onto the frame around the patio.

When the sun was low in the sky, he brushed his hands together for the last time and began collecting his tools.

Junie pulled off her gardening gloves with a casualness that belied her thrumming pulse. "I'm going down in the cellar to do a trial tasting to see if last year's vintage is ready to bottle. Want to come along?"

Manolo snapped the lid on his toolbox shut and turned to face her. "If last year's wine still hasn't been bottled, then what is it we've been drinking?"

"Come on. I'll show you."

With every step into the cellar, the air grew chillier on her skin. When they reached the bottom, they were surrounded by the yeasty smell of fermenting grapes.

Manolo sniffed. "Smells like my nona's fruit cellar. She used to can fruits and vegetables for the winter. When climbing stairs got too hard for her, she'd send me down to get what she needed. I could never forget that sweet, earthy smell."

First, Junie took him into the bottle case room. "This is the wine we're currently selling. It's two years old. This is also what I'll be promoting at this fall's crush."

"That's a lot of wine to keep track of."

She waved a tablet. "It's all here, on spreadsheets going back to when I was a teenager."

Then they went into the larger barrel room. "This is the wine from last fall's harvest. It's been down here fermenting all year. The wine is the baby, the cask is the mother. It cradles the wine until it's ready to be born.

"These past few weeks, I've been running trials, tasting it almost every night. Timing's everything. It's like 'Goldilocks and the Three Bears.' If I bottle too soon, the wine will lack spice and earthiness. Wait too long, and it'll lose its fruitiness. The moment it reaches perfection, it needs to be racked—filtered from these barrels into a big, stainless steel tank—and then bottled."

"What happens if this wine's not ready before the crush?"

"A nightmare, that's what. Because I need these barrels," she said, giving a curved wooden side a fond slap, "to be cleaned and sterilized by then. I'd rather not be doing everything at once."

Junie collected two glasses and a long plastic tube from a corner table. Handing him the tube, she opened a port on an oak barrel. "Now. I want you to gently insert the thief into the opening."

"Yes, ma'am."

"When it's full, withdraw it and press the tip against the side of the glasses until the fluid flows out."

When he'd done that, they clinked glasses. "To the crush," said Manolo.

It took all Junie's concentration to look away from his black eyes. But she'd promised to teach him about wine and so far, she had barely scratched the surface.

"I'm going to ask you to make five decisions. Tell me, is this wine ruby, garnet, or purple?"

"What's the difference between ruby and garnet?"

"Garnet is more orange."

He studied his glass. "I'd say it's more garnet."

"Now, I want you to savor a sip. Let the wine wash over every taste bud on your tongue. Which berry flavor do you taste? Red, black, or blueberry, or raisin?"

"Red."

He slid his foot forward a few inches, enveloping her in his warm aura.

"You're not paying attention," she scolded weakly, inching backward till she was brought up short by the table.

"Sorry, teacher."

With a growing uneasiness, she followed his hand as he reached around to set his glass on the wood with a soft *tick* that echoed through the cavernous room.

"Ahem. Question number three. Is the fruit tart, ripe, jammy, or dried?"

"I love it when a woman's smarter than I am." Now he relieved her of her glass as well.

Her pulse pounded, and she didn't know what to do with her empty hands. "We're not finished."

"You got that right."

Now her chest was visibly rising and falling. Knowing he saw the effect he had on her only made her breath come harder.

He planted a foot on either side of hers. She looked up to see his eyes finishing a circuit of her body just before colliding with hers.

"You know it's going to happen." Manolo peered down at her from his superior height. His posture was erect, his shoulders squared, his elbows poised like a gunfighter, ready to draw. He had a feline alertness about him, as if he might pounce at any second. His hands clenched and unclenched, worrying Junie with their indecision.

Junie's moist palms gripped the table edge behind her, her breath fast and shallow. Words failed her. The silence expanded until it filled the room with anticipation.

Then Manolo's jaw twitched and his mouth tightened into a line. He turned away. "What was the question?"

Junie let out her held breath. "Um . . ." And she thought she knew this routine by heart.

"Fruit. Tart, ripe, or jammy."

To her relief and disappointment, he retrieved their glasses. "I need to refresh my memory."

The test ended with Junie pronouncing the wine still not ready. "Not quite spicy enough."

"It will be, soon," said Manolo with a meaningful look. "You know it as well as I do."

* * *

A week later, Manolo met with the painters at the consortium in the morning, then drove out to Junie's. He had to remind himself to back off the gas when his speedometer edged too far over the limit. He had a premonition that in the years to come, whenever he thought back to this summer, he'd cherish the days he'd spent at the vineyard most.

From some five hundred yards away, Junie raised her pruning shears in a wave.

Knowing she might appear at any moment, combined with the panoramic views of the valley and the mountains, made his job anything but a chore.

But, apparently, Junie's work ethic surpassed her need to see him. Hours passed and she was still out there, babying those vines. The anticipation was getting to him by the time he finally glimpsed her little orange tractor putt-putting toward the barn.

He rose from where he was trimming away the protruding parts of a large stone and watched her dismount.

But his happiness faded when he saw the agitation in her eyes.

"What's wrong?"

She handed him a small tool. "Look."

He turned it over in his hands. "Looks like my nona's potato peeler."

"You put a drop of juice in and the reading tells you the Brix— how much sugar's in the grapes."

Manolo squinted into the end. "It's like reading a thermometer. Says fifteen."

"Do you know what that means?"

"By the look on your face, it's not good."

"The grapes aren't ripening fast enough. The Brix should be climbing into the twenties by now. Twenty-five before I can pick."

"What's that mean in the big scheme of things?"

"This could be a bad vintage."

The worst-case scenario that Sam described to Manolo might be coming true.

She opened her gloved palm. "See all these hens and chicks?"

"I see a bunch of grapes."

"Notice how they're all different sizes and shades of green and purple? To get a good yield, every grape in the cluster needs to be the same size and color. These aren't maturing at the same rate."

"Don't worry. Maybe the weather will break before the harvest. No sense in panicking—"

Vertical lines etched the space between her brows. "I'm not panicking!" She yanked her hand back. "Just because last year's vintage isn't bottle-ready yet and this year's harvest isn't ripe, and if they wind up both being ready at the same time the pickers are going to be falling over the bottlers and I'm going to go nuts keeping an eye on everything at once, doesn't mean I'm panicking!"

"Junie—"

"And what will I do if the ovens don't get here in time? What if they *do* get here and, still nobody comes to my grand opening you worked so hard on? *What if none of this works?*"

Manolo's hands encircled her toned, slender arms. His breath caught at her vulnerability. He was a soldier. Soldiers hid their feelings. But this was no time to pretend he didn't care. "Junie! Stop doing this to yourself. Stop getting yourself so worked up."

What if she found out his bistro idea might not even be legal, on top of all her other concerns?

She tore free from his grip. "It's not your winery!" she exclaimed. "You don't get it. You're not the one with everything to lose!"

Manolo's thoughts leaped to Hoboken, to the restaurant he'd thought would always be there. But he'd think about that later.

He grabbed her again, steadying her. "I *do* get it."

"How could you?"

"Because my own family business is slipping away!"

Some soldier he was.

Junie frowned. "What are you talking about?"

"Forget that." He pointed down the road. "Look what's coming."

Junie's head whipped around to see the white truck. "The pizza oven! The grills!" She turned to him, her face radiant. "We're in business!"

Manolo returned her high five.

Now what, though? He'd been hoping against hope that he'd be the only one present when the boxes came. His plan had been to store the appliances unopened in their original cartons until Sam gave him the word on whether their use was permissible. Now Junie was going to want him to install them right away.

He helped the delivery man unload the boxes.

Junie led the way. "Over here, on the patio."

Before the driver even got back in his truck, Junie asked Manolo if he had a box cutter in his tool box.

"Nope. Sorry."

"That's okay. I'll go get mine."

"Uh, hold on."

She stopped and sniffed. Just minutes ago, she'd been close to tears. "Why? I can't wait to see them!"

The thought of disappointing her was killing him.

"I was just about to wrap up here." He put his arm around her and turned her in the opposite direction. "Why don't you go in and take a warm shower? You'll feel better after you've cleaned up."

She frowned, looking over her shoulder. "Don't you want to see what we got? At least make sure the order's right?"

"That can wait. I brought something." He jerked his chin toward the house. "How'd you like to do a wine and pizza pairing tonight, to figure out what we should serve for the crush? I brought some green and red and yellow peppers, some fresh pineapple, ham, pepperoni. . . . How's that sound?"

"But . . ."

"Go on now. I'll be in as soon as I get this cleared up."

He went to the barn and got a tarp to throw over the appliances in case it rained.

Then he sped through his clean-up ritual. He wanted to be ready with a confidence-boosting smile and an appetizer when Junie came downstairs, post-shower.

Later that night, Manolo and Junie sat around her kitchen table, laughing at all the variations on pizza and wine they'd tried. Barely an inch of table wasn't covered with crumbs or bits of toppings or half-empty wine bottles.

"Okay," Junie said, waving her pencil around in a tipsy circle. "I've got your Margherita for my rosé, the Hawaiian with the Riesling, and white pizza with the pinot. Is that what we decided on?"

"That's it."

That bistro just had to be legal. Junie would be a basket case if it turned out not to be, after all this. Not only that, he would have sacrificed her trust.

Junie dropped her pencil, drew one bare knee up under her chin, and craned her neck toward the window. "When did it get dark outside?"

Manolo glanced outside out of deference, then returned his gaze to her, sitting there in her cut-offs and T-shirt.

Junie played with the fringe on her napkin. Shyly, her soulful eyes met his, and he knew beyond a shadow of a doubt that if he took her hand and led her upstairs, she would go willingly.

Ever since the day he moved her mom out, Manolo had carried the memory of a blue patterned comforter lying in a tangled heap on Junie's bed. In his imagination, it still held the warmth of her body.

Junie's damp hair was twisted into a simple topknot. Her face was squeaky clean from her shower, without a trace of makeup. He pictured loosing that hair, getting lost with her in those warm, blue covers, sampling her from head to toe.

The tension in the room was palpable.

Run, he told himself. *Run while you still can.*

He rose and scraped back his chair. With shaking hands, he started gathering up the dirty dishes. "I'll get this," he said.

Chapter Thirty-two

Saturday and Sunday nights after maneuvers, Manolo usually hit the hot spots surrounding Fort Belvoir. But this weekend he begged off.

His buddies didn't take it well. They coaxed and cajoled. "Your flight doesn't depart till Monday morning. You just going to hit the rack?"

But the thought of yet another night of carousing left him cold. He found himself sitting at a sedate bar, having a quiet beer with a couple of married officers.

One of them pulled out his phone and showed Manolo a picture of a rosy-cheeked woman in a ski jacket. "This is my wife, Grace," he said fondly.

"I call her Amazing Grace," chuckled the guy on the bar stool opposite him. "'Cause before her, he was a wretch."

A wretch like me . . . His phone vibrated, interrupting the old song lyric playing in his head.

"I'm calling from the hospital. I thought you might be out on drill, but I knew you'd want to know," said Izzy across the line.

Fear shot through Manolo. He got up from the bar and strode to a secluded corner where he could talk in private. "What is it?"

"Mom fell. She broke a rib, and it pierced her lung."

Manolo sat at Reagan National Airport in his camos all night, waiting to nab a stand-by seat into Newark.

Late Monday morning—Labor Day—he rushed into Hoboken University Medical Center. Far down the hall on his mom's floor, he glimpsed the back of an old man meandering, as if lost. The man's gait looked eerily familiar. Manolo hadn't seen his dad for two years. But that couldn't be him. Dad's walk was directed, purposeful.

In his quest to find Mom's room, Manolo ignored the stranger. But when the man reached the end of the hall, he turned and walked back, toward Manolo. As his features came into focus, a cautious hope sprouted in Manolo. *Might Mom's fall have a silver lining?*

"Dad?"

His father looked up, and Manolo's hopes were dashed when, instead of joy at seeing his son, his father's eyes held only bitterness.

Hope vanished, and guilt, Manolo's constant companion, filled the void. He steeled himself for a frosty reception.

"Who told you?" Dad growled in place of a greeting.

"Izzy. How's Mom?"

Dad resumed his pacing. "They got a tube down her throat so she can breathe."

"Is she—can she—?"

"Any luck, she can breathe on her own in a coupla days."

Thank god. "Too bad it took a fall to convince her she needs a knee replacement."

"You know about her knee?"

"I try to stay in touch." Didn't Dad know he called his mother once a week?

Manolo pictured his mother when he was growing up. "She's always on her feet," he mused, half to himself.

Dad stopped and barked, "You act like she works because I make her!"

"Where'd that come from? I never said that!"

"That's why you left, isn't it?"

"You think I'm afraid of hard work?"

A woman in scrubs passed, giving them a disapproving look.

His father lowered his head and walked on.

Manolo followed him. "Yes!" he spat when they were alone again. "You made me feel like being born into this family came with some kind of obligation!"

"Poor you." His dad dismissed him with a wave of his arm. "The only son of a successful businessman, having a profitable business handed to you on a platter. But no. That wasn't good enough. You had to go off to Timbuktu, to do who knows what."

"I wanted my own life. I've tried explaining it till I'm blue in the face. What will it take to make you understand, to stop taking it personally? It's nothing against you."

"Easy to say, when you left me here with four women, one of who is now an invalid."

It was like this every time he came home. His father was implacable.

Dad paused outside a door. "This is it. You goin' in or what?"

It was another twenty-four hours before they took the tube out of his mother's esophagus. Manolo timed his visit so that he could be alone with her.

She was dozing when he sat down next to her. He gazed down at her sleeping form. She was the only person who had never rejected him for pursuing his dreams, never withdrawn her affection. Izzy tolerated his impulses, but even Izzy had suffered as a result of his abandoning the family. Mom was the one constant in his life of continual change. Her love never wavered. Even in a hospital bed, barely able to breathe on her own, she was still the center of his universe.

Finally, her eyes flickered open. "Manolo." Grinning, she took the hand he offered and kept hold of it. "I'm so happy to see your smiling face. Did you come just for me?"

She'd been so out of it yesterday, she didn't even recall his being there. "Of course. I got here as soon as I could."

"You know I cherish our phone calls," she rasped, hoarse from the ventilator. "But it's so good to see you in person. You look wonderful. You look—" She adjusted her vision. "Different. Like you've found whatever it is you've been looking for all these years."

If she saw something in him, he owed it to her to pay attention. To discount it out of hand would be a violation of something sacred.

He tried to see himself in his mother's eyes. And what he saw was a lonely man, still living the self-imposed life of a vagabond after all these years.

Mom patted his hand. "Stop punishing yourself, Manny. All you did was search for what would make you happy. Your father didn't understand. But I knew you didn't mean to hurt his feelings. You deserve to be loved." She closed her eyes, tired out by the effort of her speech.

Love? What's love but a noose around your neck?

He hated to disturb his mom further, but who knew how much longer he would have her? There was something he had to ask.

"Mom."

"Hmm?" Her eyes opened a crack.

"Why'd you do it? Sacrifice your whole life to Dad, to the restaurant?" In the end, all it had gotten her was this—lying in a hospital bed.

"Because I love him," she said without hesitation. "It's not a sacrifice when you're in love."

Of course. She'd gotten that love too—and a family he knew she loved with her every breath.

Everything in his life had been going as planned. He'd thought he could keep running from his feelings forever.

Then came Junie. It had started with her side porch, then escalated until he'd gladly spent half his summer and half his savings on her property. He'd chalked up his behavior to nothing more than his usual desire to be helpful, combined with common lust.

Soon, he'd be facing yet another major transition—an escape he'd carefully crafted. Why, this time, was he resisting running?

A very pregnant technician appeared in the doorway, rolling an awkward piece of equipment.

Automatically, Manolo jumped up to assist her, reality snapping him out of his sappy thoughts.

He was getting all cornball because his mom was hurting. The reason he was feeling so out of sorts lately was simple. He'd violated his own principles. Let his feelings for a West Coast farm woman build up until they spiraled dangerously out of control.

Mom's head lolled toward him on its pillow. "One day, you'll realize it's not where in this world you lay your head. It's whose head's lying next to yours that's important."

He turned to the pregnant lady bending to plug in an electrical cord as his mom's prophecy sank in. "Here, let me help you."

Chapter Thirty-three

Junie examined her farmer's almanac. Tuesday. Only five days till the crush. Tonight's moon was waxing, almost full. Grapes picked at the full moon retained their juice better than at any other phase.

Her pickers were on stand-by. She'd been checking the sugar levels in her grapes morning, noon, and night, hoping against hope that the moment the Brix hit that magic number, her crew wouldn't already be tied up, picking at another vineyard.

When she wasn't checking the grapes, she was tasting last year's wine and trying to keep up with data entry and cleaning the tasting room for her increasing tide of visitors over the Labor Day weekend.

She paused outside on the new patio to look helplessly at her appliances, sitting forlornly in what was supposed to be a bistro. She'd install them herself if she could. But there were limits to her abilities.

Where is Manolo? Normally, he flew back from Reserves on a Monday. She'd hoped to have heard from him by now. But he was always guarded about his plans. And she had too much pride to call. Her emotions toggled between wishing she'd never met the man and counting the minutes until she saw him again. She tried to stop thinking about what he looked like in his uniform, grinning that fourteen-karat grin.

Halfway out to the vineyard with her refractometer in hand, she noticed something unusual. Shielding her eyes, she looked up. A bank of gray clouds drifted slowly eastward, leaving behind a swath of pure sapphire blue.

It was a sign.

She picked a handful of single grapes from random bunches and tested their combined juice as usual. With growing anticipation, she tested from another row, and another. Then, trembling, she whipped out her phone and punched in the speed-dial number for her crew chief.

"Adrian? How soon can you get out here? My Brix is at twenty-five!"

"We'll see you at three a.m. sharp," Adrian replied.

Junie punched the air and let loose a squeal she was sure could be heard all the way to Rory's orchard next door.

This called for a celebratory glass of wine—as soon as she checked her barrels. With a giddy blend of excitement and apprehension, she skipped down the cellar stairs, pulled up her spreadsheet, and snatched the wine thief. Forcing herself to remain calm, she withdrew a sample and deposited it in her glass.

She'd been waiting patiently for this wine to reach maturity for a whole year. It was ironic that she didn't want it to happen today. Not today, when the pickers would be arriving within hours!

But wine didn't adhere to anyone's schedule. Like a developing baby, it was ready when it was ready.

She sipped, noting its crucial characteristics, as she had been doing for months.

Then she sipped again.

With trembling hands, she pulled out her phone.

This wine was ready—*now*.

"When can you come?" she pleaded with the bottling man.

"First thing Thursday."

Junie hung up, her heart pounding. This was exactly the situation she'd been hoping to avoid. There would be no sleep tonight. She needed to start racking her wine immediately to be ready for the bottlers. The pickers would be arriving even sooner—before dawn.

But before the onslaught of people and machines and activity, there was something that couldn't be put off.

Solemnly, she poured two fingers of her best vintage and carried her glass out to the vineyard.

"Here's to you, Dad," she said, raising her glass to the heavens. Then, in accordance with tradition, she poured half the wine onto the ground. "And here's to a good harvest." She downed what was left. "Let the festival begin."

Chapter Thirty-four

Following the next-to-the-last inspection before the consortium's grand opening, Manolo held open the door of Sam's old house for him.

"Soon as you figure out an alternative for that shrub that's unavailable, I'll get it ordered and the landscaping should be done just in time for the final walkthrough on Friday," Manolo said.

Sam pulled off his yellow hard hat. "I'm just thankful this weather finally broke in time for the weekend. In fact, I'm inclined to start celebrating early with a beer when we finish here. Join me?"

"I should get out to Junie's, now that I know we're a go. I appreciate your help with that."

"Easier than I expected. All I did was get the county interpretation of the state law."

"Clock's ticking. Junie's probably getting antsy to get her new pizza oven put in."

"You didn't call her and let her know about your mom?"

His answer was a sheepish expression.

Sam shook his head. "Don't tell me you're still keeping with that asinine rule not to call women that you made, years back."

"It's served me well. Guess it's ingrained in me now."

"Anyway, I'm glad your mom's going to be all right."

"As soon as her lungs are strong enough, she's going to have that knee replacement she's been putting off."

Holly appeared from a back room. "I've got news," she said, eyes twinkling. "Brendan Hart Vineyards is starting to pick."

Sam pulled up short on his way to his desk. "That *is* news. Junie tell you?"

"No. I heard it from Rory. He got it from Heath, who heard it from Poppy down at the café. Poppy's friends with Sage, who, rumor has it, has been seeing Junie's crew chief."

Manolo's head spun. "Are there *any* secrets in this town?"

"Stick around," Holly said. "You'll be surprised."

"Well," said Sam, "it's official. Looks like the circus has begun. After months of relative calm, now comes the fifty-yard dash that will determine every winemaker's reputation for the next couple of years."

"There's more. Junie called Haggarty's, too."

"Who's that?" asked Manolo.

"Chris Haggarty and his wife run a mobile bottling operation."

Manolo felt his heart skip a beat. "Junie's picking and bottling at the same time? That was always her worst-case scenario."

Sam huffed a dry laugh. "The wine wants what the wine wants. Trust me, it's going to be unabridged chaos. She'll be racking twenty-four-seven until the bottler gets there. Then there's the big festival on Saturday. Thanks to Keval's promotional know-how, Clarkston's expecting record crowds this year. Even hired extra cops to manage the flow of traffic in and out of town."

Manolo headed toward the door.

"Where're you going? Thought we were going to look at some alternatives to that dogwood the landscapers can't find."

"I'll get back to you. Right now, Junie needs me more than you do."

"I know about plants," Holly said. "I'll help Sam."

"You sure?"

She brushed him off with a wave. "Go. We'll figure it out."

Watching Manolo sprint down the steps to his truck, Holly sighed. "Junie Hart's a lucky girl."

"The Lieutenant's one outstanding individual," said Sam. "But don't tell him I said so. His head can barely fit through the door as it is."

Holly just smiled.

On his way out of town, Manolo took a detour through the Clarkston Market and sprinted through the aisles, tossing peanut butter and sandwich fixings into his basket.

When he got to Junie's house, he refrigerated the perishables and left the rest sitting on the counter while he made a beeline for the tasting room, but she wasn't there.

He went over to the patio and held a hand over his eyes to shade them from the afternoon sun as he scanned the vineyard. But there was no sign of her bright orange tractor.

In the tasting room, mechanical sounds rumbled under his feet. He skipped down the cellar steps.

Yards and yards of hoses lay coiled over the rows of wooden barrels, some feeding off a portable pump that was the source of all the noise, others hooked to a piece of equipment that he recognized from his engineering background as an ozone machine.

Junie was lifting a huge barrel by herself.

"Hold it! Let me do that."

"Don't worry," she called over the noise of the pump. "It's empty. You got here just in time for the fun." She gave him a droll smile. "The wine's ready. I'm getting ready for the bottler. These hoses take the wine out of the barrel into the pump, then into the filtration tank. It'll go through a light filtration, then into another tank."

Now she attached a metal wand to the next barrel in line. There was a sense of urgency in her movements.

"What can I do to help?"

Without stopping, Junie replied, "As soon as each barrel is racked, the empty has to be flipped over and washed out with hot water, then filled with ozone to sterilize it." She turned to him hopefully. "Want to be my barrel washer?"

It took only seconds for him to size up the situation. He stepped into position, relieving her of the barrel.

"Try to keep up. I have to get all this racked by the time the bottlers get here on Thursday morning. On top of that, the grapes are ready, too. The pickers are coming at three—"

He frowned. "It's already past three."

"Not three this afternoon. Three tomorrow morning!"

They worked side by side through the night, with only a short break to eat the sandwiches Manolo hurriedly threw together. At two-forty-five, they went upstairs to wait for the pickers to arrive.

Manolo sat on the edge of the patio next to Junie to catch his breath. The air felt humid and warm after the cool of the cellar. "Can I ask you a stupid question?"

"Sure," Junie said, panting.

He reached over and brushed a lock of hair from her eyes.

"Why the hell would anyone want to pick grapes in the middle of the night?"

She wiped her brow with her arm. "It's cooler for the workers than working under the hot sun. They can work longer and more efficiently. Plus, it's better for the grapes. The sugar's more stable and they're cooler at the time of picking, which means I don't have to cool them artificially before I crush them.

"Look." She pointed across the dark valley, where a sprinkling of lights bobbed and dipped like fireflies. "We're not the only ones picking tonight."

They watched for a moment; then their eyes shared a moment of satisfaction at the hard work they'd accomplished together. Junie rested her hands behind her on the bench that he had built, leaned back her head, and closed her eyes.

Manolo studied her starlit profile, amazed at what fate had thrown together on this sultry late summer night, at this intimate hour: a city boy and a country woman, as opposite as the coasts they were born on. He thought of what his mother had said to him only hours ago: *You look like you've found whatever it is you've been looking for.*

All summer, he'd been stuffing his emotions, keeping things on a friends-only basis, believing it was best for Junie in the long run. He'd had a lot of catching up to do.

But if there was ever a moment made for romance, it was this one.

He leaned over and kissed her.

She responded cautiously, first leaving her hands behind her, flat on the bench.

Misgivings overtook him. He'd known this was a bad move!

But the dam had broken behind the force of his pent-up feelings.

Like a flower unfolding, she came to him, wrapping her arms around his neck.

He moved his hands along her sides, sliding his thumbs across her lowermost ribs. He marveled at how she could be so fragile, and yet so resilient.

Her hands tangled in his hair as their breathing came faster and stronger.

Then—*dammit*—the sound of approaching vehicles broke the silence of the country night. Manolo tore his mouth away from Junie's to see headlights streaming toward them.

The pickers swarmed out of their vans wearing fluorescent safety vests and headlamps strapped over their red and blue bandanas. Each grabbed a plastic bin and headed right out to the middle of a row. By the time the pans were loaded, the tractor hauling a flatbed was wait-ing. When it was stacked high with grapes, the tractor hauled them to the crush pad in back of the tasting room, and the process began again.

Now Manolo realized why Junie had been so meticulous about keeping the canes trained up, the ground between the vines so clean. It was so that her pickers didn't trip over canes or roots in the dark.

He swelled with admiration for her. All those brightly painted ladies in his past paled in comparison with Junie's many talents, her thoughtfulness.

He followed a single picker down a row to watch him work, mar-veling at the speed with which the man used his sickle-shaped knife.

When the man rose and carried his pan of grapes to the flatbed, Manolo gazed up at the pre-dawn sky. The full moon had set hours ago. Now blues, pinks, and violets swirled above the ripening earth. One by one, the stars blinked out.

And that's when he knew: He could plant roots here.

The thought was fleeting. Easy to say, now—when he was con-tractually bound to start his new job in Belize in exactly five days.

"What happens to the grapes?" Manolo yelled to Junie over the noise of the generator powering the portable lights.

"They get crushed, stemmed, and sent into a vat for a month of skin contact."

"Skin contact?"

"The skins are what gives red wine its color. The first load is on its way to the crush pad. Let's go."

Junie showed him how to pour the plastic bins full of grapes into the crusher/destemmer and where the berries—pulp, skins, and all—went into the open-top, stainless-steel vat to soak. These were the same hard, green berries he'd seen on the vines last April. He was fascinated to see the process by which the now fat, purple berries were turned into wine.

The pickers kept up their efficient pace until the sun was over-head. Then, they seemed to vanish as quickly as they'd come. Shortly after the last bins of grapes had been crushed, all was once again quiet.

Junie sagged onto a bench.

"That it?" Manolo asked.

"I should go back down and rack some more."

"Forget that. You've been going nonstop for, what? Twenty-eight hours?"

"So have you."

"And believe me, I feel it. Come on." He reached for her hand. "Time for a break."

Reluctantly, she let herself be pulled up. Manolo wrapped an arm around her, propped her up against him, and dragged their tired, aching bodies into the house.

Junie could barely keep her eyes open, but he sat a plate of apple slices hastily smeared with peanut butter under her nose.

She didn't have the strength to protest when he picked her up and carried her up the stairs to her bedroom.

"Thanks for everything," she mumbled.

"Goes both ways. I'm getting private lessons in winemaking."

She was limp as a rag doll when he deposited her on her bed in the fetal position and arranged the covers over her. "I'll be back," he said softly, though she was already fast asleep.

Chapter Thirty-five

"Come and get it!"
Junie woke up ravenous to the smell of home cooking and the sound of Manolo's deep voice. She checked the time. Five o'clock! She'd been sleeping for four hours.

She stumbled into the kitchen to see a plate already on the table. "What's all this?" She drifted over to where Manolo stood at the stove, spooning red sauce onto a second plate. "Chicken cacciatore."

She grinned up at him. "Where have you been?" she asked, still groggy. "Did you get any rest?"

"I had to check on something for Sam. Then I showered and took a power nap."

"You didn't have to do this," she said, tasting the sauce with a fingertip.

He held his spoon poised, waiting for her reaction.

"Mmm. Amazing."

"Got to keep up your strength. Damn, girl. I thought my family worked hard."

After supper, they went back down into the cellar and racked some more, until neither could drag one foot in front of the other.

One day rolled seamlessly into the next. Following a few hours of sleep, Manolo returned to the farmhouse at dawn, fried some eggs, and worked next to Junie until all the wine had been filtered from the wooden barrels into the steel tank, just in time for the bottlers' arrival the next morning.

Junie staggered from the tank to where Manolo was still washing and sterilizing barrels and picked up the hot water hose.

"I got that," said Manolo.

"I'll help you finish—" Her words trailed off. She staggered.

"Go on in and go to bed."

Junie felt like she had only just closed her eyes when her alarm went off at dawn. She stumbled downstairs in the oversized T-shirt she used as a nightie to make coffee, smiling when she saw that the task was already done. She poured herself a cup and took it out to the front porch, where Manolo was admiring the sunrise, as alert as if he'd been up for hours.

"There she is," he said, eyeing her appreciatively. "Morning, Buttercup."

"It's nice getting up to coffee already made," she said, suddenly shy. "I'm starting to get spoiled."

"You deserve someone to spoil you." He walked over, took her mug from her hand and set it on the windowsill. Then he picked her up and set her down on the porch railing, facing him.

"What are you doing?" She giggled.

His response was to move in between her legs, making her night-shirt ride up to her panty line. Then he reached under her naked thighs, pulling her in until his hips pressed flush against her.

Instinctively, she clamped her legs around his waist and threw her arms around his neck, returning his surprising, delicious kisses until they were both breathless.

Junie felt the warmth of his hands through the thin cotton as they traveled over her body. She arched toward him, and he placed his right hand over her breast, tentatively at first, as if it were a sacred object. She moaned, and his touch became urgent, molding her small breast to his large hand, centering his palm over her erect nipple. He dragged his mouth down her neck and cupped her rear end with both hands, kneading and pulling her in closer and closer until she felt his unmistakable arousal between her legs.

When his mouth left hers abruptly, she felt bereft.

His attention was fixed over her shoulder.

She turned to see the Haggartys' shiny, mobile bottling plant rolling toward them.

She hopped off the railing and made a dash for the door. "I need to go get dressed," she breathed.

"You go ahead," said Manolo, his eyes on the road. "Where do they work?"

"The trailer's self-contained. Everything happens inside it. I just need to get it as close as possible to my tanks."

"I'll guide them back to the crush pad."

Junie and the Haggartys confirmed the day's plan and the process quickly got underway.

Haggarty and Manolo took an instant liking to each other. Maybe it was because they both kept their facts plainspoken and their emotions bottled up.

Manolo stroked the silver exterior of Haggarty's custom semi. "Quite a rig you got there."

Haggarty lit up. "Want a tour?"

Manolo stepped up into the trailer.

"We run a crew of eight," Haggarty yelled above the continual rattling of glassware. "The bottles travel through a series of machines on their way from one end of the trailer to the other. This here high-tech machine sucks all the air out of the bottle so no oxygen gets into the wine. See?"

Manolo nodded in the din.

"After the bottles get filled, they pass along this conveyor to the labeler, then to the pack-off table."

Junie met him when he exited the trailer. "Pretty impressive, huh? Way more cost efficient than installing my own bottling line."

"Amazing. Looks like there's nothing for me to do here. I'd like to go get that pizza oven installed now, if you'll let me."

"Let you? I've been waiting all month!"

He grinned. "What's the matter? Didn't you trust me?"

"You're infuriating, you know that? If you weren't so handy, I'd . . ."

"You'd what? Now, don't get all excited, because I'm a busy man. I don't have time to be pleasuring women today."

"Excited?" she huffed. She took a swing at his arm and missed when he arced his body out of the way. "Who's excited? *I'm* not excited!"

"Now, if you'll excuse me, I've got to go show these fixtures who's boss."

Beaming inside and out, Manolo headed off to put the finishing touches on Junie's bistro. When he glanced behind him a moment later, he caught her looking after him with an exasperated expression.

He loved knowing he flustered her.

As when he worked on any humanitarian project, it occurred to him how it made no sense—a selfish bastard like he was, getting such a kick out of fulfilling someone else's dream. That was what he did, though, wasn't it? Helped out strangers to make up for letting down his own family. But he'd have time enough to dwell on that, soon enough. He might be a coward when it came to relationships, but right now he was on a high. Just for today, he didn't want to acknowledge that storm cloud gathering in his peripheral vision.

He worked quickly, hoping to finish while Junie was still preoccupied with the bottling. When the oven and grills and fridge were installed, he jumped into his truck and drove to town, where he'd been keeping the surprise extra touches he'd ordered at the same time he'd bought the consortium fixtures.

Later that afternoon, Chris Haggarty came over to say good-bye and admire Manolo's handiwork. "Good luck with the crush. I'll be sure and pass the word about the pizza oven here at Hart's. I get around some in my business."

As the semi drove away and Manolo was erecting the last colorful umbrella, Junie appeared. He stood up straight, planted his hands on his hips, and waited for her reaction.

She stopped at the edge of the patio. Her eyes met his briefly before flickering over his handiwork.

Then, in sharp contrast to the rush of the past few days, she floated as if on air beneath the pergola, trailing her hand across the stone, steel, and wood surfaces. She peered into the oven, the spotless fridge. When she finally looked at him again, her eyes were shining.

"You like it?"

Her mouth worked, but no words came out. She swallowed. "How can I ever repay you?"

"That look on your face just did."

She went back to examining and fingering everything in sight. "This is—wait until everyone sees it!"

"I need to do a food run tonight. The crush is in two days. Don't want to be buying groceries tomorrow, when who knows what fires I'll have to put out. That's the final walk-through of the consortium."

"What can I do?"

"You have a few volunteer baristas, don't you? You worry about the wine and inside your tasting room. I'll tend to everything that happens out here on the patio . . . the food, the music, the money. What time's the market close today?"

She looked at the time. "Less than an hour."

He picked up his tool box, strode over to Junie, and pulled her roughly toward him. Her breath came out with a rush. She pressed her hands into his chest and looked up at him with soft eyes, her lips open in invitation.

He looked down at her face, desire engulfing him like flames. If he caved to his ball ache now, it would be game over. He wouldn't let her out of bed for days. Those groceries would never get bought. And then there'd be no food for the crush—hell, no crush at *all* at Hart Vineyards—negating the whole point of this passion project.

He released her with a teeth-rattling suddenness and took off at a clip toward his truck.

This story wasn't over. He wanted to savor it, not jump ahead prematurely to the end.

When he was safely beyond arm's reach, he turned to see Junie watching him.

He charged on toward his truck, heart thudding with anticipation of what was yet to come.

Chapter Thirty-six

As usual, Manolo hadn't seen fit to inform Junie when he was coming back. Who knew when he'd show up? Tonight? Tomorrow? Not until Saturday?

I hate him, Junie thought as she took one last inventory, transferring cases from storage to the tasting room.

I love him, she thought every time she looked at her brand-new bistro. She'd forgotten how great it was to have a partner, someone to share the good and bad parts of a tough business. It didn't hurt that he had big muscles, either. He was attentive to every detail—as long as those details were tangible, concrete things. When it came to relationships—not so much. She couldn't get rid of the nagging suspicion that he might disappear for good at any moment.

But wasn't she equally at fault? She was too proud to ask. Or maybe she didn't want to know. There was something immediate . . . ephemeral about what they had. They lived purely in the present. Every moment with Manolo was like walking a tightrope high above the earth. Her heart was pounding with exhilaration at the freedom, yet she knew she could fall and suffer unthinkable pain. When there were no expectations, anything could happen. Every time they kissed, he took another little piece of her heart.

When dark fell, she gave up hope of seeing him that day. She trudged into the kitchen and opened a cupboard. To her surprise, she found enough food to get her through a siege. Six jars of her brand of peanut butter, soups, pastas, and fancy crackers. Familiar things that needed no preparation, and unfamiliar ingredients she presumed were for his recipes. She picked up a jar of artichoke hearts and smiled. Without meaning to, he'd given away a secret. He must be planning to do more cooking there, in her kitchen.

* * *

The day before the crush, Manolo was up at zero six hundred hours to plant shrubs at the consortium. He was to meet with the building inspectors at noon.

In anticipation of the flock of tourists, barricades were already being erected along Clarkston's Main Street to block it off for foot traffic only. The rainy weather pattern had broken, and the forecast for the weekend was nothing but blue skies. There was talk of an actual grape stomp and a pie-eating competition and a barrel roll.

No wonder Sam and Junie were so optimistic! The excitement was infectious.

He got the plants in and went home to shower, then met with Sam for the final walk-through before the inspectors arrived.

"You did a fantastic job," said Sam.

"This summer was way more than I thought it would be," said Manolo. "This is a special place you got here. Good people—even if they do dress like blind dumpster divers. I can almost see why you moved back here."

"Almost?"

"You know me. I don't let grass grow under my feet."

"What'd Junie say?"

"What do you mean?"

"About you leaving."

He shrugged. "She didn't say anything."

"You didn't tell her."

Manolo couldn't meet Sam's eyes.

"That is messed up. You got to tell her, man."

"I will."

"No, I mean, soon. What time's your flight Sunday?"

"I'll be out of here by dawn. It's an hour's drive to Portland, and I have to return my truck to the rental place."

Manolo spent that evening typing all his family's handwritten recipes onto his computer using the time-consuming hunt-and-peck method, and then he went to the additional trouble of sending the document to a print shop and driving several miles to pick it up.

Chapter Thirty-seven

Manolo was at Junie's place by ten hundred hours.

Wearing her shoulder-baring yellow sundress, Junie thumped a bottle onto her new bar. "Let's christen this place," she said.

Manolo grabbed the opener and did the honors. "Say when."

"All the way to the top."

He raised an inquiring brow. "Nervous?"

"Maybe a little."

"Trust me. It's going to be great." He raised his glass. "Buckle up, Buttercup."

There it was again—the T word.

But there was no time to worry about that today. They clinked glasses just in time before the flow of people began.

Poppy snuck out of her parents' café to support Junie, arriving with a gift of sticky buns cut into appetizer-sized bites. "Have you seen the bistro?" Poppy asked.

"I'm too busy behind the counter, selling wine."

"It's packed!"

Rory and Heath included her in their rounds, too.

Junie barely had time to breathe. The tasting room was jammed with people, talking, laughing, and drinking her wine. And before they left, many of them bought bottles.

Mid-afternoon, Manolo came through the door and joined her behind the bar. "How's it going?"

"I can't believe it," she said, raising her voice to be heard above the crowd. "It's all because of you."

He gave her a one-armed squeeze. "Without your wine, nothing I did matters."

"What's it like outside?"

"Why don't you take a break, come on out and have a look?"

Junie left her help to man the bar and followed Manolo outside to see people everywhere, seated at the tables and on the stone benches, or standing, looking out at the magnificent view. Some curious guests were even checking out the vineyard.

Keval arrived with Sam and Holly and a van full of avid wineaux who had signed up for a crush tour months ago.

"OMG. Love what you've done with the place!" Keval exclaimed, snapping photos left and right. "This is like your very own she shed."

"She shed?"

"Like a man cave, but for a girl."

She shook her head.

Manolo kissed her on the cheek. "Congratulations," he said above the music.

"Congratulations, indeed."

Manolo and Junie whirled around to see Tom Alexander standing shoulder to shoulder with Junie's mother.

Keval leaned over and whispered, "Uh-oh. I'm getting a bad feeling about this."

"Mom!"

Mom wore a swingy dancing dress that Junie hadn't seen in years.

"Look at you!" she exclaimed. "You're glowing. I'm so glad that you didn't give up on your dream."

Manolo said, "Nice to see you again, Dr. Hart."

"Have you met my friend Tom Alexander?" asked Mom.

"I have," he said coolly.

"Cheers." Tom bowed and lifted his glass to Manolo and then to Junie. "Looks like the crush is a success."

"I'm blown away," Junie said, fanning herself. "Today's been phenomenal."

Mom said, "This bistro is beautiful. Manolo. I understand you built this yourself?"

"I used to be part of a PRT. Provincial Reconstruction Team. We coordinated construction projects and provided humanitarian assistance, post-military action. Fancy way of saying we mopped up."

"But the food . . ."

"I grew up working in my family's pizzeria."

Sam appeared with Red on his arm.

"Pizzeria?" he repeated to Manolo. "Is that what I heard you say?" He turned to Junie. "Manolo's too humble. Santos's isn't just a pizzeria. It's a famous Italian restaurant. A landmark in the New York area. I've been there. There are pictures of celebrities with Manolo's grandfather and thank-you letters from presidents lining the walls."

Junie looked at Manolo, dumbstruck, while Tom glared.

Then her mom spoke again. "Junie, I have a surprise for you."

She pivoted gracefully on one foot, and from behind her appeared a slender, long-haired man.

"Storm!" Junie threw her arms around her brother.

He hugged her back stiffly, his hands cool and clammy on her exposed skin.

"How'd you—"

"I told him," said Mom, beaming. "It was Tom's idea."

"Where's your girlfriend? I mean your partner? Mom said you were living together."

"This is a business trip. I didn't see why she should come."

"Oh. Okay."

Junie saw her momentary hurt reflected in Manolo's eyes.

He reached for Storm's hand. "I'm Manolo Santos."

They shook, and Storm blanched, cradling his crushed right hand with his left when they were finished.

Then a familiar piano melody filled the air.

Mom extended a graceful hand, index and little fingers elongated, thumb tucked under, ballerina-style.

"What's this?" Junie wondered aloud.

Mom's eyes glistened. "Your father would be so proud of you. I know he would have danced with you today. But since he can't, would you dance with me instead?"

Junie glided into her mother's arms. The crowd parted as mother and daughter twirled around and around, surrounded by a panorama of friendly faces.

When the song ended, there was a smattering of applause and more than one person dabbing her eyes.

Sam approached Junie with a stranger in tow. "There's someone who'd like to meet you. This is Dan. He works for Northwest Distributing."

Dan handed Junie his card. "My company is interested in making you a proposal."

Junie lit up. "Are you serious?"

"I certainly am." He smiled. "Can I call you next week?"

A woman holding a fancy camera tapped her on the shoulder. "Excuse me, Juniper Hart?"

"Yes?"

"I'm with *Wine Spectator*. May I have a picture for the magazine?"

"Of course, sure!" She posed for the shot.

"After all this fuss dies down, would you consider sitting down with me one-on-one for an interview?"

Keval stepped between them. "I'm Ms. Hart's publicist. All interview requests go through me."

Junie and Manolo looked at each other and laughed.

Then Jed Smith approached her. "Juniper, your dad would be thrilled. Your wine is excellent. Serving complimentary pizzas is genius. There's only one thing missing."

"What's that?"

"Humble pie for me, for not giving you that increase on your credit line."

"I know I was a long shot."

"I'd like to personally invite you to come back to the bank and meet with me."

"Well, I—"

Movement over Jed's shoulder caught Junie's eye. It was Storm and Tom being edged out of her growing circle of well-wishers. On their faces were matching counterfeit smiles.

A local reporter holding a tablet angled for Junie's attention.

"Let's see what happens," Junie called to Jed over the commotion. The press of people and gushing were taking a toll on her. She brushed away a lock of hair that had escaped from her topknot.

Manolo took Junie's arm possessively. "That's enough for now, folks," he said, leading her through the throng to the quiet of her office.

"Thanks," she breathed when they were alone behind the closed door.

Manolo picked her off her feet and twirled her around. "You did it!"

"*We* did it," she replied.

"You okay?" he asked, still holding her close.

She smiled shakily. "Yeah! This is all a little overwhelming, but in a good way."

He let her feet down but kept his arms loosely around her waist. "You have a lot of supporters out there."

"I know. I'm so lucky."

"You deserve it. Every bit of it." He pulled back to look down at her. With one fingertip, he traced the demarcation line along her shoulder where her sun-browned arms met her milk-white shoulders. "You got a farmer's tan," he murmured.

She shuddered at his light touch.

He continued the line along the top edge of her strapless sundress. "I remember this dress."

She'd only ever worn it one time, with Daryl.

As he languidly traced the outline of her clavicle, up her neck to her earlobe, her eyelids fluttered and her head fell to the side.

"When you walked into that pool party, I—I won't tell you what I wanted to do to that poser."

They both knew who he was talking about. Junie opened her eyes and straightened her shoulders.

"Where is he? You'd think he'd be here for you, today of all days."

"How many times do I have to tell you? Daryl doesn't care about anyone but Daryl."

"Guess Daryl and I aren't so alike after all."

Wait. Did Manolo just admit he *cared* for her?

She plumbed his eyes for answers, but their black depths were unfathomable. That trademark chandelier smile was nowhere to be seen. The hard line of his jaw twitched. He looked like a man grappling with a life-or-death decision.

She shivered at his frank inspection. He made her feel naked. Vulnerable. She held her breath, waiting . . . for what, she didn't know.

He took her by the shoulders, gently turned her around, and nudged her toward the door. "I've monopolized you long enough. You belong out there."

She stumbled forward, then stopped, turned, and saw him standing there alone. Outside the office door, the sound of raucous merriment went on unabated.

"Go on," he said with a toss of his chin.

She felt like she was being thrown out of her own office. "Aren't you coming?"

"This is your place, and those are your people."

She frowned. "What about you?"

He hesitated. And then he said, "I don't have a place."

The sun set over the hills, and still, people came. They drank, ate, laughed, and danced throughout the tasting room and outside, under the pergola.

Finally, everyone seemed to vanish at once.

Junie watched the red taillights of the last car bounce away from the estate. With a surreal feeling, as if she were walking on clouds, she went back inside the tasting room, her mind still reeling with snippets of conversations, visions of friends old and new, and well wishes.

Chapter Thirty-eight

Manolo worked his way around the outdoor tables, closing up the market umbrellas for the night.

The day had gone even better than planned. The party had been perfect. The press would be talking about it for days. Junie had even got a meeting with a distributor.

Now the consortium had its approvals. Satisfied, Sam had cut Manolo a check, replenishing his savings.

His work here was done. Tomorrow, he was moving on. All he was taking with him were his memories. In the future, whenever Oregon came up in conversation, he'd say, *I was there, once.*

He had to hand it to himself, he thought smugly. It had gone against the grain, but that hands-off policy he'd adopted with regard to a certain farm girl had worked.

It'd been touch-and-go at times. Without even trying, she'd managed to wrap herself around his heart like a vine, twisting and tightening almost imperceptibly. Then good old inductive reasoning and logic had kicked in to hold those rogue feelings in check.

As he fastened the strap around an umbrella, the flash of red taillights caught his eye. He looked up and he saw the silhouette of Junie waving good-bye to the last car driving off the property.

And like a rubber band that had been stretched too far for too long, he snapped.

Suddenly his feet were carrying him to the tasting room.

Junie had barely begun wiping down the bar when Manolo came striding toward her like a man on a mission.

Without a word, he took the bar rag from her and tossed it in the sink, clamped her chin with his strong hand, and took her mouth with his.

There was no time to think. She kissed him back and hung on for what some instinct told her was going to be the ride of her life.

He bent her backward over the bar, his hands everywhere at once.

"Junie," he said raggedly, dragging his lips over her ear.

That alone, even without his hands on her waist, now her back, now her hips, would have made her day. Even a day as sweet as this one.

"Junie."

His hands were under her sundress, under her panties, his fingers spanning her ass, digging into her flesh.

She caught a glimpse of his face and gasped. He was like a man possessed. His fevered expression was contagious, making her insides liquid and eager for more. More, more, *more.*

Her panties dropped to the floor in a puddle of pink ruffles.

He looked down at the sight of them and clucked with disapproval. "I don't think those are OSHA-certified."

Before she could think of a reply, she was being lifted onto the oak slab by the same hands that had hammered and sawed and nailed it into place, as if in preparation for this moment, this grand event that eclipsed all else.

Manolo opened her legs and drew her into him like he had done on the porch railing. But the bar was counter-height. This time, her breasts were aligned with his head, her hips with his chest.

He shoved his thumbs into the top of her dress and shimmied it down like he'd done it a thousand times before.

Fort Bliss, Fort Belvoir, New York City . . . he probably *had.*

No bra shielded her breasts from his intent gaze. She trembled with anticipation; then her head dropped back in rapture when he covered first one breast, then the other with his mouth.

She heard a *zzzip* and lifted her head to see his chinos hanging open with a heavy burden.

Oh.

"This is gonna be quick. I apologize ahead of time. Promise I'll make it up to you."

With that, he slung his hips onto a stool and Junie's off the bar and onto his lap in one masterstroke, filling her almost beyond endurance.

Junie cried out.

But he took no mercy on her. He was relentless in his need.

He *was* quick. But afterward, he held her in place so long, she thought his arm muscles must surely be ready to give out.

Hours later, in Junie's bed, Manolo stroked Junie's hair where it fanned out over his chest.

How many times had he pictured the two of them right here, tangled up in Junie's blue comforter? Now that they actually were, he still couldn't see her. It was pitch black. The moon had set long ago. *It's true,* he thought, *that saying about the darkest hour being right before dawn.*

He'd kept his promise. He'd more than made up for his urgent first performance, pleasuring her again and again until she'd begged him to stop.

Time was his enemy. The time he had left with her was too short. Once he was gone, the time it would take to forget about her would stretch out endlessly.

She snuggled closer to him. "What are you thinking about?" she asked in the husky tone of a woman thoroughly satisfied.

After a pause, he said, "You. How you're so strong and resilient. How, no matter what happens, you always land on your feet."

She giggled. "You sound so serious, all of a sudden."

"This, coming from the most industrious woman I know."

"Thought you said your sisters and your mom were the most industrious."

"They don't count. They're not women, they're my relations."

She laughed sleepily. "What's your idea of the perfect woman?"

"What kind of a question is that?"

"Humor me."

He considered. "Soft, yet strong. Smart. Independent. One who has interests, whose life doesn't revolve around me."

"That first day you came to my run-down tasting room, I had you pegged as a man who needed to be the center of attention."

"I'm pretty selfish. And a flight risk. I like the freedom to pick up and go at the drop of a hat. I warned you about that the day we met. And did I mention I'm selfish?" There was one thing good about the dark—Junie wouldn't be able to see his face when he said what he was about to say.

"But no one can whip up a mean omelet from old cheddar and expired eggs like you can," she said.

He huffed a soft laugh. The circles her finger drew on his belly felt way too good. He didn't want to start something he didn't have time to finish. Gently but firmly, he removed her hand and tangled his fingers with hers.

"When I stay in one place too long, I feel trapped. Then I leave, and someone gets hurt. That's why it's best not to form attachments."

"What happened to you, to make you like that?"

"I was the only son. It was taken for granted that I'd take over the family business. But I wanted to be a builder. I told my dad I wanted to go to college to be an engineer or something. It wasn't a matter of not being able to afford it. He wouldn't even consider it. So I left. I'm just like your brother."

"That's not why Storm left. Storm didn't have any ambition. He was looking for something to do with his life that didn't take a lot of effort."

"Our family didn't even take vacations. We couldn't leave the restaurant, because it never closed. I wanted to explore the world beyond Hoboken."

"Well, you've fulfilled that goal. Didn't you say you've been to almost every continent?"

"Five out of seven. It's unrealistic to think I'll ever make it to Antarctica, but Australia? I'd do just about anything to go there. Even have a head hunter working on it.

"My next assignment's not too shabby though," he said as lightly as though he were talking about the weather.

There was a pregnant pause.

"Well. Aren't you going to tell me where it is?"

"Ever hear of Belize?"

He felt the comforter shift as she propped herself up on an elbow. "As in Central America? *That* Belize?"

"There's only one, so far as I know."

She laid down again, withdrawing her leg from where it had been wrapped around his.

He felt like a spark plug that had lost its contact point.

"Good timing," she said brightly.

By the sound of her voice, she'd turned her head to the wall.

"While I'm bundled up in my hoodie in the next few months, you'll be wearing board shorts."

Manolo lay on his back with his arms at his side and tried to pretend that he wasn't a world-class cad. It wasn't like he was breaking any promises. She'd known the rules of the game going in.

From the other side of the bed, he heard a single sniff.

Junie said, "Your lease is up soon, isn't it?"

"You remembered."

The covers rustled. "Did you honestly think I could forget?" came her voice, now closer to his ear.

He rolled onto his side, his hand inadvertently brushing across her breasts. Delinquent that he was, he couldn't restrain himself from stroking their gathered tips with his knuckles.

The thing that really got him was, she let him.

"How soon?" she whispered.

He rolled onto his back, interlocked his wayward fingers across his chest, and stared up at the ceiling. "I leave tomorrow."

The light had subtly changed without him noticing. He was able to make out the shadowy corners where the ceiling met the walls.

He turned to search for her face, expecting to see tears, but there were none.

"This *is* tomorrow," she said in a voice that did not crack.

Chapter Thirty-nine

Manolo shuffled his feet as he walked in the warm sand, the gentle trade wind ruffling his hair. To his left was the white-crested Gulf of Honduras. To his right, a woman in a bikini.

His orientation week had just ended.

"Do you have any lingering questions?" Amanda asked, cocking her head provocatively.

"I'm good," he replied absentmindedly, looking out to sea.

"I was thinking of going to the beach bar and getting another Carib. Want to join me?"

"Do you think they got any pinot over there?"

The tinkling sound of her laughter came to him on the sea breeze. "Belize and fine wine aren't words you usually hear in the same sentence."

"Sure, I'll have another beer. Why not?" He shrugged. He didn't have anything better to do.

At the bar, Amanda made an admirable effort at small talk. "A proper infrastructure is crucial for the local community here. You're providing a great service."

"Great," replied Manolo, peeling the label off his Carib.

"Manny?"

"Huh?"

"Did you even hear what I said?"

"Yeah. I'm providing a great service."

"That's right. I'm really excited you'll be here for the next six months."

"Me too."

"Are you?"

He scowled. "Sure I am."

"Because you seem to be a thousand miles away."

Two thousand six hundred seventy-three miles, to be precise. He couldn't help it. All he could think about was Junie.

He wanted to violate his number-one policy, to call her up and ask her how the first full week of crush was going, if the guy she'd hired to man the bistro was working out, her impression of last year's vintage now that it'd been safely bottled and stored, and a hundred other details.

But if he was going to forget her, he had to cut himself off, cold turkey.

"Manny?"

"Yeah."

"What'd I just say?"

"Something about the catch of the day. What were the choices again?"

"Queen lobster or grouper."

"You order for me."

For once in his life, food was the last thing on his mind.

Chapter Forty

When Manolo left town, Junie felt as if she were sinking gradually to the bottom of a well.

He'd never promised her a thing he didn't fulfill. He'd said he would make her tasting room the talk of the town, and he had. He'd promised to have the bistro finished in time for the crush, and he had. He'd told her he was a vagabond, and he was.

Work was her salvation. There was a break in the vineyard chores, but the crush season had only just begun. Hart Vineyards was the star of the show this year, with Sam bringing busload after busload out, and carsful of thirsty tourists arriving from dawn to dusk.

Keval convinced her to formally change the name to Broken Hart Vineyards, saying that it hinted at a melancholy yet intriguing story.

Broken Hart Vineyards, indeed.

Keval set up interviews with the local press and *Wine Spectator*.

Northwest Distributors sent one of their managers to wine and dine her at the Radish Rose, Clarkston's bastion of fine dining.

She was grateful for the distractions. They kept her from thinking about Manolo.

Best of all, she met with Jed Smith at Clarkston Savings Bank and crafted a plan to pay off Tom Alexander and write a check to Manolo, even though he hadn't asked for it.

Once those debts were paid, she breathed a sigh of relief.

The next challenge was to buy out Storm. But that shouldn't be too hard. He'd only bought out Mom's half interest to help her afford her townhouse.

Or so Junie thought.

And then, one day in early November when the grapevines were withering and the air held the promise of snow, Jed Smith called and asked Junie to meet him at Poppy's Café.

The crush was just winding down. It had been a record year, not just for Junie, but for the entire Willamette Valley.

Poppy took their orders and pretended not to eavesdrop.

"So. What's new?" Junie asked, biting into her sticky bun. She still didn't cook, despite Manolo having left a folder with all his family recipes in it on the tasting room bar, along with detailed instructions for the seasonal cook she'd taken on.

"I heard from your brother, Storm," Jed replied with a grim expression.

Chapter Forty-one

November, Hoboken, New Jersey

Manolo bent over and kissed his mother's cheek. "How's the knee?"

He'd managed to incorporate a side trip to visit his mom at the rehab hospital following November drill.

"Coming along. They had me up walking the very first day."

"Amazing what modern medicine can do, isn't it?"

"It sure is. Hand me my glasses, will you?"

She put them on and studied his face. "Where are you these days?"

"You know, Mom. We talked about it. Belize, remember?"

"That's right. It's all these medicines I'm on that makes me forget things. You didn't like it out west, then?"

Manolo looked at the floor. He tried not to think about the wide open spaces, the big sky, and, most of all, the unique people. "Liked it fine. It was just time."

"You looked so happy the last time I saw you."

He threw out his arms and pasted on a smile. "I don't look happy now?"

"I don't know. I suppose you do. There was a spark you had, the last time you were here. . . ."

"Well, I should look happy. Because I just got word from my headhunter. She thinks she found me a new job. You'll never guess where."

"Hard to tell. Haven't you been just about everywhere under the sun by now?"

"Australia!"

"Australia. You always talked about going there."

"That's right. I got an interview this week for a project in Sydney."

"How are they going to interview you, all the way down there?"

"It's all done on a computer nowadays, Mom."

"Now, when would that start?"

"Soon as the Belize job's over, in February."

She shook her head on her pillow. "All this change . . . I can't keep up. You know your father's selling the restaurant."

The news was a bolt of lightning through his chest. "No. I didn't."

"Our customer base is fading. Everyone's going to those new places. Sushi and vegetarian and gluten free and who knows what else. Talk about change. . . ."

Manolo laid his hand on her shoulder. "I know, Mom. I know."

Later, he ran into Izzy in the hall.

With no preamble, he asked, "What's going on?"

"Mom told you? Business is dropping off more and more. There was a time when the name Santos was worth something. But now the real estate's worth more than the restaurant. The liquor license alone will fetch a pretty penny. Wait till you hear this: Dad's been looking at condos in—wait for it—Miami Beach."

"Florida?"

"I know, right?"

"Well, it'll be good for Mom."

"That's for sure. That woman deserves to bake on a beach for a change, instead of in the kitchen."

Manolo frowned. "But what about you and the girls? What will you do?"

"Paloma needs a break. She's ready to stay home with the kids— Anthony's practice is doing well enough. Maria's thinking about going back to school, now that her rug rats are old enough."

"What about you?"

Izzy had never married. All she lived for was the restaurant.

"Who knows?" She shrugged.

To Manolo's horror, tears filled her eyes. He couldn't handle women crying. Especially women he loved.

He gave her a brotherly squeeze and peered over her shoulder, down the hall of the hospital, without seeing it. "Don't worry about it," he said. "Something will come up."

Everything's disintegrating, he thought. *Soon there won't be anything left to come home to but my storage units.* And, like Junie had said, a storage shed was hardly a home.

Chapter Forty-two

In early December, Manolo got a phone call from Sam.

"I've been trying to call you, man. Finally got through!"

"Reception's touch-and-go down here."

"How's Belize?"

"Awesome. Hot sun, hot babes . . . what's up with you?"

"Forget it. Can't compete with that."

"Try me."

"I'm planning to do some skiing over Christmas break. Wondered if you want to come up and hit the slopes, assuming you *have* a Christmas break."

With his family split into pieces and his staff jetting off to their various hometowns, Manolo had been resigned to spending Christmas alone.

"Sounds great."

"You sure the local hotties can survive without you for a few days?"

Even under threat of waterboarding, he'd never confess to Sam that the last woman he'd laid a hand on was Junie Hart.

"It's a chance I'll have to take."

A couple of weeks later, Sam picked Manolo up at the PDX airport.

They drove south out of Portland, toward the Willamette. The cityscape disappeared behind them, replaced by suburbia's mishmash of houses and small businesses. Gradually, fields outnumbered developments. At a distance, snow blanketed the high ground.

"How'd your interview go?"

"Nailed it."

"Australia?"

"February fifteenth."

Sam whistled through his teeth. "That's a long way away. Think you'll ever get tired of running and settle down some day?"

"Nope."

Neither man spoke for a mile or so.

Then Sam said, "We've driven halfway to Clarkston. So far, you've asked me how the consortium's doing, about the relative success of this fall's crush, and what's the latest between me and Red."

"Your point?"

"When are you going to quit skating around the subject and ask me the thing you're dying to know about the most?"

Manolo gazed out the window, feigning ignorance. "I don't have a clue what you're getting at."

Sam thumped his chest as he drove. "Are you forgetting who this is you're talking to?"

"Okay. You win. What's going on with Junie?"

"She paid off Tom Alexander. But Storm still owns the half of the vineyard he bought from their mom. Junie naturally assumed he'd sell it to her, now that she's in the black, but instead of playing nice, he jacked up the price. When Junie balked, Storm offered it to Tom Alexander."

Manolo was seized by fury. "How do you know this? Did Junie tell you?"

"Poppy overheard Jed Smith telling Junie about it."

The Clarkston gossip mill is alive and well.

"What was Alexander's response?"

"He hasn't responded yet, far as I know. And when he does, who's to say Storm won't turn right around and jack the price up again, to see if he can bid Junie up?"

"Storm could play this game forever. That's not right."

"No, it's not. Junie doesn't deserve this, after all she's been through. You haven't talked to her?"

Manolo looked at his hands, which were lying impotently in his lap. "She won't take my calls. My bad. I never used to call her. Now it looks like it's too late." Filled with regret, he pressed his lips together. "Why didn't *you* tell me?"

"Don't think it didn't cross my mind. A certain counselor advised me to stay out of it."

"Or," said Manolo, "you thought you'd invite me out here to go skiing, and should it happen to come up in the course of conversation . . ."

Sam grinned. "Something like that."

"Well, at least Junie got herself a distributor. That was the reason I built her that bistro."

"Uh, think again."

"What do you mean? I was there when you introduced him to her at the grand opening!"

"If you remember, Dan said Northwest was offering her a proposal. It wasn't a done deal. They don't want her unless she owns a majority of her operation. Think about it. Northwest can't be signing deals with someone who isn't in control of her business."

Manolo's head fell back against the seat. "I can't believe this. I thought everything was good when I left. It was all supposed to be settled."

"One more thing. Do you remember Junie's mom's mystery boyfriend?"

"Kind of."

"You won't believe who it is."

"Let me guess. Tom Alexander?"

The look Sam gave him was his answer.

"I never liked that guy. And that Storm character may be Junie's brother, but he rubs me the wrong way, too."

"Remember what I said about him back in April?"

"Soup sandwich." Manolo scrubbed a hand over his face. "Too bad he's not here instead of Colorado. I'd like to wring that little twerp's neck."

"He *is* here."

Manolo whipped his head around. "Storm's here? In Clarkston?" He set his jaw. "Sorry to break it to you, Cap'n, but doesn't look like I'll be making that ski trip after all. I got some business to take care of."

Sam grinned gleefully. "I was hoping you'd say that."

"You didn't invite me out here to go skiing, did you?"

"Like I always say, we take care of our own."

"Mind if we stop by Junie's on our way to your place, Cap'n?"

"Roger that," Sam replied.

When Manolo knocked on Junie's front door, her mother answered.

"What a surprise! Is Junie expecting you?"

"No, ma'am. She around?"

"She's out in her office with her brother. Let me grab my coat, and I'll walk you out."

They heard Junie's raised voice before they even entered the building.

Manolo hastened his steps. Instead of holding the tasting room door for Junie's mother he rushed past her and headed straight for the office.

Behind her desk stood Junie. In front of it, with their backs to Manolo, were Tom Alexander and Storm.

Junie thumped her fist on her desk's wood surface. "Manolo Santos and I worked our asses off to get this property in shape for the crush so that I'd have a better venue to sell my wine out of. You know how much it means to me, Storm. Meanwhile, you haven't worked here since you were eighteen years old. You never cared what happened to this winery. Why are you wielding your share like it's some kind of trump card?"

Tom lifted his chin haughtily. "Storm can sell his portion to anyone he wants."

"That may be true. But why can't he do the decent thing and sell it back to me?" She turned from Alexander to Storm with a pleading look on her face. "For God's sake, Storm. I'm your *sister*."

"Because I'd be stupid to not get as much as I can out of it, now that it's the hottest little property in the valley, that's why," Storm replied with a snide chuckle.

Jennifer Jepson-Hart marched straight past Manolo, into her daughter's inner sanctum.

"What's going on here? Storm, what have you done?"

Storm shrank under his mother's question. "Nothing. Don't worry about it."

"Is what I heard true? You won't sell Junie's land back to her?"

"It's mine to do with as I please."

"He's right, Jen. This is a business matter. Let us handle this," said Alexander.

Jennifer turned to Tom and yelled, "This is *family* business. You stay out of it."

Then she stepped into her son's personal space. "And you listen to me, Storm. I've had it with you. You've known how attached Junie was to this land since the two of you were children. Why are you so greedy when you don't need the money? What's happened to you? Your father would be appalled."

At that last comment, Storm flinched and averted his eyes from his mother's probing glare.

Jennifer leaned in for the kill. "You're going to sell your sister's land back to her at the price she paid for it."

For a moment the only sound was Jennifer's breath, rushing in and out of her lungs.

Slowly, Storm lifted his head and drawled, "Or what?"

Manolo moved to Jennifer's side. "Or I'm going to rip off your arm and ram it down your throat, nuts-for-brains."

"Touch him and I'll have you arrested," said Alexander coolly.

Jennifer whipped her head around. "Who's going to arrest him? Everyone in this town knows what Manolo Santos did for Junie. They know what her father's dream was for her. That includes his fellow lawmen."

Junie pointed across her desk to Tom. "And you're going to stay out of my way, starting right now, or I'm going to see that everyone in town knows how you've been trying to manipulate me for your own gain."

"How dare you threaten me?"

"Don't you know?" cried Junie to her mom, "Tom's been using you, too. He knew I didn't have enough money to buy you out. He convinced you to get me and Storm to buy your share of the property, knowing I'd have to take his loan at his exorbitant interest rate. He was sure I'd default and he'd end up majority shareholder of the vineyard."

When Jennifer regarded Tom again, there was a new clarity in her eyes. "Well, you were wrong about that, weren't you?"

"Say anything you want," replied Tom. "Who's going to believe you?"

Then Sam appeared, and immediately Manolo knew his old comrade had been listening from the tasting room. He could always count on Sam to have his back.

"You relish your reputation as the local doctor-slash-vintner, don't you, Alexander?" said Sam. "It's a variation on the 'big fish in a small pond' theme. I happen to have a little bit of influence, myself. If I should let word of this matter slip out to my consortium members, I guarantee you'll be persona non grata at every wine event in the valley from now on."

"Think I'll hang around here a little while," Manolo told Sam after everyone but Junie had gone.

"Call me if you need a ride. Tonight, tomorrow, whatever," said Sam on his way out.

When they were alone, Manolo followed Junie into the house. "Still no living room furniture, I see."

"It's not a priority. I never have time to sit down. Want to come out to the kitchen?"

He followed her, devouring every detail of her body from the top of her head, over her slender curves, to her boots.

"Hungry?" she asked.

He scrubbed a hand over his eyes. "Starving. I came directly here from the airport. I haven't eaten all day."

"Let me make you something."

"You? When did you start cooking?"

"I didn't. But there's pasta in the cupboard, and I inherited some good recipes."

He eyed her hungrily while she moved around the kitchen. He hadn't realized how much time he'd spent alone since he left this place, now that he lived by himself in the apartment in Belize. He cooked alone, ate alone, and slept alone. It was good to be in her company.

"How'd you know what was happening with Storm?"

"Sam told me."

"Is that why you're here? To check up on me?"

"Sam invited me out to go skiing. He filled me in after I got here."

"Is that the only reason?"

Manolo scraped the chair aside and crossed the floor to stand behind her. He cupped his hands over her shoulders like he was warming them over a campfire, basking in her aura. After a moment they settled on her like a butterfly landing. He bent his head to inhale the hippie-dippie scent of her hair.

She stopped stirring, turned the burner off deliberately and turned around.

His hands stroked down her bare arms.

She melted into to him in a warm embrace. "I can't believe you're standing here, and I'm touching you, and you're real. Just this morning I was afraid I'd never see you again, and now, here you are. It's a miracle."

"You're the miracle," he said.

They kissed, and it felt like a homecoming to Manolo.

"Stay?" she whispered.

He nodded and they went upstairs, the half-cooked food forgotten.

And when the new day crept over the windowsill, Manolo felt a peace he'd never known.

The next day was the winter solstice. Manolo helped Junie dig through the frozen ground in the middle of the vineyard. She thrust her gloved hands into the hole and pulled out the cow's horns and brushed the soil off the wine bottle they had buried last summer, when the birds had been singing and the sun shining on their shoulders.

Inside the farmhouse, before a crackling fire, they drank to the earth's bounty.

And when the bottle was empty, they made love again.

Chapter Forty-three

Mid-February, Belize

Manolo smiled as he watched a ragtag clutch of kids shuffle down the dirt road to the one-room school in cliques of two and three, whispering and shoving and singing the way school-children did, the world over. Now, thanks to the village's new water filtration system, they could spend more time learning instead of hefting heavy buckets up the hill from the river multiple times a day.

He thanked his team, filed his reports, and packed up his gear.

Then it was wheels up.

Halfway through the long flight, he patted his breast pocket containing the heirloom passed down to him by virtue of being his mother's only son.

When he landed, he rented a car for the final leg of his journey.

But the view outside his car wasn't of the Sydney Harbour Bridge or the Opera House.

And in place of the Southern Hemisphere's bronze-tinged autumn leaves, he was surrounded by flocks of robins digging in the newly turned earth, field hands bundled up in hoodies wielding long-handled pruners, and fuzzy willow catkins along the quiet two-lane roads . . . the unmistakable signs of a Pacific Northwest spring.

Junie bounded down the porch steps to meet Manolo.

Though they'd spoken on the phone every night, it had been two months since he'd held her in his arms. He dropped his bags and swung her around, loving the joyous laughter that bubbled out of her throat.

Arm in arm, they entered the farmhouse.

"I have a surprise for you," said Junie.

In the living room sat an inviting new couch flanked by matching chairs.

Manolo eased his body into the plump cushions.

"You like?" she asked, beaming.

Manolo patted the seat next to him. "I'd like it better with you here, next to me."

She plopped down by his side and he slung his arm around her.

"Feels like home sweet home," he said.

"That's the best thing you could have said to me," she replied, smiling up into his face.

"I have something for you, too." He withdrew the tiny box from his pocket, cracked it open, and took out the ring, tilting it to watch the stone's facets reflect the light.

Since December they'd worked out all the details of their future plans. But he only intended to get engaged one time. He wanted to do it right.

"This was never supposed to happen," he began. "Growing up, I felt trapped, chained to a family business. All I ever wanted was to break free . . . to run as fast and as far as I could, building something as my hallmark at every site. If I managed to make some lives a little easier along the way, so much the better. And then I ran into you."

He withdrew his arm from around Junie's shoulder, picked up her hand where it rested on the couch and cradled it in both of his.

"When I landed here last summer, at first I thought it was only about creating this amazing space for you to sell your wine. Then when I went to Belize, I had this nagging feeling that I'd left behind unfinished business. I kept dreaming of ways to make this place even better, thinking that it was just like all the other jobs—all about the work. But in the end, I realized what I'd really left behind was my heart."

Manolo slipped his grandmother's ring onto Junie's ring finger, drew her hand to his lips, and kissed it.

He drew in a breath. "After all the things we've said over the past two months, you may think this is just a formality, and I guess it is. Something about me that hasn't changed, that will *never* change, is I don't make promises I don't intend to keep. And this is one promise I want to make in person."

He slid down on one knee in front of the couch and looked up at her.

"Juniper Hart, I promise to stay by your side through everything that is to come . . . through seasons of want and seasons of plenty, forever and ever, no matter what."

Junie's face crumpled and she tucked her chin into her chest.

"What's wrong?" he asked with alarm, dipping his head, seeking her eyes with his.

"I'm an ugly crier," she apologized, wiping a tear from her cheek.

Gently, he lifted her chin with a fingertip, then chuckled, pulled her to her feet and gathered her into a bear hug.

"You're beautiful, Buttercup. And I'm crazy about you."

He pulled back to show her he meant it by the straightforward look on his face.

Eyes the turquoise of the Mediterranean sparkled into his. She looked down at the ring glittering on her finger. "If I said no, I'd have to take this off, wouldn't I?" she laughed through her tears.

"Pretty smooth, how I did that, huh?" he laughed with her.

He kissed her then, and their tears mingled, washing away their loneliness, welcoming something new and strong and whole.

Loved THE CRUSH?
Then keep reading for a sneak peek at
the next crisp entry in
An Oregon Wine Country Romance series:
INTOXICATING

Chapter One

"Thanks for coming! Good seeing you again."

Poppy Springer scooped the coins left on the crumb-littered table into her pocket as she watched Sandy and Kyle wheel their stroller out into the September afternoon.

Behind them, a stiff gust of wind sent the bell above the door clanging like a fire alarm. A page torn from a coloring book soared off the table and landed at Poppy's feet, only to skitter out of reach when she bent to pick it up.

Outside the café window, the couple didn't get far before Sandy paused the stroller to pull up the hood on her toddler's jacket.

Must be a storm brewing.

Poppy remembered the day Kyle had balked at holding Sandy's hand in line at Clarkston Elementary. Now those two were expecting their second baby in May—though just this morning they had come to a mutual decision to wait a bit before telling anyone.

When Poppy was growing up it had never occurred to her to do anything but work at the café on Main Street that her parents had named after her. Her mom always said Poppy was a people person, and the café provided a comfortable living.

But sometimes Poppy couldn't help but feel like the residents of Clarkston had become blind to her . . . discussing personal matters between bites of toast while she stood inches away, neglecting the small courtesy of looking up when she topped off their coffees.

Poppy gave Sandy and Kyle the benefit of the doubt. They weren't rude, just preoccupied with their full lives. Besides, Poppy's dad had always called her his human barometer. That was his teasing way of saying he thought she was too sensitive to others' moods and emotions.

She slid the high chair out of the way, squatting to scrape up the congealing yolk of a dippy egg. Then she strode to the other side of the café, knelt, and picked up the cartoon picture of a princess whose face was scribbled almost beyond recognition.

She was still gazing at it when the doorbell jangled again. When she looked up to see Heath Sinclair, Junie Hart, Keval Patel, and Red McDonald blustering through the door, her insides warmed like one of those rare autumn days when the sun filtered through the Oregon mist onto the vineyards and the pickers' carelessly discarded jackets were bright spots of color on the ground between the rows.

Half an hour later, Poppy rested her tray on the table edge and began distributing drinks and sandwiches. She felt the strain in her back and arms more than usual today, thanks to a late night of studying. For Poppy, book learning had never come easy.

Heath snapped shut the large, hardbound volume he'd been leafing through and shoved it in his backpack.

"Red, here's your spicy Italian wrap. Junie, sticky bun. Keval, are you sure all you want is spring water?"

Keval sighed. "I'm on a cleanse."

"Heath—turkey BLT and lemonade." Poppy's eyes flickered to his, then back to the food she handed him.

She felt like she was walking a tightrope whenever she was around Heath. She could tell she made him feel off kilter, too.

"Thanks," he murmured, cramming his backpack onto the seat behind him.

Poppy was much better at reading faces than pages. But anyone could see that Heath was hiding something.

"How do you do that?" asked Junie, as Poppy deposited the empty tray on an adjacent table. "Always remember everyone's order without writing anything down?"

Poppy just smiled and slid into the vinyl booth next to Red.

"Poppy has a great memory," said Heath.

She flushed with pleasure. She was used to getting compliments on her looks, not her brains. Heath wasn't a man of many words. If he made the effort to say something nice, you could bet it was sincere.

She sought out his hazel eyes to make her appreciation clear, not caring if it made him umcomfortable. "Thank you," she said point-edly.

But he was already intently working out the best angle from which to attack his BLT.

At twenty-eight, Heath's angular face was still boyish. He had a naturally trim build beneath his fitted plaid shirt, and wavy hair the golden-brown of the filberts that had been ubiquitous to the Willa-mette Valley—until the pinot boom came along and farmers up-rooted the nut trees and replaced them with wine grapes.

Poppy folded her arms on the table and observed her companions as they ate and drank. Who would have believed that the brewery Heath had started in his parents' basement would become so suc-cessful? And Red, known to the public as Dr. Sophia MacDonald, had been voted Clarkston's best therapist for the past two years. Keval did I.T. for a local wine consortium, plus a few select clients on the side. Junie had taken the reins of her faltering family vineyard, and her work was paying off in increased sales.

All of them had made impressive strides over the past decade. All except Poppy. How did she even get to sit at the same table with the likes of them? With every step forward, she took two back.

A few months ago, the little wine shop where she'd worked for four years had been sold. Her main source of income was gone.

She couldn't help but think that maybe the prediction written about her at graduation was destined to come true.

"I saw your dad at the vet this morning," said Keval. "He told me your news. Exciting!"

"What news?" asked Red.

Poppy hesitated. She hadn't decided how much to tell her friends about her long shot for the future, in case it didn't pan out.

At first when Cory Anthony—*the* Cory Anthony, one of Port-land's top chefs—mentioned he might be able to put her knowledge of wine to good use at the new place he was opening up, she'd been ecstatic.

Then, during the formal interview, Chef told her the elaborate renovations were going to take longer than he'd originally thought. The target opening date had been pushed back until the end of the year. But the real clincher was that even though he was impressed by her having taught herself about wine, his job offer was contingent on her becoming official—earning her sommelier certificate.

Her elation had given way to panic. She was a terrible test taker. To this day, she still had nightmares about school.

"First I have to pass that exam," she told her friends.

"You'll pass. You've got a great bedside manner," said Keval. "Besides, it doesn't hurt that you look like that classic painting of Venus on the Half Shell."

"Thanks—I think," she told Keval. *Another well-meaning comment equating her worth with her appearance.* "And it's called table service. The parts of the test are wine theory, tasting, and table service."

"Ex*cuse* me," said Keval, waving his fork in the air. "Do I know all those fancy wine terms? Promise me one thing. Once you're a famous lady somm with your face plastered all over, you won't forget your roots."

She chuckled. "I can safely say that's not something you'll ever have to worry about."

"You've *heard*, right?" exclaimed Keval to the others. "Poppy's been, quote unquote, *discovered* by a talent scout who happened to be having dinner where she used to hostess. Not only is she going to be a wine steward at Cory Anthony's latest place, she's been tagged to be the new face of Palette Cosmetics!"

"Easy," said Junie, dodging Keval's utensil. "Here, Keval, eat part of this sticky bun. I can't finish it. Poppy, what's he ranting about?"

But Keval couldn't seem to help himself in his frenzy to be the one to spill the beans. "Am I making this up? Her father told me himself. He was leaving the vet's office with Jackson, and Miss Sweetie and I were on our way in. Miss Sweetie *adores* Jackson. Anyhoo, between the fabulous new restaurant, the modeling, the private parties, and the jetting off to who-knows-where—well, I'm just saying. Take a good hard look at her. We might as well say sayonara *right now* to the Poppy we know and love."

She was going to kill her dad first, and then Keval.

From the corner of her eye she thought she saw Heath's healthy complexion pale.

Then Red chimed in. "Details, please?"

Keval opened his mouth, but Red cut him off with a look. "From *Poppy*, if you don't mind."

Poppy wrung her hands in her lap, her excitement tinged with nerves. "Well, it's far from a sure thing. The Palette people are waiting to see if I pass the test and get the wine steward position. Everything hinges on that. So, I guess we'll just have to wait and see."

"It's a thing now for companies to use a so-called real person with an authentic career in their ads instead of a full-time model," added Keval, stuffing the wad of cinnamon-encrusted dough Junie had given him into his mouth. "What's hotter than a lady somm?" he asked around his mouthful. "Everybody either *wants* one or wants to *be* one."

Keval might have a flair for the dramatic, but he was right. The day would soon come when a somm was a somm, but for now, flaunting women sommeliers was a way for restaurants to get buzz.

Red squealed and hugged Poppy as best she could in the narrow space between the table and the booth. "That's fabulous!'"

"Go Poppy!'" said Junie from her seat by the window, raising her mug in a salute.

Poppy looped her ponytail around her hand again and again until she noticed the right angles poking against the canvas of Heath's backpack. She pounced on it as a way to change the subject.

"What's that?" she asked playfully, craning her neck.

"What?" replied Heath.

"That book."

"Nothing. Just a book." He drained his lemonade and wiped his mouth with his napkin.

"Our old high school yearbook," said Red.

Poppy's smile dissolved. "That's ancient history." She had long since thrown her yearbook in the dumpster. But not before the senior superlative that yearbook editor Demi had managed to sneak by the advisor had become fixed in her mind.

After all these years, it still felt like a stab to the heart. Anyone else would have been content to stick with the traditional lines: Best Dressed, Most Likely to Become President, and so on. Not Demi. She'd had it in for Poppy since seventh grade, when she found out Daryl Decaprio, the guy she had a crush on, was playing Poppy sappy love songs over the phone at night.

In a small town, your senior superlative defined you like an epitaph carved in stone. Except unlike an epitaph, you weren't dead when you got it—you had to live with it for the rest of your life. Demi had used her creative writing skills to create the ultimate, parting gibe.

"What made you haul that out of storage now?"

Junie said, "You know Heath. He doesn't get rid of anything. Our tenth reunion's coming up. Didn't you get the Save the Date?"

"I haven't checked email for the past couple days." Poppy had been spending every free minute studying.

"We thought it'd be fun to look at faces. You know, jog our memories. Guess who'll show and who won't."

Heath pulled out his phone, tapped something in and handed it to Poppy. "Here. Read this."

Poppy's body stiffened like a corpse.

Heath knew her impediment better than anyone. How could he put her on the spot like this? Surely everyone could see the panic on her face.

You're not stupid, she told herself firmly. But her shame at being dyslexic was still paralyzing sometimes, especially when she had to read out loud, in public. And not being able to control her shame made her feel guilty. Inadequacy, shame, guilt. A vicious cycle.

For once, Heath held her gaze. "Poppy," he said evenly. "You've got this."

She felt his strength seep into her, igniting a warmth that stole through her body. Gingerly, she reached for the phone and bowed her head over the screen. The letters of the alphabet swam and shifted before coalescing into a pattern of rune-like shapes.

"Deep breath," Red said gently.

Dutifully, she inhaled. "Clarkston High School Ten Year Reunion. Saturday, December 15, 8 pm," she read haltingly. "The Radish Rose. Dinner and dancing. RSVP to Demi Barnes, Reunion Committee Chairman."

"So, who's in?" asked Red.

"I am," sang Keval with a wave of his fingers.

Of course Keval would go to the reunion. Reunions were made for people like him. Following four years of exceptionally awkward adolescence, Keval was a walking "it gets better" ad.

"It'll be good for business," said Junie. "I don't get out enough as it is, what with running both the vineyard and the winery."

Red looked at Poppy. "What about you?"

"Think I'll pass." She handed Heath's phone back and attempted to bolt, but Red stopped her with a hand on her forearm.

"Aw, come on. It'll be fun! Dancing, seeing people you haven't seen in forever . . ."

"That's after Poppy's test. She might be chillin' in some Portland penthouse overlooking the river by then," said Keval.

Maybe not a penthouse, but she'd better have some place in her sights. Because if she didn't, that would mean she had flunked the test and failed to get the sommelier position. And that Demi had been right about her all along.

"She can come back for it," said Red. "It's only an hour's drive."

Still perched on the edge of the booth, Poppy asked Heath, "Are you going?"

He shrugged. "Don't know."

Heath had come a long way since his own senior superlative: *Most likely to blow something up. On the watch list of the Clarkston F.D. since sixth grade, when his attempt to build a geyser with a pack of Mentos, a liter of soda, and duct tape worked a little too well.*

Poppy smiled to herself, forgetting her own problems for a moment. Heath had always been somewhat of an enigma.

Their teachers murmured to each other that he was a science prodigy. Who could forget his Edible Skin Layers Cake made from Fruit Roll-Ups (epidermis), Jell-o (dermis), and mini marshmallows (hypodermis)? Rumor was, he'd aced his college boards. Yet he'd tossed out all those scholarship letters without opening them. And now beer drinkers all over the Pacific Northwest couldn't get enough of his ales with names like Newberg Neutral and Ribbon Ridge Red.

But when it came to social skills, there was a sweet innocence about Heath that made him hard to get close to.

Junie didn't waste her breath pressuring Heath to go to the reunion. Everyone knew he'd rather face an angry rattlesnake than make chitchat at a party. Instead she focused on persuading Poppy. "Don't you want to see all the people we went to school with?"

"I've never stopped seeing most of them," replied Poppy. Even during the four years she worked in Portland, she'd still lived with her parents. "For everyone else, there's Facebook."

"A lot has happened over the last decade. Some people went away, some got married, had kids, got divorced, won and lost jobs . . ." mused Red. "People change."

"Exactly. That part of my life is behind me. I don't feel the need to see how I'm measuring up."

"But how can it hurt?" pleaded Keval. "Come on, Poppykins. It won't be any fun without you."

She set her jaw. Finally, she said to Heath, "Hand me that year-book."

Rain pelted the windows, and there was the rumble of distant thunder.

Poppy thumbed through the pages until she found what she was looking for. She laid the open book in the middle of the table and pressed her index finger to the passage that had never stopped haunting her.

Red, Junie and Keval tipped their heads and read silently, while Heath looked around the room like he'd rather be anywhere else than there.

Most likely to still be a Clarkston waitress at our tenth class reunion: Poppy Springer. Poppy's most endearing talent is writing her name backwards. She is a true golden retriever at heart, as evidenced by her blond mane and a mind refreshingly free of deep thoughts. Poppy's hobbies are organizing individually wrapped tea bags and leaving a trail of smiley faces wherever she goes. Why change?

Following a brief pause, everyone started talking at once.

"Are you serious? Who cares about an old senior superlative?"

"That doesn't define you."

"Who's going to remember that? It was the freaking Stone Age."

Lightning flashed. The café door opened and a tall woman in a silk blouse and pencil skirt blew in, shaking the rain off her umbrella.

Demi Barnes had started out in the typing pool at the statehouse down in Salem and worked her way up the ladder until Senator Hollins appointed her to run his newly-opened Willamette Valley satellite office.

She paused just inside the entrance, combing her fingers through her windblown hair, waiting to be seated.

Poppy was the only server working until the dinner shift came in at three. But somehow her butt was glued to her seat.

When Demi spotted Poppy she started walking toward her, her heels clicking ominously with every step.

From the corner of her eye Poppy saw Heath slam the yearbook shut and slip it into his bag.

"Well, look who." Demi stared down at the splashy, orange flower on Poppy's apron. "Back working at your parents' cafe?"

"For now," she replied meekly.

"Things didn't work out in Portland?"

Why did Demi always make her feel so inferior? It was her own fault for letting Demi get to her. Inadequacy, shame, guilt.

By some miracle, she managed to mask her inner turmoil. "Things worked out fine. I'm just . . . just back home temporarily, until my new job starts."

"Oh, really? What job is that?"

There was a roaring in Poppy's ears. She felt like she was in the middle of a circus ring and everyone was waiting for the show to begin. Five sets of eyes homed in on her, projecting every emotion from encouragement to empathy to disdain.

From somewhere deep down, defiance welled up in her. She was tired of being talked down to. Underestimated.

She squared her shoulders and lifted her chin. "I'm going to be a sommelier at Cory Anthony's new restaurant in Portland."

Her heart pounded. *What was she saying?*

Demi's jaw dropped.

She was speechless.

And Poppy was loving it!

Keval caught Poppy's momentum. A haughty grin spread across his face. "And a model. *Boom.*" He punctuated the syllable with his fork.

Demi's eyes swung back to Poppy's, seeking clarification.

"You've heard of Palette Cosmetics?" Poppy tossed her ponytail and stared straight into Demi's treacherous green eyes.

She was already in over her head. Might as well go all the way.

"They've hired me to be their spokesperson."

What alien being had taken over Poppy's body?

But as swiftly as Demi had been caught off guard, she recovered. "Isn't that special? You'll definitely have to come to the big class reunion, then! I'm sure everyone will be fascinated when they find out we have a sommelier *and* model in our class. In fact, spreading the word ahead of time might get more people to come."

The faces around the table froze.

Demi sensed weakness like a shark smelled blood. "That is . . . unless it's not a done deal?"

Keval said, "Oh, it's a done deal. Done as a dog's dinner. Tell anyone you want. Tell the world! Poppy Springer has evolved. Our golden retriever's going to compete at Westminster. Instead of sorting teabags, she'll be sorting French Chardonnay. In place of smiley faces, she'll be the face of—"

"Poppy's going to be a great somm." Compared with Keval's rising hysteria, Heath's voice sounded rock solid.

Poppy wanted to kiss him—even if it did make him squirm.

Red took advantage of the lull to start gathering up her belongings. "Nice to see you, Demi. Poppy, could I scoot out and pay? I have an appointment to get to."

"I should get going, too," said Junie.

Poppy let Junie out and remembered that for the time being, her job was pouring nothing stronger than Stumptown's Hair Bender. She offered Demi a nearby table.

"Actually, I'm not as hungry as I thought," Demi said, backtracking toward the exit. "But we're having a reunion meeting here next Tuesday evening. I'm sure every person on the committee will want to hear all the details about your new job then."

"I look forward to it," said Poppy.

Her smile felt as phony as a three dollar bill.

She watched Demi walk briskly out the door and down the sidewalk, umbrella in one hand, phone in the other.

If only she'd kept her mouth shut!

There had never been any expectations of Poppy. She could have gone on working at her parents' café forever and no one would have thought less of her.

But now, if her fabulous new life failed to come to fruition, she was going to be the laughingstock of Clarkston.

Heather Heyford learned to walk and talk in Texas, then moved to England. *("Y'all want some scones?")* While in Europe, Heather was forced by her cruel parents to spend Saturdays in the leopard vinyl back seat of their Peugeot, motoring from one medieval pile to the next for the lame purpose of "learning something." What she soon learned was how to allay the boredom by stashing a *Cosmo* under the seat. Now a recovering teacher, Heather writes romance novels set in the wine country. She is represented by the Nancy Yost Literary Agency.

HEATHER HEYFORD

A Taste of Chardonnay

THE NAPA WINE HEIRESSES

Join author Heather Heyford as she uncorks a sparkling new series following the St. Pierre sisters, heiresses to a Napa wine fortune who are toasting the good life and are thirsty for love . . .

Chardonnay St. Pierre's father is as infamous for his scandals as he is famous for his wine, and it's up to Char to restore the family name. The Challenge, an elite charity competition held in Napa, seems like the perfect opportunity for the socialite to cement her image as a philanthropist. But all eyes—including Char's—are on the Hollywood heartthrob who's also entered the race . . .

Long before his face was splashed across the gossip magazines, Ryder McBride grew up in a working-class family in Napa. He knows all about the St. Pierre sisters and their notorious father, and when he learns he'll be up against Char in The Challenge, he assumes the grape doesn't fall far from the vine. But the more they get to know one another, the more they begin to realize that nothing pairs better with a heated rivalry than a healthy pour of flirtation . . .

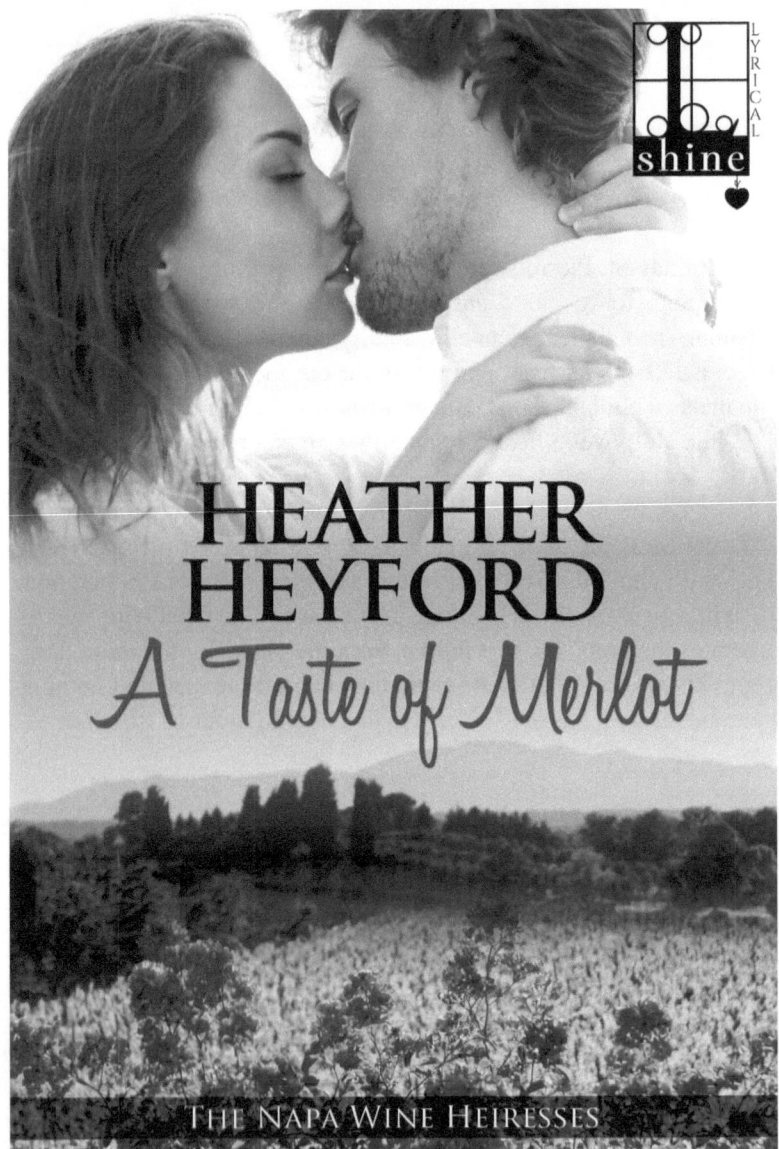

HEATHER HEYFORD
A Taste of Merlot

THE NAPA WINE HEIRESSES

Raise your glass and join Heather Heyford as she pours a second serving in her series following these headstrong wine heiresses in their quest to strike out on their own . . .

Merlot St. Pierre is struggling to break free from her family name. Her college classmates whisper behind her back that her passion for jewelry design is little more than a hobby, since she'll always have her father's fortune. But Meri is determined to prove them wrong, and with the help of a handsome jewelry buyer, she just may taste her first sip of success—as long as she can hide who she really is . . .

Mark Newman's family owns a chain of high-end jewelry stores, and he's working hard to get out from under his aunt's thumb and prove he has a good eye *and* a head for business. He's certain Meri's designs could be the next big thing, but he'll have to convince her that she can use her famous last name to her advantage. As their business partnership takes root, an attraction begins to flourish—but they'll both find that love, like wine, takes time to perfect . . .

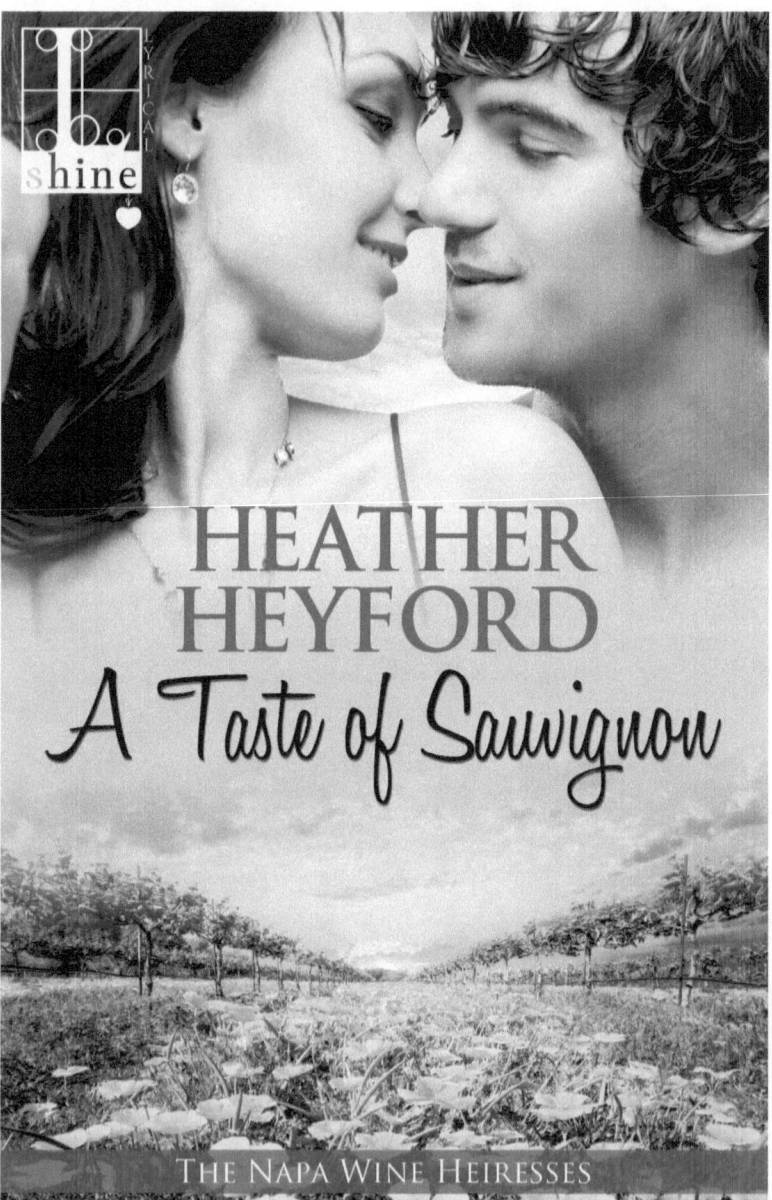

HEATHER HEYFORD

A Taste of Sauvignon

THE NAPA WINE HEIRESSES

Join Heather Heyford as she returns to Napa for a third taste in her series following three wine heiresses, each as vibrant and unique as the grapes for which they were named . . .

Sauvignon St. Pierre has always been fiercely ambitious. She easily could've cashed in on her family's fortune, but instead she struck out on her own, breezed through law school, and landed a job at a small firm in Napa. Savvy's life is as tidy and straightforward as her sizable collection of little black dresses, and she likes it that way—but every now and then, she can't help but long for her first sip of love . . .

After a chance encounter with Esteban Morales, the *caliente* son of Papa St. Pierre's long-time rival, something inside Savvy wakes up. It could be that Esteban's interest in cultivating lavender appeals to her passion for perfumery. But there's something else about the charming but down-to-earth farmer that she simply can't resist. They both know their families are an unlikely pairing, but together, Savvy and Esteban just may be the ideal varietals for a perfect blend . . .

HEATHER HEYFORD

A Taste of Sake

THE NAPA WINE HEIRESSES

As author Heather Heyford pours a final glass in her series follow-ing three Napa wine heiresses, a newcomer must work her way into a tightly-knit family whose bond has been fermenting for years . . .

Though they each have their own ambitions and are known to be competitive—even with one another—the St. Pierre sisters are fiercely loyal. Chardonnay and Merlot are thrilled about Sauvignon's wedding day, and it's slated to be the soirée of the decade among Napa's most elite residents. Given the family's notoriety, it almost stands to reason that their eccentric father, Xavier, would arrive by helicopter. But no one could have anticipated the wedding surprise he'd brought along with him . . .

The product of one of Xavier's many affairs, Sake is introduced as the half-Japanese sister the St. Pierre girls never knew they had. She struggles to break into clique-ish Napa society—and getting in with her sisters is proving more difficult than nabbing a '74 Cabernet. It seems only high-end realtor Bill Diamond can tell there's more to Sake than meets the eye. Afraid of repeating her mother's mistakes, Sake just hopes that getting drunk on love won't leave her with a hangover of rejection . . .

www.ingramcontent.com/pod-product-compliance
Lightning Source LLC
Chambersburg PA
CBHW031359250626
47155CB00004B/1334